DATE
WITH A
PLUMMETING
PUBLISHER

ALSO BY TONI BRILL

Date With A Dead Doctor

DATE
WITH A
PLUMMETING
PUBLISHER

a Midge Cohen mystery

Toni Brill

St. Martin's Press New York

Library of Congress Cataloging-in-Publication Data

Brill, Toni.
    Date with a plummeting publisher / Toni Brill.
        p.   cm.
    ISBN 0-312-08753-5
    I. Title.
PS3552.R478D39   1993
813'.54—dc20   92-21221
                                                                   CIP

First Edition: April 1993

10 9 8 7 6 5 4 3 2 1

to Bubby, again. Thank God.

1

PEARL, my mother, crossed her ankles and tilted her head at me, tenderness blunted by her fear I would get even madder. "Still, it *is* odd . . . that it should happen again, I mean."

"No, it is *not* happening again! Not to me anyway, because this time I'm not getting involved!" I slapped my hand on my mother's coffee table, bouncing brownie crumbs around.

Pearl perched uncertainly on her 1988 tax materials, stored on the Italian side chair she and my dead father Max had bought in Venice two years before I was born; she wrapped her left hand tightly around her middle, right hand covering her mouth for a moment, before she patted her hair with it, then finally dared to say, "Involved? Who said anything about involved? All I said, it's strange, you go out with the poor man on Wednesday and *bang,* here he is in the obituaries in Friday's *Times.*"

"What's strange? It's my new line of work! Hit dating! Dial M for Midge! Get rid of the inconvenient people in your life, arrange an evening with Midge Cohen, blind-dating's angel of death!" I snapped, then jabbed at the channel changer, which scrolled a surreal jump cut of programs—talking heads, cartoons, Beaver Cleaver, a truck with tires bigger than Pearl's whole apartment pouncing down on an already flattened automobile.

Pearl reached over for the channel changer, poked another button shutting off the TV, and then stood to go around the Formica bar that separates her kitchen from the living room, while I slumped back into the sofa, nausea washing up onto me like hot swamp water.

Pearl washed dishes for a moment, making I'm-not-saying-anything noises through her nose. Then, as if she had lost an internal battle, she straightened her back and looked at me almost daringly. "Maybe you have mystery on the brain, you know what I mean, sweetie? Those books you write, and then . . . oh, you know, that other thing? The dead proctologist? Plus your troubles with that policeman, Mark. It's no wonder you're maybe a little, well . . ."

"Crazy?" I snarled. Then, turning angrily the other way, I punched one of Pearl's throw pillows, hard enough to give my knuckles a rub burn. "Anyway, his name is *Mike,* and this isn't about Mike," I muttered, feeling that wet prickly tingle that presages crying, so I punched the pillow again. My mother was *not* going to see me cry! "That's over. It didn't work. Like you said, we're . . . different."

"*Overreacting,* sweetie, not crazy. Just overreacting. And I never said that Mike wasn't a perfectly lovely person."

"No, you said he was Italian, and you said that he was a Catholic, and you said mixed marriages don't work, and you said that the physical fades and then what do you have. But you never ever said he wasn't a lovely boy."

"Okay, Midge, honey . . ." Pearl came back around the counter to brush something wet from my cheek with her rubber-gloved thumb. "So it's just the rain and maybe her period that makes my I'm-a-grown-up-damnit-mother daughter suddenly turn up at my door, collapse crying on my couch."

"Crying? I'm not crying, I came to watch your TV."

"TV you don't have in Brooklyn, of course."

"Not cable. I told you, I want to watch something. A fight, there's a fight . . ."

"You and your boxers. You know what your grandmother would say about a nice Jewish girl who likes to watch sweaty naked men dancing around in shiny underwear, muscles on them like on a police horse?"

"Joyce Carol Oates wrote a whole *book* about boxing!" I shouted, before curling up in the corner of the sofa, where maybe mother wouldn't see the tears trickling down my face, the salt stinging the inside of my nose when I inhaled. "Any-way," I snuffled after a bit, because even I knew I looked ridicu-lous, "you know I'm always kind of down in September."

My mother made an indefinite snort of disbelief, then walked over to stand at her window, where she feigned intense interest in what some workmen in yellow oilskins were doing to a glistening asphalt roof over at NYU, on the other side of Wash-ington Square.

"Well, since my divorce anyway," I added after a bit, to the silent rebuke of her back. But even if teacher's-pet, twenty-eighth-in-her-Midwood-High-class, Cornell-grad, professor-of-Russian Margaret Cohen had loved September all her life, ever since I had finally decided I wanted to live in New York City and be a writer so badly that I even walked out on my veterinarian husband, our hundred acres and his seventy cows, all those back-to-school sales and bright yellow school buses are like a month-long question, saying "Did you do right?"

I sniffed hard, giving my septum another jolt of salty tears, then sat up, brushing off the crumbs of Pearl's palliative brownies.

Pearl gave up the window and went back to plucking glasses from her dishwasher, storing them in her cupboards. "Uh, Midge, sweetie . . ." she said hesitantly, after some minutes of clinking, clanking silence.

"Yeah, Ma?"

"I've been thinking . . . there's that nice Valentino I found for you last spring, when Loehmann's was clearing their back room. It has red piping, but I think that would be okay, as long as you accessorized in black, and make sure to pin the neck up high. You claimed the dress was too tight, remember? So you hid it way back in the closet . . . just like that plaid with the Mary Jane collar I sewed for mother-and-daughter night, remember? You thought I wouldn't find it under your dresser . . ."

"That was for *Brownies,* Mother," I said dully, pushing my sproingy hair behind my ears and smoothing my damp cheeks with the palms of my hand, trying to get myself into adequate enough shape to permit both of us to pretend I hadn't been sobbing like a preschooler. "I was *seven.* And anyway you always left pins in the seams."

"All I meant, with that five pounds you've lost, I'm positive that that Valentino would look stunning."

"*Fourteen* pounds, Ma," I snarled, proud enough of the weight I'd dropped to be exact about it even if the loss hadn't come through willpower, but because ever since July my insomnia had me knotted up so badly that I had been living on nothing but bran nuggets, bowlsful of what looked like the stuff my veterinarian ex-husband used to feed to his calves, and tasted like what insomnia would taste like if they could figure out how to put being sleepless at 3:47 A.M. into a box. "And stunning for what? I'm going somewhere?"

"The funeral, of course."

"But I'm *not* going to the funeral!"

"Midge, a man you are dating throws himself out a window, I think the least you can do is show up at his funeral." My mother pursed her lips and shook her head, as if we were arguing over what color shoes went best with a plaid skirt. I inhaled, to erupt at my mother again, but then my anger suddenly collapsed. I hauled myself from Pearl's couch, came around to stand beside her at the sink.

"I wasn't dating him. I only went out with him once," I murmured, feeling miserable, and wanting to be held.

After a moment, Pearl obliged. I even dropped my head onto her shoulder, trying to pretend that I wasn't a grown-up myself, an inch taller than my mother.

"Don't worry, baby doll," Pearl even did what she could to stroke my hair, though it kind of hurt, because I hadn't given her time to take off her rubber gloves. "It's not like it's your *fault* he killed himself, you know."

I snorted, stood erect, and pulled myself free. I studied tiny, salt-and-pepper–haired Pearl for a minute, who was as puzzled by my sudden appeal for caressing as she was by my equally abrupt withdrawal, while I wondered why it was that my mother had *never* been very good at the lap-cuddling, boo-boo-kissing part of maternity.

"Mother," I tried to sound calm, not querulous, "you really want to know why I'm upset? It's because I'm scared, okay? Because I don't think Simon Brent-Waterhouse killed himself *at all!*"

2

IF you've never heard of Simon Brent-Waterhouse, then nothing in his *New York Times* obituary would have explained why, when I read that he had committed suicide, I couldn't have been more surprised if he had come whistling down out of the sky in person, to break his head in my soup.

It wasn't even one of those obituaries you'd particularly notice. Neither so old that you'd marvel at what a full life he'd had, nor so young you'd wonder about AIDS, the premier publisher of emigré and dissident Russian literature had been worth only a couple of inches of *Times,* and most of that was a list of the now-famous Russian authors whom Simon Brent-Waterhouse had been first to publish. In addition to the facts that Brent-Waterhouse had been fifty-seven years old, born in the Midlands somewhere, educated at Leicester University and London School of Slavonics, that he was survived only by a mother, the *Times* made discreet reference to an "apparent suicide," but provided not even the slenderest of motivations on which to speculate, nothing about failing health or failing business, unrequited loves or unloved spouses, anything at all which might have induced Brent-Waterhouse to put himself out a window *ever*.

To say nothing of committing suicide about four hours after a dinner at which he had taken enormous relish in making the rest of the table feel like fools, because he was about to make himself very rich.

It would be misleading to say that I hadn't expected to loathe Simon Brent-Waterhouse, because that would give you the idea that I had somehow expected to *meet* him some day, which I never did, because who in this life ever actually gets to become personally acquainted with her heroes?

Which he was one of mine, because out of all of us who were besotted by Russian literature, Brent-Waterhouse was just about the only one who figured out how to make that passion pay. When the rest of us Slavic drones were trudging to yet another screening of *Potemkin,* memorizing irregular verbs, and struggling through *August 1914* in the original, Brent-Water-house was hunched over a primordial computer typesetter he had had the brains to buy, laboriously tapping into it all the manuscripts that washed over the Russia of the 1970s like melt-water in spring. In those years no Russian-speaking foreigner ever left an all-night drunken poetry reading, a sodden week-long wedding, a tippling weekend out mushrooming in the country, or even a simple afternoon wine-and-tea without a manuscript or two or three, barely legible tenth carbon copies of hand-bound, pathetic homemade novels, poems, philosophical treatises, and exposés. It was only Brent-Waterhouse, though, begun as a junior lecturer in Slavonic studies at some grim red-brick university in the Midlands, who had the brains to smuggle those hopeful, pitiable *cris du coeur* out to the west and his waiting typesetter. Later a secretary and a shipping clerk were added, to make up the entirety of Sirin Press, which published the books in Russian, generally with cover artwork that also had been thrust upon Brent-Waterhouse by Russian artists made as desperate as his volunteer authors by censorship and oppression. Then, often as not, Brent-Waterhouse translated the books into English and published them again. Maybe Sirin Press never got big enough to give Random House cause to fret, but in just a couple of years Brent-Waterhouse was out of the red brick and living in London, in a manner I could only dream about. Every university library bought Brent-Waterhouse's books, and some of the larger bookshops in New York did, too, but where I think he made most of his money was selling to us—the graduate students and young faculty of a marginal and shrinking academic discipline. I mean, how many dissertations (which you need to get degrees), articles (to get jobs), and books (to get tenure) can you squeeze out of Tolstoy? So we soaked up Sirin's books, on the basis of which some of us at least got degrees, and jobs, and even tenure.

Brent-Waterhouse got something much better though. He got rich.

However, it was not because of his *money* that I said "yes" when Pearl called to ask whether I would consider being a last-minute replacement at a "terribly, terribly important business dinner," for this man who had just brought his first-choice date ("fairly pretty, if you like those tall blondes with legs like race horses and the rest more like on a cow, if you know what I mean") into Kornbluth, Kornfeld, and Singh, D.D.S. P.C., where my mother was the receptionist, because the poor woman had just shattered a back molar on a baby olive at Cucina Partinico, a very upscale pizza place around the corner from my mother's building at Two Fifth Avenue, the kind of place you go if you've ever wondered what a black caviar and chevre pizza on stoneground unbleached would taste like, baked in a wood oven heated with olive logs flown in special from Sicily.

In fact, I almost didn't say yes at all. Normally when my mother calls from the dental receptionry with her latest root-canal or gingivitis-cursed dream date, I snarl something like, "Damnit, Mother, I'm trying to work, I don't need a blind date, would you stay out of my love life?" and my mother says something on the order of, "It's not a date, it's just to get out; what are you, a nun that you sit inside, the sun never even touches your cheeks?" Then I slam the phone down, after which I stare at it for three days, until one of us—usually me—calls to apologize. Because after all I had *had* a husband. A perfectly good husband, almost a doctor even—a veterinarian with rich parents—but I still had to walk out on him or go nuts. So I am in no hurry to get another husband. Especially one upon whom my mother has stumbled across simply because his gums are receding.

"Too bad for the girl, Ma," I said, "but I don't get it. The guy can't just go alone?"

"Midge, from what I understand, this gentleman is hosting a terribly high-level dinner, and he feels it is imperative to have an escort."

"An escort he can find on Forty-second Street, Ma."

"The gentleman is right here, Midge, and he says he needs someone that speaks Russian, and knows Russian literature. Isn't that right, Mr. Brent-Waterhouse?"

"*Simon* Brent-Waterhouse?" I squealed. You know, I don't think I actually *ever* said "yes," but ten minutes later I was groveling in the clipped curls at my hair girl Julie's feet, whining and begging and bribing her to let me pay her $152.95, plus tip, for a razor cut, a brightener, a full facial, and a nail wrap.

This was *me*? Midge Cohen, normally with the T-shirts and the pencils behind my ear and Wite-Out flecks on my fingernails? Now racing around my apartment humming "Will You Still Love Me Tomorrow?" preparing to cram myself into a gold silk Ungaro that even after I had lost fourteen pounds was still so tight in most places I had to get into the cab on all fours, but so loose on top that I could practically check for lumps without undressing.

I blush, but it was me. What was I hoping for, that frantic afternoon, made unbearably long by anticipation? What does *anybody* hope for on a blind date? Love, marriage, romance. A London townhouse where I could become Margaret Cohen Brent-Waterhouse, literary lioness, witty conversationalist, and *soirée savante,* a society beauty with brains who though neither tall nor blond was remarkably leggy for someone only five-foot-four, and with the sort of cleavage that would inspire the designers who would frequent my *levées* to begin making clothes for real women again.

All right, so maybe I let my hopes get a little high.

On the other hand though, when Pearl called I was only a few weeks away from slipping over the Alps that stand between "early thirties" and "nearing forty," and my third young-adult novel (*Tammy and Tanesia and the Purloined Painting,* for Girl Scouts ages eight to eleven) had a few months ago sunk beneath the waters of oblivion without so much as a ripple, and once a month my literary agent returns my new manuscript (a *real* novel this time, for adults, that I have worked on almost five years) with ever curter and more exasperated suggestions for the changes she'd "like to see, before I'd be comfortable sending it out. The adult market is much tougher than the young-adult market, you know," and since before Labor Day already I can't make myself even get started on a crummy little one-thousand-word book review (of four new young-adult novels) that an old friend who I only recently discovered is now a junior editor at the *New York Times Book Review* said I could try to do for him (but with no, repeat, no guarantees he would publish it), which meant it probably won't ever get printed even if I should manage to write it, and even if it does, all the *Times* would pay is $250 tops, less than I have spent already on the lunches I take this editor friend out to so I could get the crack at a piece in the first place. Not to mention that all the men I know—which you could count on one hand and still have fingers left to scratch with—seem to be mad at me at once, and then, last week in the shower, when I plucked three of those little hairs that grow around your nipples . . . *two* of them were white.

What I mean, who *wouldn't* want a totally new life, that would let me pretend that my first three decades had been simply a bad dream?

Which is probably why I hadn't disliked Simon Brent-Waterhouse immediately; that had taken nearly half an hour. Time for Brent-Waterhouse to tread on my foot, bruise my arm in an attempt to steer me around a waiter that he pushed me into instead, splashing coffee on my Ungaro, and then ask me, as he lifted the curtain into the back room of the half-empty, rather dirty chop house that occupied the address Brent-Waterhouse had given my mother, whether I had brought a credit card with me.

"Strictly just in case, you understand, Midge my dear. I chose this place as much because it's cheap as anything, but cheap in this Manhattan of yours is any other man's dear, you know. Heh-heh."

"Heh-heh," I agreed, grimly, before trying to set the first of the evening's ground rules. "Except I'm not Midge. I'm Margaret."

"*Margaret?*" Brent-Waterhouse said, raising where his eyebrows would have been if he had had any. "But I believe your mother referred to you as Midge."

I have visions of that cursed "Midge" carved in granite on my damn tombstone, for all eternity. Short for "Midget," of course. I hate the nickname, but I let my mother use it, partly because it was she who invented it, back in 1961, when I tottered downstairs to watch JFK's inauguration wearing her mink and high heels, and partly because even though I am an inch taller than Pearl, I am still only five-four (well, almost five-four).

"I am *Margaret*" I repeated, probably too firmly, so to add a little friendly, I grinned. "Like Margaret Rose. The Princess."

But I don't think he heard me, because Brent-Waterhouse was six-six if he was an inch, which meant that as long as we were standing I was going to do most of my conversing with Brent-Waterhouse's belly—a wobbling bulge that pushed a few gingery hairs through the soup-spotted fabric of his shirt and made alarming pussy-whisker puckers around his buttons.

Brent-Waterhouse was a good reminder that they are called "blind dates" because that generally is what it would help to be, when you are on one. He looked a lot like Daniel Patrick Moynihan would, if the senator were in the final stages of cirrhosis. His face behind his W.C. Fields honker was high-blood-pressure pink, with turgid mottles blotching up into a fuzzy straw-yellow tufting of hair so pale that he seemed not even to possess any eyebrows at all. Technically the publisher wasn't bald, because most of his scalp was dotted with little islands of something mosslike, spaced so regularly he must have been being reseeded. Brent-Waterhouse also spoke like a Monty Python skit, all British chortles and grunts and oblique little asides that don't quite fit with whatever you just said, but make you feel vaguely stupid.

Fortunately, though, we didn't have to make forced chitchat over cheap red wine for very long, because Brent-Waterhouse's three other guests arrived, and, after a brief moment trying to decide whether my mother had misheard or had made up the scale of this "high-power business supper" that in fact could have been held in the back of my Volkswagen, I was able to get started on what I spent the rest of the evening doing—feeling seriously inadequate as I compared myself to the guest of honor, and the latest Russian literary sensation, Polina Volkova.

Volkova was a Russian Germaine Greer with a healthy swirl of Erica Jong, mid-forties to at the most early fifties in age, and well preserved, for a Soviet woman. She was tall, almost six foot, and lithe, not thin, a distinction she made more than adequately with a raspberry body stocking and a black-and-white polka-dot Minnie Mouse skirt that barely covered her tush, and the yards of jangly bracelets she clanked every time she waved her noodle-thin arms. Even my clear advantage in the *zaftig* department was nullified by the downward swoop of her Danskin, which revealed so much your eye automatically assumed there had to be even more breast, someplace. After a couple of hours of really catty effort, the only consolations I could muster for myself were Volkova's hair—a frizzy hennaed triangle long ago martyred to Soviet hair-dressing technology—and her face, an incredible network of tiny wrinkles that in another five years would leave Volkova looking like Lillian Hellman.

Nor was it enough that her looks made me feel like the Pillsbury Doughboy, deafened by the creaking of my Ungaro's seams with every bite I took. Volkova was funny and quick-witted and bright and so absolutely shameless in her flirting that within twenty minutes the only place in the entire restaurant where you could find a waiter was within ten paces of her.

Making it entirely believable that Volkova was precisely what the title of her future book claimed she was—*A Hooker for the KGB*.

"Oh, yours is going to be a *glorious* book, Polina!" Brent-Waterhouse crowed, for the seventh or eighth time that night. "Just imagine, a book by Yuri Andropov's mistress! Hooking in the bloody Kremlin! High Party steambaths, all those corpulent swine being patted about by lovely sweating naked beauties, bands of lovely bare things skinny-dipping in the Black Sea, and more pillow secrets than a collective farm has broken tractors! My God, this book has bestseller written all over it, eh Petuh?"

"Petuh" was Peter O'Connell, who sat on Brent-Waterhouse's left. "I'm sure Miss Volkova's book sounds all very interesting," he grimaced with what seemed physical pain, "but there have been other books about sex in Russia, you know, and none of them has excited much commercial interest. All that sweaty tittie-in-the-bathhouse thing, Ian Fleming did that first. And better."

Roly-poly, and short enough to look me in the eye, with a sparsely clipped graying beard and glittering blue eyes, O'Connell fumed and sulked through the whole supper like a boy denied a piece of birthday cake. This is not the behavior I would have expected from someone whose most recent book had been on the front page of the *Times Book Review,* and a bestseller besides. Whom Queens College had subsequently given a scandalously well-endowed chair in Russian Studies, and then— life's little cherry on the cupcake of his existence—only last fall had gotten a MacArthur genius grant.

But then, it seemed to have been an evening for shattering the clay feet of my heroes.

Also English, O'Connell had first risen to prominence as a translator and active advocate of dissidents. It was in that capacity that he met and charmed the most irascible of the Soviet dissidents, Shura Kostoglotov, whom rumor said made Solzhenitsyn seem a pussycat by comparison. When he was chucked out of the U.S.S.R., Kostoglotov insisted that O'Connell become his exclusive Western biographer, but then was so offended at O'Connell's final result—a thousand-page slab of a book that caught every wart and bristle on the old jeremiah's soul—that Kostoglotov had sued, trying to halt sale of the book.

Naturally this made the biography into front-page news, and O'Connell into a hero. A *rich* hero. Which was why it was so odd, and quite-soon distressing, to find O'Connell as petulant as a maiden aunt at the wrong end of the month.

As the evening dragged on though I began to understand that miserable was exactly what Brent-Waterhouse wanted O'Connell to be; in fact, that was what he wanted *everyone* at that dinner to be.

Even Volkova.

Maybe *especially* Volkova. What I picked up over that fragmented and inexplicably tense evening was a general understanding that Volkova had been on the verge of concluding an enormous contract with Piper-Wilkey Publishing, when up popped Brent-Waterhouse, to remind her that at some earlier, and far more thoughtless period of her life, she had signed her entire literary future over to Sirin Press.

"Damnit, Simochka," the former hooker had purred, tapping her inch-long, blood-red claws on the table, "I keep telling you, this book is not just sex, it's serious. I'm going to show what kind of man Andropov was, the dangerous things he planned, the way he is influencing Russia even today."

"Preposterous," O'Connell snapped at her, then focused his irritation on Brent-Waterhouse again. "Not that it matters, because with everybody but the cleaning woman at the Kremlin publishing their accounts of the coup and all that, the market is what you might call saturated, old boy."

To which Brent-Waterhouse had crowed, "Oh, sour grapes! Sour sour grapies! You know perfectly well that's nonsense, or why else would Piper-Wilkey have been so quick to send you down here when I called, if they didn't hope somehow to snatch Miss Polina back, right out from under my poor old nose? It *galls* you, doesn't it, that Polina's book is going to make *millions?* For me!" Brent-Waterhouse guffawed again, ordered more cheap red from one of the half-dozen waiters who were hovering over Volkova, and then tapped O'Connell on the chest. "Polina names names, don't you dear? Places, faces.

. . . And there'll be considerable dirt about our boy Gorby, and dear Mister Yeltsin, and one or two other surprises besides, eh? Oh, we're going to have such a *lovely* little book, we are, dear Polina! The readers are going to absolutely *kill* to get hold of this book!" Then Brent-Waterhouse splashed the fresh carafe of ice-cold burgundy around and on the table, insisting we all drink to Polina's—and Sirin's—incipient success.

"Well, emm . . . that's actually a concern, for my client. Distribution, you know?" Victor Pedlar, the fifth of our merry band of diners, and apparently Volkova's agent, had inserted into the silence after that self-satisfied toast. "The relatively modest resources of Sirin Press leave us with considerable . . . emm, concern about your ability to market a property of this . . . emm, scope."

Pedlar was much younger than the other two men, and not British. I would have guessed him for American, except that there was something funny with his English vowels, a kind of high-pitched nasal something that made me wonder whether Pedlar might be South African. Though he was curiously reluctant to speak it, and he pedantically anglicized all the business words, Pedlar's Russian was excellent, better than mine, and much better than Brent-Waterhouse's. He was a big fellow, with a quick, pleasant smile, green-gray eyes, and a tan too light to be artificial, as if he spent a lot of time in the Bahamas, but hadn't been able to go this month. I suppose it is some sign of how disappointed—and bored—I was by Brent-Waterhouse that I gave some thought to letting myself be attracted by Pedlar, especially as he reminded me of someone, though who I couldn't place. Gerard Départieu on a diet, after rhinoplasty? But I decided against flirting over the gelid prime rib and rock-hard potatoes, because Pedlar also reminded me of a car salesman— pinstripe suit, enormous gold cufflinks, fifty-dollar haircut, and an engraved business card that declared him a "literary representative" at one of the enormous, and very hot, agencies uptown. The sort of agency that can get you a seven-figure, four-book contract for an idea scribbled on the back of a napkin, provided the napkin came from the right restaurant, and last week you had been on Oprah Winfrey.

Brent-Waterhouse, though, had been utterly unfazed by hardball agentry.

"Oh, I'm sure *everybody* will see the wisdom of Polina publishing with me, dear boy! Sirin Press may be little, but it's many a Goliath has learned the folly of size, what? Besides, Polina, my love, in your line of work it's first served, first come, isn't it?"

Polina's green eyes had glittered with a chill that would have been icy five miles north of Murmansk, and Pedlar turned an uncomfortable shade of eggplant.

"Well, actually, there *is* some question of just how binding that kind of blanket assignation of rights can be . . ." he began cautiously, drawing swirls on the tablecloth with his fork.

"*Blanket assignation!*" Brent-Waterhouse flapped his arms in delight. I ducked, so Brent-Waterhouse's thin, bitter red wine splashed over most of O'Connell's lovely leather coat, which couldn't have cost much less than my dress. "Blanket assignation, the apt term indeed, eh, Polina?"

Then, just in case any one had failed to eat his portion of wormwood and gall, Brent-Waterhouse had laid out the document which proved his claim on Polina, stroking the letter smooth as if it were a beloved cat.

" 'I, Polina Volkova, hereby designate Mr. Simon Brent-Waterhouse to be my publisher for ever and always, in all English-speaking countries,' " Brent-Waterhouse read gravely aloud, in English, then, pausing, added the date. "One January 1978." Then he smiled. "There are witnesses, too."

At which Volkova had apparently had all she could bear.

"*Witnesses!* You bloody bastard! Everybody was drunk! *I* was drunk! It was New Year's and I was *drunk!*" she screeched, snatching the paper up and ripping it grandly into shreds.

Brent-Waterhouse had beamed over his half-glasses, looking like a dissolute Santa Claus.

"A lovely paper, isn't it, Polina? So nice that a man would make any number of copies. Can't have us damaging Sirin's original, can we? Wouldn't be good business, would it, Petuh? Eh? So, we're keeping that nice and safe, in our special place, aren't we, Midge?"

I think that was the only question anyone actually asked me that evening. What I will never understand, as long as I live, was why—fool that I am—I smiled, and nodded yes.

As if I worked at Sirin Press, and knew something about where the original of that letter was kept.

Which, of course, I didn't. But whoever they were who had broken into my apartment that Friday afternoon, while I was around the corner at the Waldbaum's, wouldn't have known I was lying, would they?

3

"MIDGE sweetie, you think somebody's been in your apartment, call a policeman, for heaven's sake!"

This was my mother's advice, when I finally unburdened myself of what had sent me sniveling across the boroughs on that wet and nasty afternoon.

Which illustrates the big drawback of asking your mother for advice. Ask, she gives, and then what excuse do you have for not *following* her advice?

"Ma, *think,* I'm going to call 911 and tell them someone broke into my apartment *to clean it?* They'll take me maybe to Bellevue, in one of those coats that the sleeves buckle through your crotch!"

"So," Pearl had smoothed her skirt, "you don't want to call

the local precinct, ask at least a policeman you know." Then she had smiled, slyly. "I mean, you *do* know a policeman?"

Yes, I know a policeman. One policeman. And before I would phone him I'd rather be chopped into chunks and deep-fried by the devil.

At least that was what I thought, until I left my mother and went back to my spic-and-span apartment, to find the red light blinking on the answering machine. The machine I had gotten soon after I started going out with Mike Russo, the policeman I know, and so had calls I didn't want to miss. This replaced the machine I had deliberately broken, in a period when I had had nothing *but* calls I wanted to miss, most of them from my mother, to inquire whether anybody else had left messages. Since June though, most of the messages were once again from my mother.

Whose apartment I had just left. Puzzled, I punched the listen button.

Click, whirr, click: "Hi, Margaret, this is Vic Pedlar, representing Miss Volkova? What I was wondering, with the . . . ummm . . . new situation at Sirin, could you contact us, let us know where things stand now? Thanks. You can reach me at . . ."

I didn't listen to the number, because my spine had turned to ice, and every little hair between my neck and my tush was standing as stiff as a Christmas nutcracker.

About two minutes later I realized I probably wasn't as over Mike Russo as I had been telling myself, because he was still number one on my speed dialer.

"Mike?"

I could hear music, laughter. I pictured his apartment, in the basement of his mother's house, in Queens. We hadn't gone there often, because of the clatter my heels made going down—or what was more embarrassing, because it was so much later, up—the wooden stairs, and anyway, why would we, since I have my own place. Besides, it was almost midnight, Friday night; why shouldn't the man be having a little fun? I felt a stinging in my eyes, in the back of the nose.

"Who is this?"

The four months I hadn't talked to him had wiped a lot of his "Noo Yawk" out of my memory. I was just about to put the phone receiver down again, before the mistake of this call got any worse, but then, suddenly, Mike Russo recognized my voice.

"Hey, it's Midge! Midge, how ya doing!"

I wiped my nose. Probably a cold, something I picked up schlepping around Manhattan in the rain.

"All right, I'm doing all right, I'm sorry if I'm disturbing you, I mean, if you're busy . . ." I mumbled, embarrassment making even my hair feel hot.

"Sorry, I can't hear you! Damn music and everything . . ."

"Mike, I'm sorry, I'll just call you back tomorrow!" I said frantically, meaning I would never call him again, ever.

"No, it's okay, just a second, I'll turn off the TV . . ."

A second later the party in Mike Russo's apartment vanished, and my heart grew warm.

"Stupid box," Mike said as he came back on the line, "All that money for that damn cable, thirty-six big-deal channels, and the only thing I can find to watch tonight is "Kojak" reruns. Can you believe it?"

For a second I was thrilled—it was Friday night and Russo was *home*. Then I remembered that that didn't mean he was alone.

"Listen, Mike, I'm sorry to bother you, so late especially, but . . ."

"Hey, it's no bother. I'm happy to hear from you, it's been a while. In fact, I've been wondering about you . . ."

"Wondering?" I asked, curling myself up in the corner of Aunt Dora's couch, just for a second letting myself pretend it was Mike embracing me, and not a fifty-year-old piece of chintz from Abraham and Straus.

"Yeah, you know . . . how you are and everything." There was a longish pause, while each of us waited for the other to start. Unfortunately, I waited a little longer than he did.

"So what, you're calling this time of night 'cause you got, like, a mouse or something?"

I sat up straight, away from the embracing sofa. "No, damnit, I don't have a mouse. If I had a mouse, I'd take care of it myself."

"All right, all right, touchy as ever. Jeez, it was a joke."

"I'm not touchy. Jokes are supposed to be funny," I hated myself for the scolding whine I could hear in my voice, but couldn't stop. Instead, as a kind of explanation, I added after a minute, "This isn't funny."

"Okay, it ain't funny. It's your nickel, so tell me what it is." Russo's voice had risen a notch too, anger on a thin and fraying leash of humor. Which means our first conversation in almost four months was beginning just about where we had left off.

There was another longish silence, and then Russo spoke, hesitantly. "Look, Midge," he cleared his throat again, "is this like . . . well, are you trying, you know, to apologize?"

"Apologize?!" If it were physically possible to get out of Aunt Dora's sag-bottomed couch in fewer than two tries, I would have been on my feet, screaming. *"Apologize?!"*

Russo must have snatched the receiver away from his ear, because now his voice came from much farther away. "Well, I mean, not apologize, but you know, like, make up. Get things . . . started again."

"Why on earth would I apologize to you? I didn't do anything to you! I called you because I need a cop, that's why I called you!"

"A cop? You called me 'cause you need a cop?"

"That's what you are, isn't it? A cop?"

"I'm a detective . . . a *detective,*" he shouted, making the receiver shrill. "And my precinct's in Manhattan. I do homicides. You want like a traffic ticket fixed or something, you call Brooklyn police."

Suddenly my defensive fury melted down into something that, if I wasn't one hundred percent over my thing for Mike Russo, I would have said was a throbbing desire to have him hold me.

"Mike, Mike . . ." I could feel a tear working its way loose from my right eye, and my voice was trembling, "somebody's been in here. In my place. Going through my stuff."

"How in the hell can you tell?" he snapped, still angry.

"Yeah, well maybe I don't vacuum the goddamned burners on the stove like your mother, spray Lysol into the phone, but I think I can tell when somebody's been searching my desk!"

Russo snorted. "What I remember, if they held the Valentine's Day Massacre in your ice box, it'd take you three days to notice. And besides, why would anybody go through your desk?"

"Goddamn, if I want somebody on my case about dust," I began, but then caught myself, took a deep breath, let it out, then sat down on the couch again, determined to make Russo understand what it had done to me to discover that a stranger had been in my apartment.

When I walked out on Paul Blank and our eleven-room Victorian with the four-acre garden outside Dryden, New York, I had done so in large part because I suddenly, wholly unexpectedly, had Aunt Dora's apartment to come to. *My* apartment, now, thanks to her will. Bedroom to the left of the front door, living room to the right, and kitchen straight ahead. The ceilings, most of the paint, and a lot of the furniture were all prewar, and the kitchen cabinets had been repainted so many times they wouldn't close, and my only additions to the place—floor-to-ceiling bookcases that a semi-deaf Serbian handyman I found through a laundromat bulletin board had built for cash and a

dy supply of slivowitz—made the apartment look and smell
I had a sideline in used books.

ut it was *mine*. I could arrange my photos however I wanted
those shelves, and leave my cups under the newspapers on
coffee table until there were brown stains in the bottom,
tch television all night if the mood to do so struck me, pick
the laundry only when I ran out of underwear, and never ever
st.

"And so you came back from the store and it was clean?"
ısso asked, voice straining not to laugh.

"Mike, a paper band around the toilet seat and the place
ɔuld have been a *motel*. Everything dusted, the books all
ranged by size, the junk on my shelves neat like in a
hotchkes shop. Even my drawers! Every damn thing in my
ɛsk was gone through and tidied up!"

Finally Russo couldn't restrain himself, and guffawed. "I'm a
ɔp almost fifteen years, never once have we had a complaint of
ackward vandalism! You're right, got to nip this thing in the
ud, otherwise you'd have like whole gangs roaming the city,
crubbing up graffiti, raking the leaves in Central Park, going up
ɔ total strangers and picking the lint off their lapels. You sure
his intruder of yours wasn't maybe the good fairy?"

"Mike, can you focus for a minute? Or are you telling me it's
how okay in New York to break into somebody's place, just so
ong as you clean up after yourself? Anyway, that's not all. This
evening I get home, and there's been a call from one of the guys
at this literary dinner I was at, the agent."

"What literary dinner?" Mike asked, with a patient kind of
exasperation that made me think I must sound like Gracie Allen.
I inhaled deeply, shook my head, and told the story of my date
with Simon Brent-Waterhouse and his sudden demise in as flat
and unemotional a voice as I could manage.

"Okay, I guess I hear you," Russo finally admitted, when I
stopped. "The suicide bit, I don't know. . . . But the letter,

4

that makes sense, if somebody thinks you have it. Something to look for, if somebody really has been going through your place . . ."

"Goddamn it," I snapped frostily, "when I tell you somebody has been going through my stuff . . ."

"Whoa, whoa, get offa your broomstick, slip of the tongue, that's all. What I meant, okay, somebody thinks you've got that letter, so they let themselves into your apartment to look for it. But what's that got to do with this agent fellow?"

"I don't *know*, but don't you think it's *weird*, Pedlar calling me here?"

"Since when is it weird that a guy calls you? Especially somebody in the book biz?"

"I never gave him my number, *that's* what's weird!"

There was a pause, and when Mike spoke again he sounded as if he were being patient. Which I hate.

"You're sure you never gave him the number? It couldn't have like slipped out? Or a business card maybe? You gave him your card?"

"I don't *have* a card, and what do you mean, 'slipped out'? How does your phone number 'slip out'?"

"Well, okay, the guy got your number somehow. But why do you think he'd have anything to do with going through your apartment? I mean, there was nothing threatening about what he said or anything, right? Just a straightforward business call."

"In the evening?" I shrilled, with a triumphant certainty that even I knew was ridiculous.

Russo contented himself with a snort, until, the silence having dragged on, he asked, with unexpected gentleness, "It's really the phone call, isn't it? That's rattled you, I mean. Not the break-in, but the call?"

I nodded, but somehow Mike understood, and waited.

Tears were again trembling on my lower lids, and ripples of shivers coursed up and down my back, but this time it wasn't emotion. This was fear, which I despaired of making Mike understand, because even I thought I was going crazy.

"Mike, Mike . . ." I tried not to whimper, but I don't think I succeeded. "I knew him. The voice. I think I knew him."

Mike waited a bit longer, but finally gave up. Puzzled, he asked, "You said you had dinner with the guy, so why *wouldn't* you know him?"

Before answering, I tested my memory again, as I had a score, a hundred times since the tape had first spun Pedlar's voice from my answering machine. Perhaps because of the tinny speaker, perhaps because the voice was disembodied now, without the distractions of the expensive suit, the well-groomed American face, whatever the reason, Pedlar's voice had sparked an arc of memory, a short-circuit that had no natural right to exist, but once established was indisputably, unquestionably *there*. And no amount of scoffing at myself, no amount of berating myself could make that certainty go away.

Not even now.

"Mike, I mean I recognized his voice. I knew him before. In Moscow. Except then his name was Vitya Korobeikin."

4

THAT phone call was a recipe for real *killer* insomnia. *Maybe* it would seem longer to cross Mongolia by camel than it did to make it through that weekend, but I'd hate ever to find out for sure. Sundays I used to hate even when Mike and I passed them by sleeping until two, and then going up to Little Italy somewhere for frettas. Now, when the only things sharing the pleasures of my empty apartment were a book review I couldn't write and a novel I couldn't sell, the minutes passed like I had to squeeze each one from stone. I sat at my Selectric making Xs and Os, or lay rigid on the bed, staring at the ceiling, wondering when I would get it through my thick head that an Italian cop and a Jewish writer need more to hold them together than the fact that my knees turned to Silly Putty when he squeezed my earlobe. On the surface we were so alike, loving take-out Chinese and pepperoni slices, laughing at how similiar our memories were, of Howdy Doody and Gerry and the Pacemakers and our parents driving us out to Coney Island on summer nights when it was too hot to sleep . . .

But it was a deceptive similarity, parallel evolution, the way a panda bear looks like a polar bear wearing a tuxedo, but you could never mate them, because one is a bear and the other is an overgrown Chinese raccoon.

Which explains why I had three almost sleepless nights. What it doesn't explain is why it is that, the first deep sleep I finally tumbled into, was shattered by a phone call.

"Hey, Midge? 'D I wake ya?"

"Mmmmm. Taimzit?"

"The time? Almost seven. Yeah, yeah, I know it's early, but you got to get up anyway."

"Whoozis?"

"What, been drinking or something? You don't recognize me? It's Russo."

"Russo?" I rolled over onto my back. The telephone cord got all tangled in my hair, and my "A Woman Needs a Man Like a Fish Needs a Bicycle" nightshirt was halfway to my neck.

"Yeah, Mike Russo, remember? The guy you called Friday night. Come on, I ain't running the five-borough wake-up service here. You better shake it if you want a chance to look at this hotel where your blind date tried to learn to fly. Couple of my pals agreed to bend the rules a little."

I sat straight up, like Frankenstein's monster when the lightning bolt hits. "Where are you calling from?"

Russo chuckled. "That's better. Meet me 'round the corner in ten minutes."

"I'll make it in five," I promised, throwing the covers aside, my hands shaking with adrenalin.

" 'ROUND the corner" was a luncheonette as old as the neighborhood, now owned by two women, Jewish refugees from Moldavia who had learned their cooking and cleaning under communism. The grease and smoke on the ceiling were so thick the Sistine Chapel frescoes could have been under there and you'd never know it, the doughnuts on their cake stands up on the counter were so stale that the flies bounced off them, the Board of Health would have ordered the griddle to be buried immediately out at the Fresh Kill landfill if they ever inspected the place, and the red-vinyl upholstery on every stool and bench had cuts in it, so no matter where you sat you snagged your nylons. On the other hand, it was the only place in the neighborhood open past eight P.M., so Russo and I had spent a lot of time here, last spring.

Mike stood and smiled uncertainly as I stumbled in, the dark glasses I was wearing to hide my baggy eyes making me trip on the mudmat. Russo was still six-one, and his close-cut brown-blond hair still sketched a W on his forehead, but his teeth were yellower, and his chin seemed less chiseled than I recalled. Too many cannolis, I told myself, convincing myself that this meant I was over Mike Russo. Even if he remained the most handsome man I'd ever seen in three dimensions.

"Morning. You want a cuppa coffee or something? Not your cappuccino, of course. Christ, I'd forgot, the stuff they make in this place, not even a cop can drink it," he sloshed the thick white mug he was holding, then added, "but you look like you could use a jolt of some kind."

I smiled, wishing I had done more to my face than wash it. "My" cappuccino, because the espresso on our trip to Sicily had been too strong for me, in those breakfasts we shared on that shaded balcony, tiles, handpainted with octopuses and fishes, running along the balcony, big clay pots of pinkish-purple geraniums, and bees fumbling among the rosemary . . .

"You woke me up to go see this hotel room, so let's go see the hotel room. I was up till like five or something." I almost snarled, demonstrating once again this gift I have for getting along with people.

Russo continued to smile, but he looked like a jack o'lantern whose candle someone had just snuffed. "Active social life, eh?" he put the mug on the counter, then rubbed his fingertips, like something was sticking to them. It was just after seven in the morning, but already Russo's tie was pulled away from his opened collar, and his beard was pushing out, the texture against his tan skin reminding me of wet sand, just after a wave has receded.

Mouth dry, I took a conciliatory swig from his cup, then made a face, smiled. "*No* social life, actually. I was worrying." We wandered outside, to the familiar low-slung red car, parked in the bus stop in front of the diner. Out of habit I bent to let myself in, then remembered that my proprietorial rights to Russo's car were a lot less defined than they had been some months before. I stood back up and looked around, watching the first of the old women creaking their battered shopping carts toward the Waldbaum's, the Pakistani news vendors across the street catching bundles of newspaper, an overweight black guy in engineer driver overalls and a Brooklyn Dodgers cap was throwing off a graffitied truck.

Russo was smiling broadly again. Keys in his hand, he waved across the top of the car. "Get in, get in. It'll take us the rest of the morning to get over there, if we don't get a little jump on the traffic." Then, seated and the car gargling its powerful purr, he asked, "Worrying about maybe this book agent guy is really from Russia?"

"Well, don't you at least think it's bizarre that Pedlar is

running around pretending to be American, when he's really Russian?"

"You don't know that's true," Russo pointed out, almost sharply. "And even if it is, so what? New York isn't exactly suffering a shortage of guys from Russia."

I conceded the first point, slightly. "I don't *know* it know it, but at dinner that night, there was something about the guy, I couldn't place it, familiar, you know? And his voice, his accent. Like he was maybe foreign. But then when I heard him on my machine, it was like I just suddenly *knew*, I could picture him there, back in Moscow."

Just as I had all night, staring at my bedroom ceiling. Vitya Korobeikin, a desperate college kid, who had sought me out in my Moscow dormitory room, fastening onto me with the grip of a drowning man.

"You knew this guy well in Russia?"

"Not really. He hung around the dormitory. He'd just sort of show up, knock on the door, and slip in before you could ask who it was, then motion, that I should follow him into the shower."

Russo looked over sharply, his expression professionally blank. "You *showered* with the guy but you don't remember what he looks like?"

"You know I'm blind without my glasses." I smiled acidly, then slapped the dashboard. "Damnit, will you be serious? Of course I didn't *shower* with him, it was so they couldn't *bug* us. He'd turn on the water, and sometimes the radio too, and that's where we'd talk."

"In the shower?" Russo was still skeptical, because ever since that stupid afternoon when I took off all my clothes on that beach in Sicily, his opinion of my morals—or more exactly his suspicions about the lack of them—has been a big part of the reason why our conversations have been more prickly than a bag full of hat pins.

"*Next* to the shower . . ." And then, unexpectedly, the memory made me giggle. "And it would get steamier and steamier, and my hair would just go *limp,* and you'd be so sweaty it felt like a jungle or something. . . ." And Korobeikin, clinging tight to my arm, a younger version of the voice I had heard come from my answering machine yesterday, whispering harsh, hot, and urgent as he vented his hatred for his government, for the limitations on his future, for the lies that smothered him and his country in one flatulent, stupid cloud. Wound so tight you'd almost think it was him spewing the steam, flailing his hands and raging away, Vitya never told me anything I didn't know— the opposite in fact, since I knew far more about his country's history than he did—and he never really *asked* me for anything either, but somehow I always gave him something. Nickel and dime stuff, that Vitya had received with gratitude so pathetically enormous it bordered on the absurd. A science fiction novel. A book about Picasso that had maybe a dozen reproductions of paintings, done as postcards that could be ripped out. Bazooka bubble gum, a couple of times. It was even Vitya who had seen me off, when I left Moscow for the last time.

For a moment the unexpected sweetness of that memory transfixed me. The robin's-egg sky flush with peach blossom behind the jagged inky stand of fir, the June air chill at four A.M. I was shivering on the curb amidst my bulging baggage, waiting for the taxi I had ordered, to take me from the university on Lenin Hills, out to Sheremetevo Airport. I was exhausted, wrenched, and drained from all the farewells, feeling not so much that I was leaving Moscow as that part of my life was about to be amputated, so intensely had I lived there, and so unlikely was it that I would ever be able to return.

And suddenly . . .

Vitya.

Proudly, shyly bearing his farewell gift, a samovar. A silly, ugly, brand-new phony electric samovar, as big as a turkey, and just as unlikely to fit into my luggage, which was approaching critical mass even without that unwanted bit of Soviet kitsch. Vitya gave me the samovar, shook my hand, then, hesitant and clumsy, hugged me, pushing the samovar's handle painfully into my breast. Then, glaring fiercely, he made me swear that if ever I were to return to Moscow, even if for a single day, I would notify him, and no matter where the cruel vagaries of Soviet fate might have cast him, he would move heaven and earth if need be, but he would come, to see me once again.

Because we were *droozya*.

Friends.

I must have thought about all this for a long silent while, because we were already thrumming over the Brooklyn Bridge before Mike asked me, delicately but clearing his throat tensely, "I still don't get it. . . . If he is the same guy, which you gotta admit the evidence is maybe a little slim for, but if he is, it was what, more than ten years ago, but you're so miffed he didn't recognize you that you kept yourself up all night? Seems kind of weird, unless . . ."

"Unless what?" I snapped, turning toward him, because the tension in his voice insinuated perfectly well "unless what." It was precisely that tension, the question Mike would not ask and I would not answer, which had kept me living on bran and insomnia ever since that cursed afternoon in Sicily, the memory of which I refuse to discuss even with my mother. Mike and I were sitting on a white-washed, red-tiled café veranda at the edge of the beach, watching all those tanned, nearly nude European bodies parading up and down the strand, the men wearing what looked like Spandex scrotums, the women joggling and woggling along with their nut-brown boobies bare. At some point Russo had grinned, looking like a cat stretching out on a sun-warmed carpet, and pointed his chin at one of the passing pin-ups.

"When in Rome, hey? Maybe you should dress more like a native, you know?"

Like a joke, but not entirely. Flattered, intrigued, and already half stunned by the heat and the voluptuaries of vacation and the second carafe of the thin, chilled, local white wine, I impulsively reached behind me, unhooked myself, and so joined the Mediterranean mammaries. At first I felt naked and embarrassed, but with a bit more sun and wine and a lot of compliments from Russo, I began to feel proud and pretty, and then a little while after that, with all that sun and sand and the sea as blue as the twinkle in God's eye, I got to feeling as randy as an alley cat in April.

Which I would like to believe is why when all of a sudden Russo started screeching I should cover up because some guys from his father's village were coming down the beach, instead of doing like he said I got mad, and called him a cowardly chauvinistic hypocrite, which is why he started shoving my beach shirt down over my head, so I got even madder and yanked on the bows that were holding me together at the hips. Thereby transforming myself into a sunburnt Botticelli, and nearly getting both of us arrested.

"Unless nothing," Russo backed down immediately, and pretended to concentrate on the FDR Drive traffic while he mastered his own anger. Eventually though he said, "What I mean is, I don't get it. So he's a guy you knew in Russia, and so he's Americanized his name, and so he didn't recognize you. So what? And what's any of it got to do with this Brit publisher that I'm taking you halfway across New York to look at where he died?"

"I don't *know,* that's why I called you!" Anxiety was making my stomach hurt; I pulled my knees up, hugging them for security, rehearsing again the arguments with which I had wasted most of the night trying to convince myself. I mean, damnit, Mike was right. Vic Pedlar, New York City literary

agent, slick as butter on ice, and Vitya Korobeikin, ardent dissident, Soviet citizen, and my long-ago friend—how could they
possibly be the same person?

Because in the first place, how could Korobeikin even have
gotten *out* of the U.S.S.R.? He was no more Jewish than Ronald
McDonald!

So he was thrown out maybe, for dissident activities? That
had seemed possible, at first. Solzhenitsyn wasn't Jewish either,
no matter what the KGB tried to make people think. And don't
you just have to love a country where being Jewish is something
you can be *accused* of, like glue-sniffing or child-molesting? Still,
Jewish or not, some of the things Korobeikin had snarled in that
steamy shower might have earned him a one-way ticket to
Munich. Except that the little dissidents, the ones who weren't
best friends with the correspondents for the *Times* and the *Post,*
those guys got sent farther east, not out to the West.

And besides, if Vitya *had* gotten out, wouldn't he have contacted me? Written, telephoned? Dropped by? Lord knows,
since Gorbachev opened the birdcage door just a little, almost
every other Russian I had ever even set eyes on during my year
in Moscow had suddenly popped back into my life. Calling
from Goose Bay, Labrador, at four A.M. to see if I would come
pick them up "for a little visit." Writing that they soon would
be in Anchorage, Alaska, on business, and would I please arrange a series of lectures for them, honorarium plus expenses
and travel, in Disneyland, New York, and Paris? Even showing
up at the door, to say that INS was going to throw them out of
the country, unless someone guaranteed them support for six
months, and would I mind doing so, as a little favor?

One day I even got a collect call from a pharmacy in the
Bronx, to verify that I had indeed agreed to pay for a year's
supply of heart medicine for the second wife of the father-in-law
of someone who had had me to dinner in 1981, and was now
delivering a paper at Columbia; stunned, I had asked at least to

talk to this man, who informed me sunnily that the CD player he had to buy for his son had taken the last of his money and that, more darkly now, "Maya Zinovievna will die without that medicine, and I know you wouldn't want that!"

Which prompted even equable, understanding Paul Blank, still my husband then, to say, "You know, if I had known these people were going to follow you home, I don't think I'd have let you go there in the first place."

I was calmed for a time by the simplicity of that syllogism—if Korobeikin had come to this country he would have contacted me, but he hadn't, so therefore Pedlar couldn't be Korobeikin—but eventually the worms of doubt began to gnaw again, as they will in the dark, well after midnight.

Suppose Korobeikin *had* emigrated, somehow, and had settled in, even made a success of himself, but had never bothered to look me up, or perhaps did not know how to go about finding me.

Okay, ten years ago I wore my hair to the shoulder and now it's clipped up past the ear, and what was glossy black then has gone maybe a third gray, and I never wore contacts then, because the fluids were impossible to get in Moscow, but I *know* I actually weigh two pounds less now than I did then, and my chin has not fallen (well, not much), and . . .

What I am saying is, even as much as Vitya had changed in looks, there was still something familiar enough in Pedlar that I caught it that night, at Brent-Waterhouse's dinner. I almost hadn't changed at all, so how was it possible that Vitya Korobeikin could have failed to recognize me, at least a little?

So either I was mistaken, and Pedlar wasn't Korobeikin, or I was right, and he was Korobeikin, and he *had* recognized me.

And *he* didn't want *me* to remember.

It was the eerie shadows cast by that thought that had kept me awake virtually until dawn.

"Anyway, I never asked you to take me anywhere. Besides,

what's to look at in this hotel room, anyway?" I growled, rather than try to explain this all to Russo.

Russo's hands were at five and seven on the wheel, giving an odd nonchalance to the way he slithered through the turgid clots of the FDR, heading north. "What's to look at you can decide. You're the skeptic, remember?"

"What I mean is, how is that there's still, you know, effects there? Don't the hotels clean up immediately after a suicide, so they won't upset the other guests? Isn't that weird?"

"I don't think the other guests in this place are so easy to upset," Mike said, but didn't elaborate.

"How come they're letting us look at it?"

"Professional courtesy," Russo looked solemn, then, after a moment, he smiled at me. "Actually, I told a couple guys I happen to know in the precinct that you're this big-deal crime writer who wants some atmosphere for a book."

"Ah, *jeez*, Mike, you know I hate that. It's embarrassing, people asking how come they've never read any of my books, and then I have to explain they're just mysteries, for Girl Scouts, the only people who read them are like ten years old, and I don't think there are even so many of *them*."

"Don't worry, these guys, Stephen King could back a dump truck up to them, drop a couple tons of his books on their heads, they still wouldn't know who he was. Only thing these two ever read is Miranda rights and pushcart menus."

The car went left just then, sharply enough that I was thrown against the door, then back against the seat as Russo accelerated, to catch the yellow light ahead; if any part of his car crossed the interchange legally, it was at most his front bumper.

"God," I muttered, "cops like you, the city is saved."

"Hey," Russo let go of the steering wheel to chop at the air with his right hand, "in this town, you don't run the yellow, the guy behind you comes up your tail pipe, parks in your manifold."

We were on 125th Street, heading across town. New York. Stores on the ground floor, fire escapes zigzagging down the stories above, garbage piled out at the curb, thickets of metal posts holding up signs. NO PARKING. BUS STOP. LITTERING IS NASTY AND DIRTY SO DON'T DO IT. All ignored by the parade of passersby, every color, shape, and age you could imagine, strolling, sitting, running, walking, against a backdrop of electronics stores and coffee shops and more graffiti, under garlands of old tennis shoes, which dangled from every wire and lamp.

The nearer we got to Brent-Waterhouse's hotel, the more nervous I got. I told myself it was the neighborhood; what it really was though was a growing certainty that I was going to look like an ass in front of Mike Russo.

Then I remembered something. "Hey! Wait a minute! You said I'm a crime writer, correct, and that's why you're showing me this place? That must mean there's a crime, right? So what you're saying, the police actually *do* think Simon's death was suspicious?"

Russo was watching street signs, so the answer was slow. "Like I told you before, Midge, we have to suppose every death is suspicious. Unless you die in your bed, a hundred and seven years old, with twenty relatives standing vigil right up through when you took Extreme Unction, the department generally likes to at least look into things. But don't ask me, ask Chuck and Bertie . . ."

We pulled over to the curb and parked, meaning we had arrived. I looked around, startled. There are lots of relatively nice stretches of Amsterdam Avenue, but this wasn't one of them.

"*This* is Brent-Waterhouse's hotel?" I couldn't help bleating. The Van Horn Hotel, for all that it bore a resonant old Dutch name, was four windows wide, made of dark, crumbly old brick, most of the front covered by a rusted fire escape; all that announced its existence was a weathered neon sign, the dangling glass tubes of which plainly could no longer light up even the modest claim of "Rooms." The milk cartons, bread loaves, and cereal boxes set against a lot of the windows in the upper floors only confirmed what the two sun-faded Hot Wheels tricycles out front and the knots of little kids shrieking and playing tag had already made obvious.

"Simon Brent-Waterhouse lived in a welfare hotel?"

5

THERE is no graceful way to climb out of Mike Russo's low-slung car, and feeling stunned with surprise didn't make me any more coordinated. Our one evening together had taught me that Simon Brent-Waterhouse had not been nearly as rich as I had assumed, but that hardly prepared me for what the Van Horn suggested so starkly—that Simon Brent-Waterhouse had been *poor.*

"The mayor's office prefers us to avoid that phrase, but yeah, the city does pick up the tab for considerable of the Van Horn's guests," said a man who was sauntering toward Mike's car. From the top of his head to the middle of his nose he looked like Arnold Schwarzenegger; from the neck south he looked like Schwarzenegger upside down, narrow shoulders flaring to impressive hips. He stuck his hand out, grinning a grin that exposed a large pink wad of bubble gum. "Hiya, Lieutenant Wolanski, but a friend of Mike's can call me Gabe. You're his girl, right? The famous writer?" He sported the same rumpled raincoat and open-collared look as Russo, but his clothes were wrinkled and slept-in looking, covered in coffee stains.

I let my hand be shaken, too numb with digesting the welfare hotel to react to "famous writer" and "his girl."

"Goddamn your mouth, Wolanski," Russo growled, his face flushing to cordovan and tendons showing along his collar. Wolanski still had hold of my hand, so I could feel him tense, too; they were going to *fight?*

I never found out, because another person I hadn't noticed stepped forward, to shove the two men apart. "Jeezus, you two, give a lady a break, would you? Hi there, you must be Ms. Cohen. Isn't this just your idea of heaven, a wop on one side and a Polack on the other, both of them with more hormones than horse sense?"

The other "guy" was a girl. She was about my age, maybe two-inches taller and twenty-pounds heavier, squarely built, dyed blond hair twisted into a tight french braid, tied at the neck with a little girl's blue bow. Her handshake was crisp, and she smiled in a not-very-amused way that suggested she had said this many times before. "Detective Bertha Inderland, 'Bertie' to most of the wits on the force. You're thinking I don't look like Joe Friday, right? What you don't know is, if I want to, I can throw Wolanski over that car. You want to see me do it?"

Wolanski cringed in mock terror, while I shook my head numbly.

"Well, thank God for that," Wolanski relaxed, grinned again, shifting his pink wad to the other cheek. "Every time some joe makes a crack about lady cops, Bertie here throws me over some damn car. I keep trying to get her to throw the wiseguy over the car instead, but she says no, then they'd have her ass in for abusing the citizenry. Nothing on the books though about cops abusing cops. So you come to see this leaper's room?"

I cleared my throat, but didn't trust my voice yet. I put on a serious face such as I hoped a writer might have, and nodded. Bertha strode off ahead of us, her pink satin baseball jacket shimmering in the sun, the script "New York" logo in baby blue. Her rear end, crammed into black acid-washed jeans, looked powerful enough that she might simply have bounced up stairs.

She almost had to, because the elevator was out of order; judging by the smell, it had probably shorted out from all the people who peed in it. The Van Horn wouldn't have been a nice place when it was new, and that was a long time ago. The lobby was covered in lineoleum scarred with long black rectangles of cigarette burns, the chairs filled with people of indefinite ages and shapes, who were torpidly watching Fred Flintstone chase Barney Rubble through the snow of the ancient black-and-white set. Kids ran about, shouting and swearing at each other, shooting alarmingly real-looking pistols. The front desk was enclosed in heavy wire mesh, festooned with crude signs on which DON'T and NO predominated, hand-lettered on old shirt cardboards. Behind them a very plump young man with coppery skin and shiny black hair slumped indifferently on a high stool, his gaze darting lizardlike after the scampering kids. Wolanski caught his attention, pointed at the stairs; the man nodded, and we went up. The stairs smelled of things that the St. Regis doesn't, but exactly what remained a mystery, because the stairwells had no light bulbs.

Even Bertha seemed a shade less ebullient by the time we reached the sixth floor; between puffs I was renewing one of my semi-annual vows to join a health club. Wolanski wiped a film of sweat from his forehead, then sniffed. "My gosh, if it's atmosphere you wanted, there's more than enough of it here, isn't there?"

In addition to winded, I was also feeling confused, overloaded with conflicting information. That Simon Brent-Waterhouse, a man whom I had spent a lot of my adult life envying, should have ended up *here*. . . . Why? Where had his money gone? Had there even *been* money?

Against all expectation, Brent-Waterhouse's room proved reasonably neat when Detective Inderlund pushed open the door, and larger than I would have guessed. A bed stood against the wall to the right, head and footboard of tin tubing spreading a hammock of interwoven springs that must have made the devil's own racket when Simon eased his bulk down onto that nubbly cotton bedspread. A bureau with a mirror that could have belonged to any of my Aunt Dora's friends, a number of photos under a sheet of glass. To the left was a kind of alcove, fitted with a compact kitchen—sink, two electric rings, under-the-counter refrigerator. Coffee cups, wine glasses, and silverware in a tiny drain rack, and boxes and tins visible through an incompletely closed cabinet made it clear that someone had lived here. A battered round table and a rubber-backed orange-and-green throw rug completed the decor. Stacked next to the dresser were three cardboard cartons into which Simon Brent-Waterhouse's effects had obviously been stuffed. If anything, those boxes were even more depressing than that threadbare little room—five decades of a man's life, taking up less space than twelve gallon jugs of Giacobazzi wine.

Conscious that I was being closely watched by the three policemen, and sorely puzzled by the vividness of Brent-Waterhouse's unexpected poverty, I wandered across the little room, idly grabbed the handle of the closet, and jumped back, as if the knob had given off a spark.

"Damnit, I shouldn't have done that, right?" I said.

The two detectives laughed. The woman put her hands on her hips. "What do you think, we didn't go through the place? Anyway, there's a lady down the hall, this Brent-whoosiwatsis paid her to kind of pick up after him. She's the one who found him, but it wasn't until after she'd already cleaned up. The window was open, she said, and she went to close it . . ."

I glanced left, at the two sash windows, which faced out onto Eighth. "Which . . ."

"Naw, not those, that window back there, in the can," Wolanski pointed the stub of his ballpoint at the sliver of frosted glass that could just be seen through the bathroom door; as with my bathroom on Ocean Parkway, the jamb had been painted so many times the door wouldn't completely close, keeping the coiled porcelain intestines of a 1930s toilet on permanent view, crouched over checkerboard tiles of black and age-yellowed white. Most horrible of all, add a plastic shower curtain with Aubrey Beardsley's designs for Salome and you would have a virtual twin of my own bathroom.

"He went through *this* window?" I walked over in disbelief, to contemplate a window the size maybe of two pizza boxes, which you had to stand on the toilet to reach.

"That's the one he was found under," Bertha said, watching me closely. "In the airwell."

"Is it okay if I look?" I gestured at the window, miming a step up onto the toilet.

"Sure, sure," Wolanski brushed with his hands, shooing me on. "We've checked everything, there's nothing you could screw up."

I wobbled uncertainly onto the tub rim, put the other leg on the toilet seat—there was only a horse-collar seat, no cover—and then tried to peer out. The ledge hit me just at the chest, so all I could see through the open window was a brick wall, opposite. Suddenly two hands grabbed me at the waist, boosting me up.

I shrieked with surprise, clutching at the smooth tile encasing the window frame.

"Quit wiggling, would ya?" Russo grunted, when I squirmed around, "you maybe got skinny, but I still got to lift you."

"What are you doing?" I managed to move so that my knees were on the sill, wedging myself uncertainly on the same ledge where at home there was barely room for my shampoo, conditioner, and bath gel bottles.

"You want to look, look." Russo was flush, but I think more with embarrassment than with the effort. "I didn't drive you across half the city just so's you can decide you're too short."

"I'm not too short, damnit," I snapped automatically, even as I inched my way around, heart hammering, a death grip on the paint-flecked frame of the lowered upper window. There was no screen. I stuck my head out cautiously, praying that whatever was holding that window frame in place against the crumbly bricks would continue to do so.

What I put my head into was not so much an airwell as an air chimney, narrow enough that an especially long-legged person might almost have straddled it. If, that is, he was crazy enough to want to stand over six floors of nothing—that shaft seemed to plummet straight down to hell. The walls of the shaft were thick with that unidentifiable urban gunk that is particularly horrifying because you can't help but wonder whether the inside of your lungs looks the same.

When my eyes got a little more accustomed to the murk, I could see that the shaft was not used just for light and air; the bottom showed an indefinite collection of junk. Parts of a chair, a shattered television, a lot of glass, bits of wood, what looked like a kid's weapon or toy, a loop of rope at the end of a pole, a dead pigeon, a sneaker, papers, rags, and lots of other things so befouled by their years in the pit that there was no longer any way even of identifying them.

"God, how could anybody kill himself in a horrible place like this?" I shivered, then jerked my head back in, and slid awkwardly off the ledge. When I felt my skirt start climbing up my legs, I pushed away from the sill, managing to stumble on the toilet and then fall onto Russo.

He caught me, then let go of me, almost throwing me. I flushed and looked down, straightening my clothes.

When I looked up, Wolanski and Inderlund were studying me intently.

"What?" I finally asked, with that horrible suspicion you get just before you realize you've tucked the hem of your skirt into the back of your panty hose.

Wolanski and Inderlund exchanged glances, then looked over my shoulder at Russo, before Bertha said softly, "Mike says you knew this guy."

"A little. I mean, I knew of him, for a long time. And then, kind of by accident, we went out. But when I see this room . . ." I waved my hands vaguely, then shrugged. "I don't think I could say I knew him."

"You didn't tell them when it was you were out with him," Russo said behind me; he was trying to sound casual, but I could hear an edge of intensity in him as well. I felt like the rabbit with the electrodes in her head, just before the scientists shut the switch.

"It was the same night. The night he . . . uhh . . ." I waved at the window. "Jumped, I guess. The night he jumped."

"You went out with him, and then he killed himself?" Wolanski asked, neither tone nor expression making clear whether the lieutenant was making a joke or asking a question.

Either way, Wolanski irritated me. "Nobody's told me a time of death, so I actually have no idea. All I know is, Wednesday evening we were at the restaurant, Friday morning I read his obit in the paper." Then, because Wolanski and Inderlund were still watching me, I added, "That was the only time I ever saw the man. And it was mostly a business dinner."

"He's dead. You didn't know the man. And yet you're convinced it couldn't have been a suicide?" It was Inderlund asking now, after a glance at the two men. Her voice was businesslike, but with an undertone of sympathy, I suppose in case I did something female, like burst into tears, or rend all my clothing, tear out my hair, and begin beating my breasts.

Which is why I got a bit tart. "How many people do you know who go home and kill themselves, just to sort of round out a big evening?" I glared at Mike, because whatever he had relayed to them about what I told him over the phone, it was too much. "You weren't there, but believe me, the whole point of that evening was to *gloat*. The woman . . . Mike told you about the Russian woman, and her book?"

The two policemen nodded economically.

"Well, okay, the woman's book is worth a lot of money, and what I understood of the evening, she signed a paper that makes most of the money his. Which would seem a more pleasant way than the window for him to get out of this," I held up my hands, meaning the room. Then, because they still seemed blankly unconvinced, I added, "Besides, the condition he was in when we put him in that cab, I don't know how he'd even *find* the window."

"So he drank a lot, and the evening was a strained one?" Still Inderlund asking.

"He wasn't *drunk*, he was almost *unconscious!*"

"Why would it be so odd, later that night, when the liquor wears off, maybe the man feels remorse or something, maybe he's frightened of success or something, I don't know. But the window is right there, and . . ." Russo asking now, ending the question with a shrug, and pointing his chin at the bathroom window.

I was pretty sure that all Brent-Waterhouse would have known of remorse was how to *spell* it, but because this was Mike, all I said was, "Simon just didn't strike me as a guy who was going to race home and chuck himself out a window. That's all I'm saying."

"Simon?" Mike repeated softly, while Wolanski sneered, much louder, "This is it? Female intuition or some shit is what makes you so sure he couldn't have jumped?"

That made me mad.

"Well, goddamn it then, you don't want to believe me telling you psychological stuff, like that he wasn't the suicide type, or that he was in a good mood, so how could he kill himself? Fair enough. So then I won't ask *you* to explain a couple of other things that cross my mind, such as like how come most people when they decide to jump off something, they seem to want to choose like the George Washington Bridge or the Empire State Building, instead of some scummy airwell, six stories down into pigeon shit? Even so, it seems like there's one point that could use a little clearing up." I pointed melodramatically at the bathroom window. "Have you *measured* that thing, to see if it's even physically possible for Simon to squeeze his tush through that hole?"

"Well, the autopsy showed the guy didn't have a mark on him, other than what you'd get going head-first down six stories of air shaft. I suppose that made suicide seem a pretty logical conclusion," Inderlund offered in a conciliatory, if ambiguous, way.

Without even thinking, I shot back, "Why would someone have to even lay a finger on him? Maybe he was still unconscious, and somebody *stuffed* him out the window! Or maybe there was a gun, somebody forced him to get up on the ledge?"

"Jesus, Midge!" Russo raised his hands in exasperation. "What kind of stupid threat is that? Commit suicide or I'm going to kill you?"

Making myself look as severe as I possibly could, I pulled the face that Pearl makes when somebody tries to squirt sample perfume on her on the first floor of Bloomingdale's. "I don't think that Simon killed himself, period, end of conversation."

Another glance was passed around among the policemen, and

then Wolanski pulled out a piece of paper from his jacket, extended it towards me. "So you wouldn't read this as a suicide note then, huh?"

I looked at the pair of them carefully, then at Russo, before I accepted the proffered page. The poor quality photocopy trembled in my hands, making the single typewritten line somewhat hard to read:

"September twenty-five, Nineteen ninety—. To all and sundry. I hereby relinquish any claim to the literary or other works of Polina Volkova."

The signature, if that's what it it was, was a huge curlicue S followed by what might have been a cardiogram, or the record of an earthquake in Australia; not only could I not say whether that squiggle really was Simon's signature, I didn't even know whether it spelled "Brent-Waterhouse."

"He made a photocopy of his suicide note?" I asked, handing the paper back to Wolanski.

He looked a little irritated, refolding the paper and returning it to his inner pocket. "That's not the original, of course. But let's say you found the original in this room, maybe stuck to that mirror there with a wad of gum." He lifted his dimpled chin in the direction of the dresser. "You buy it as a suicide note then?"

New York City has given Western civilization many things. Egg creams. The Macy's Thanksgiving Day parade. Donald Trump. None of these is as useful as the City's most characteristic invention—the question that you use to answer a question.

"Do I buy it? The question is, do *you* buy it?"

But Wolanski was a New Yorker too.

He smiled, his eyes flat gray. "You tell me, you see a typewriter around here anywhere?"

My eyes widened in surprise, as I understood that all of my objections had only confirmed conclusions they had already drawn.

I guess because she understood what was going through my

head right then, Detective Inderlund put an arm around me. "See, the problem for us is, even if this Brent-Waterhouse didn't commit suicide, he's still dead, which kind of points us toward the idea that somebody else killed him. Logical, right? So what Mike thought, when he called, was since you're so sure this Brent-Waterhouse person wouldn't kill himself, maybe you have some idea about who might have, and why."

6

THE detectives let me do all the speculating, of course, denying or confirming nothing, but it didn't require tremendous brains to work out that if the publisher had been killed, then the reason would be something to do with Volkova's manuscript. From there it was no leap at all to the suspicion that that something, whatever it was, involved Pedlar.

Who was really Korobeikin. A Russian, who was an old friend, only he hadn't acknowledged that he even recognized me. *Recognized me?* He hadn't even acknowledged he was Russian!

From which it was a fast scary slither down the chute into all *sorts* of horrifying speculations, of a kind that a lot of bestsellers are built on; variations on *Three Days of the Condor,* except that in most of the scenarios I could imagine, instead of getting to be Robert Redford, I seemed to end up dead.

That wasn't why I was chewing my knuckle almost raw, though, too preoccupied even to make small talk with Mike Russo.

When we left the Van Horn the sun was inching toward a swelling wet sponge of clouds above the Jersey side, gold and red beams bouncing around Manhattan, giving the city the sparkle of Oz, but doing nothing to make the wind less chilly and raw. The people on the streets all seemed to be scurrying somewhere, glancing about nervously before they ducked into doorways, or scuttled into stores.

Russo offered to take me home, or out to lunch, or if for some reason I wanted to, even up to the Cloisters or over to Grant's Tomb, but after the Van Horn, all I knew for certain was that I would never go to sleep again if I didn't find something out.

"Just where in the devil did Brent-Waterhouse's money *go?*" I demanded of Russo, for maybe the hundredth time.

"How in the hell do I know?" he growled back, glumly studying the Broadway traffic ahead. "Do you know for a fact that he even *had* money?"

"He had to have had money, he *had* to!" I insisted, even as I remembered that dreadful dinner in the restaurant, his asking about my credit card. Somehow I was more shattered by the dreariness of the Van Horn and what it said of Brent-Waterhouse's finances than I had been even by his death. I mean this was a man who hobnobbed with all those good Russian writers, who got to travel the world selling books he cared about, who could contribute articles to the *New York Times Book Review* and the *New Republic* and *Harper's* and *New York Review of Books* just about whenever he wanted to! Who had everything I had ever dreamed of having, plus a lot that I never dared dreamed about besides . . . and he had ended up living at the Van Horn?

Call it being a novelist (my preference), or call it being a nosy-parker (Pearl's usual reaction to my curiosity); I was not going to go back to Brooklyn until I got some idea of why Simon Brent-Waterhouse was broke.

Even if that meant that my tender new detente with Mike Russo was withered by my demand to be dropped at West Forty-third, so I could talk to Walter Goldberg, junior assistant editor at the *Times Book Review,* literary maven knowledgeable to the point of insufferability, and, we both had been shocked to learn, a friend from upstate.

"You have a friend at the *New York Times?*" Mike had been first surprised, then suspicious.

"An acquaintance, somebody I know," I said, hoping my voice made clear I was sorry I had mentioned it.

Russo looked straight ahead, his jawbone knotting and un-knotting while he tapped his thumbs on the steering wheel. Then, reluctantly, he asked, "A girl friend? I mean a good friend?"

I let another block or two slide by before I answered, "He's a friend, that's all, somebody I knew from upstate." Meaning, "mind your own business, Mike Russo."

Which he did, until Times Square, where we got seriously bogged in traffic. Then, his voice almost as tense as the first time the subject of sex had come up between us, and his eyes straight ahead, he said softly, "Just what I was thinking, at the paper and all, maybe this guy could give you a little help, get your books reviewed?"

"What help?" I snapped, "I don't need help."

"With your career. Your writing. I mean, you've done three books, so where's the reviews?"

Ever since I had chanced across Walter Goldberg last summer I had wondered the same thing myself, whether he could help me, but I wasn't going to tell Russo that. Instead I let myself out of his car, slammed the door, and walked away, leaving only an airy "Thanks!" as a possible link to ever speaking to him again.

I had stumbled over Wally at a party my agent was throwing on her terrace overlooking Central Park, for another of her clients whose book had just moved onto the *Times* bestseller list. Sixteenth position, with an asterisk, which meant that it was only on the list because it was indistinguishable in sales from number fifteen, and the book was stupid besides, some space fantasy about over-hormoned women warriors who couldn't have looked less like the dumpy, nearsighted, and now suddenly wealthy author, who was smiling nervously near the punchbowl, pulling up her sagging panty hose. It was not the sort of party where I would have been in a good mood even if Mike Russo and I had not just recently come back from a trip to Sicily together, which had made it seem like a good idea that maybe we shouldn't even go to the corner store together. My life, artistic and personal, was just entering what my future biographers will know as The Great Bran Period. Do yourself a favor and come, my agent had said. There'll be lots of people from the industry there, come mingle, network a little. You'll kill yourself if you miss this chance.

So I went, did some grim mingle, mingle, mingle, wishing most of the evening that I had chosen killing myself instead.

Until I mingled into Wally. Head back, eyes cold, and face sporting a mustache that was all that had survived from his Cornell beard, wearing Brooks Brothers tweeds and worsted cut to emphasize a new slimness that he hadn't had when he was an associate professor of comparative literature at Cornell, Walter Goldberg was scarcely to be recognized.

Except for his laugh.

It was that crowlike raucous derisive *noise* that had brought us together in the first place, way back at some regional Dostoevsky conference at SUNY Binghamton we were both indifferently and torpidly attending. Resigned to the slack-jawed boredom to which the stupidity of most of the papers delivered at such conferences usually reduces me, I was electrified by a guffawing laugh, a glorious mocking noise, which managed to imply somehow that not only was the speaker an insufferable moron, but so were his parents, his children, and the neighbor boy who mowed his lawn. I had sought out the laugher at the first coffee break.

We became lunch friends. Nothing more, because I was married, and he was married, he was tenured at Cornell and I wasn't, at Ithaca, and probably also for lots of other reasons too. But both of us read a lot, and enjoyed making fun of our colleagues who didn't, and, I suppose, we shared a great deal of New Yorkness, which among all that Upstate stuck out like high heels in a cowbarn. It was enough in common to let me look forward with real excitement to the two or three lunches a month we managed to meet for.

Until my Great Aunt Dora dropped dead, leaving me her three-room co-op on Ocean Parkway and just enough money to make it worth risking becoming a writer. Which, after a lot of indecision and staying up all night torturing myself, I did, so suddenly that I didn't even discuss it with my husband, let alone some guy I had lunch with on alternate Thursdays. That probably explains why Wally dropped his wine glass, when I shouted in his face.

"Wally!"

Eyes icy and sharp, face scowling. "Please, my name is *Walter* . . ." Then, face paling, recognition. "My God, *Midge!*"

"Please, my name is *Margaret*," I had laughed, as he steered me around his puddle of zinfandel and over to a corner of the terrace, behind a boxed juniper.

His naked ring finger, his sudden nervous urgency, and the glittering, gusty glamour of shivering on a parapet about a thousand stories above Central Park West misled me in interesting directions about why he wanted our conversation private, for about ten minutes. Then I understood that Wally's—sorry, Walter's—nervousness didn't originate in his heart.

"You mean nobody *knows* you're a lit. prof. from Cornell?" I had blurted out, when it dawned on me what was being begged of me there behind the potted plants.

A nervous lick at the canapé cream cheese stuck in his spiffy new mustache. "The paper knows, of course. Everybody there knows, it's not exactly a secret, but for *them* . . ." He waved his hand at the terrace and library behind him. Men in silk sports coats and no ties, with ponytails, being urgently quizzed by willowy beauties wearing gold earrings the size of kitchen appliances. Swarthy, grizzled old men who looked like Haganna veterans or rug merchants or philanderers, being courted by fresh-faced graduate students of indeterminate sex. Here and there, befuddled-looking types with thick glasses and ill-fitting suits, uncomfortably cradling wine glasses and longing for the exits. And the talk, a buzz of "A hundred grand for *that* piece of . . ." and "She's, what, the fifth one now, and they're always the same age . . ." and "Of course Sue Faludi would have a cow to hear me say this, but . . ."

Your average literary cocktail party. Jealousy, sex, money, power, and—here and there—real talent. In a word, the whole literary world, every part of which lives and dies by the *New York Times Book Review.* At least some of the editorial decisions for which, I had just found out, were being made by a guy who two years ago was still red-penciling blue books.

You can see why Walter wouldn't want people to know that, can't you?

If so, then you can also see why I would do what I did, which was, very graciously and over a lot of lunches that I paid for, blackmail him into letting me try a review.

Which would probably also explain why Walter always called me, never giving me his telephone extension.

"Mr. Goldberg expecting you?" the uniformed and muscle-bound guard asked indifferently from his desk behind the barrier, not even bothering to look at me; instead his eyes scrutinizing the pass of each and every one of the people who were streaming through the metal-detecting gate. Every few seconds he checked something off on a paper he clutched to a clipboard.

Having to stand at a barrier explaining myself while everyone around me is let in does not bring out my best side, especially when what the guard is protecting looks more like a liquor store and check-cashing *bodega* in Spanish Harlem, than what you'd expect of the *New York Times.* The *Times* you would expect to have a lobby like maybe the Plaza Hotel, or at least the *Daily Planet,* in the Superman movies, instead of this scuffed linoleum floor, the walls painted mental-hospital green, and the floor-to-ceiling bulletproof glass separating the front door from the stairs.

I had already made Mike Russo hate me, probably forever, so I wasn't about to be nice to this rent-a-cop. "If you'd been listening the first time, you'd have heard me say, no he isn't. Not specifically today, anyway. In general, yes, he'd be expecting me, because I am doing some work for him."

"Call him then, make an appointment."

I was just about to explain—in a roundabout way—that Walter was such a pompous ass about working at the *Times* that he would only give me the telephone for the main receptionist, not his own extension number (in retaliation for which I had given him Pearl's number, not mine, saying she was "my secretary"), when the guard suddenly shot to his feet, beamed ear to ear, and barked, "Morning, sir!"

Someone who looked a lot like my Great Uncle Izzie—short, bald, big ornate ears, and a figure that wouldn't have been out of place on a snowman—walked into the lobby and past the security desk; unprepossessing as the man looked, all foot traffic halted, and people in the gate actually scurried to get out of the man's way. The chipped gray doors of the elevator gaped, the man disappeared, and the lobby returned to normal.

Which reminded me what the *Times* was like. A trifle status-conscious.

"I can't, somebody just broke the window in my Jag, swiped my Rolodex," I said, making my New York accent so world-weary and nasal that I think I hurt something. "So can't you just at least *call* Mr. Goldberg, to ask him to meet me down here in the lobby?"

"Sorry, miss. . . . Can I help you?" He looked over my shoulder.

I turned; it was a member of New York's most terrifying social group—a bike messenger. Wind-tangled blond hair hung below his shoulders, sweat-corroded gloves with the fingertips cut away, Spandex shorts to the knee, clutching legs so thin he looked as though putting on the pants had made him six inches taller, like when you squeeze a toothpaste tube. Chewing gum to some internal rhythm that clicked over at several hundred RPMs, the messenger flashed the label of the packet and then bounded through the gate, taking the stairs about three at a time, like a Visigoth on his way to sack Rome.

"Him you let in and I have to wait?" I couldn't help snarling at the guard.

The guard didn't even shrug. After a bit more silent raging, jostled by the streams of people in and out, I took a gamble, and went over to Hyman's Delicatessen.

Guaranteed Double Glatt, half the customers with beards and earlocks so long they can't keep it out of their buckwheat kasha and stuffed derma, every table with two kinds of horseradish (regular and purple), and a faded sign over the cash register that I'm sure is supposed to rhyme—"Send a Salami to Your Son in the Army."

"Jesus, Wally . . . Walter," I couldn't help asking, the first time I took him out to lunch, at his choice of places, "all of

Manhattan to pick from, couldn't you at least find one maybe that the waiter doesn't put his thumb in your beef-and-barley soup?"

Walter had paused, challah in one hand, soup spoon the size of a hubcap in the other. The gold aviator glasses he wore would have made his face look severe, even bellicose, except that the left corner perched up higher than the right; then, with the faint jerk of his neck that always made Walter seem surprised, as if he had just noticed you in front of him, he said, with great solemnity, "This place is a *tradition* with the guys at the paper, Midge. All of us eat here, if we're not on a story or something."

Which is why I hoped that I would find him there now. It probably also is why the food in Hyman's tastes like marinated pizza box to me, because whenever I'm in there I can't forget that where *my* midlife crisis had gotten me to a three-room co-op in Brooklyn and a writing career that seems doomed to remain "promising" until I die of old age, *Walter's* midlife crisis had landed him on the staff of the *New York Times*.

Which he enjoyed with such thorough, pompous zest, such a solemn air of having been with "the paper" ever since he was born in Ben Hecht's bottom drawer, that at least it seemed worth sloshing down all the soup and tea I had to order so that the waiters wouldn't chase me away from my rear table at Hyman's, for the almost two hours it took until I finally spotted Walter, peering and craning on tiptoes in search through the lunch crowd for a stool at the counter.

I stood and shouted his name, relieved and very waterlogged.

"Midge," he acknowledged my exuberant wave, with a look that didn't seem precisely pleased.

"Hi, Walter, look, I was waiting for you, I've got a table . . . hey! I *said* don't clear that stuff away! . . . Come on, back here . . ." I took Walter's arm, glaring at the age-spotted waiter who was trying to shovel my plates into a busboy's tub.

Walter resisted.

"Uh, look, Midge, I've uh . . ." he looked over his shoulder.

"You're working? Look, I won't bother you . . . you even *touch* that table again and I'm never ordering another cup of soup in here in my life! Walter, please, just give me a minute, okay? There's some things I've got to ask you."

Now Walter actually jerked his elbow away, turned to another man who was on his left, and said, "Madison, just a second, okay? This is . . . someone I know."

Madison was thin, immaculately groomed, crisply tan, and a good foot taller than Walter. Khaki suit, yellow tie, and the sort of sunglasses you would wear if you were going to bomb the bridges at Toko-ri. I smiled, half-expecting to be introduced; instead Walter stepped into me, almost knocking me down.

"*Jee*zuz, Midge," he hissed, glaring. "You want to talk to me, you phone and set up an appointment, you *don't* just accost me in a public place."

"What are you, Madonna? You don't want to be bothered in a deli, I suggest you pay for some bodyguards, okay?" I hissed back, the cannonball of soup in the bottom of my gut reminding me how long I had been waiting for him to show up.

"I'm sorry I ever took you to this place, if that's how you're going to be. It's abusing a confidence, that's what it is. I wouldn't ever have taken you to the paper's deli, if I'd known you weren't going to respect the fact that our work requires anonymity. Christ, we let it get out that people from the paper eat here, next thing you know every agent and author in town would be hanging out here, and then how would we ever get any work done?"

"In the first place, it's you that's bellowing about being from the paper, not me. In the second place, this is work? Picking up a tray of sandwiches is work?" I pointed at Madison, who looked like some sort of WASP anthropologist preparing a display in a museum of Jewish life, as he checked the white bags, neatly arrayed in a cardboard box that once had held Dr. Brown's Diet Cream Soda.

"Walter, you get the drinks, okay?" Madison ordered. "I'll be outside."

Walter's shoulders fell. "It's Monday," he explained, then put his dark glasses on again. I guess I looked blank, because he added, "The day we close the section."

"And they send you two out for sandwiches?" I was stunned. This is Walter's big-deal job, that I was dying of envy over?

Walter shuffled, looking over at the counter, where a harassed-looking woman, half-specs on a cord dangling over a bosom the size of Mount Rushmore, had just set down another cardboard carton—this from Mother's Whitefish Balls in Lo-Cal Broth—and was now looking around for someone to take it.

"It's kind of a tradition, the paper pays for lunch on Monday . . . everyone stays in the office, talking about what we're going to run, where stuff is going to be positioned . . ."

"Yeah, but why don't they just have a messenger bring it up?"

"Coffee's getting cold, boychik," the woman observed, her voice managing to imply that Walter was also a clinical moron.

"Yeah, yeah, I'll take the box, just a minute," Walter barked. "Anyway, your coffee's lousy even when it's hot," he added, then made a face at me. "Paper's trying to save money. The editors managed to hang onto the sandwiches, because it's a tradition. But the damned pencilheads up in accounting, they won't spring for the delivery boy to bring it over."

"And so they make you new boys come get the food, right?" I couldn't resist a grin, which I knew was at Walter's expense.

He knew it too. He shrugged, turned away, picked up the box. Everything from the faint flush on his neck to the way his shoulders were hunched told me he knew he was a sandwich boy, but that it still beat being a professor, by very long yards.

Who was I to argue, especially if I needed a favor from Walter?

Which I did.

"Hey, listen, I'm sorry, Walter. I didn't mean to, you know, cause problems. I just have to ask you something."

His back to me, Walter struggled a bit trying to decide whether to be an old friend or an arrogant son of a bitch. I guessed I had about thirty seconds to hook or lose him, probably forever.

"It's about something kind of strange, actually," I babbled. "Maybe even something that might make an item. For the section."

Walter turned around, his entire body making plain how unlikely it was that I might know something suitable for "the section" that he didn't know.

So, panting and wondering whether my nerves would make me barf my liters of barley soup, I gave as quick and coherent an account as I could, of Simon Brent-Waterhouse's curious demise and Polina Volkova's book.

Someone jostled into Walter, nearly knocking the coffee from his hands. He righted the box, then asked, "You know this Volkova or something?"

"No," I answered, a little mystified that it was only to this part of my story that he had responded. "I mean, I met her, at that dinner, and we had a pretty good . . ."

"So you wouldn't know who she's going with?" he interrupted.

"I only spoke to her that one night, Walter. Anyway, it was business, so nobody had dates or anything." Except me, I didn't add.

Walter barked his boy-are-you-stupid laugh. "With, with. Who's she *signed* with? Who's going to publish her?"

"From what I could tell that night, that's an awfully complicated question. In fact . . ."

"What complicated?" Walter interrupted. "I remember right, she's a client at International Creative, correct?" Walter shrugged. "Those guys're so hot right now they could get an ape in print. What I hear, though . . ." he thought for a moment, as if trying to recall something he had heard. "This is the hooker from the Kremlin, right? Yeah, there's been a lot of buzzing about the package, now that you mention it. Big money swinging in behind her, if I am thinking of the right people."

"Well, yeah, and that's why everybody thinks it's so weird that Brent-Waterhouse would want to kill himself, if he was going to make a lot of money off this."

"Everybody? You're saying it's not just you, the cops aren't buying that it's a suicide either?"

I shook my head, then, upon further reflection, nodded. "They seemed pretty suspicious," I finally said, unable to decipher the grammar of Walter's question well enough to answer it.

"Are they saying that Brent-Waterhouse was *murdered?*" he asked then, the scorn making it pretty plain that if they weren't, then I was wasting his time.

So I just raised my eyebrows and looked solemn, before whispering, "Actually, it could be worse than that. There's some things about the case, that, well. . . . This *could* be an issue of . . . national security."

7

I don't know what it is—maybe having done their bar mitzvah training and hearing their voices break at just about the same time as the New Frontier and James Bond and the Cuban missile crisis and the Green Berets and JFK boffing Marilyn Monroe in Mary Lincoln's bedroom—but there is nothing that gives men like Walter a rocket in the pocket faster than those two words—"national security."

"Walk back with me," Walter said through clenched teeth, his expression such that I could practically hear "The Battle Hymn of the Republic" in the background. "I better jot some of this down."

So I did get into the *Times* building, finally. The biggest pleasure, though, proved to be smirking at the guard as Walter ushered me through, because the rest of the building made the lobby look elegant. Maybe there are nice parts someplace, but where Walter took me the *Times* looked like it had been decorated by the same guy who had done Humphrey Bogart's office in *The Maltese Falcon*. Dusty metal slat venetian blinds, banks of wooden desks that I swear to God must have been bought surplus from my junior high school, and long strips of fluorescent tubes overhead, each of them buzzing louder than bees in clover. There was even a real water cooler in the corner, like you usually see only in comic strips.

"Walter?" a man put his head out of a corner office. He could have been a waiter at the deli—the sort of complexion you get from decades of fluorescent lighting and pastrami, the kind of body you only find on old accountants, and silvery eyes with all the snap and sparkle of one of those garlics you find at the bottom of pickle barrels. "What's with the coffee? We're waiting . . ."

Poor Walter twitched like a galvanized mouse. "Just a sec, damn place was . . . you know how it is at lunch, here, here's the box. . . ." Flustered, he balanced the box on one hand, unhooked his glasses with the other, leaving them dangling from one ear as he raced into what was obviously his superior's room, but different from the large room where I was standing only because it was partitioned off. I could see a clutch of people sitting around a cluttered conference table, those nearest the door eyeing me. I tried to look as authorial as I could, at least until Walter's boss gazed at me. His glance suggested that even if Cervantes and Sholokhov had come in to announce they were collaborating on a joint sequel, *The Quiet Don Quixote*, he would have asked them to wait in the lobby.

"Okay, okay, okay," Walter was reciting, like a mantra against panic, as he scurried back, flung himself down at a desk in the middle of the room, and started tapping at a computer. "Let's get this down . . ."

He made the keys go "pokata-pokata-pokata" for a bit, giving me time to reflect on the difference between Walter's new desk, and his old one, which was in a corner office at Cornell, with a view of Cayuga Lake and the changing foliage of campus. Where he had graduate students who brought *him* coffee, and sandwiches too, if he wanted.

"One thing I don't get, though," Walter looked up, "let's say the guy *was* killed, and I guess I can buy that this Pedlar is who you say he is, a Russian. But what's that got to do with national security?"

Trust Walter to put his finger on the soft spots in my news item. I mean, since when does a perfectly ordinary person such as myself stumble onto a KGB assassination? In actual real life, wouldn't the chances of an everyday person accidentally uncovering some sort of deep and devious Kremlin agent be about the same as I would have for getting hit by a meteorite, or winning the Publishers' Clearinghouse Sweepstakes? Especially *now*, when the KGB is practically having to sell fudge in Red Square to keep itself in operating funds?

"Well," I slid into the chair at the end of Walter's desk, "that's where I was sort of hoping you could help me."

Walter's hands dropped from the keyboard, the silliness of having his sunglasses still dangling from his right ear not doing much to dilute his irritation. He glanced at the corner office, where people seemed still to be eating.

"You want *my* help?" Walter almost shouted. "I thought you were *giving* me something."

"You give, you get. It's that kind of town," I said, trying to sound like Lauren Bacall. "I've got some ideas, but . . ."

"Ideas," Walter repeated, making it sound like something I should put ointment on.

I ignored him, instead describing the Van Horn, and the squalor in which Brent-Waterhouse had shuffled off his mortal coil. When I was done, Walter seemed more interested, even if he was still affecting indifference.

"Where did his money go? Who the hell knows? Girls, or up his nose, or . . ." Walter shrugged, sneaking a peek over his shoulder at the meeting I was keeping him from. "Besides, what makes you think he had any to begin with?"

"Jeezuz, Walter, Sirin Press . . ."

"Sirin Press, Sirin Press!" Walter laughed. "You knew anything about Sirin Press, you'd wonder why Brent-Waterhouse didn't take up indoor skydiving about five years ago."

"Things were really as bad as that? I got the idea that night, at that dinner, that Brent-Waterhouse had big hopes for Volkova's book . . ."

Walter's smile made me feel like he was beating me badly at Jeopardy! or Scrabble. "If he published it? Look, for the sake of argument we'll pretend all the *ifs* are out of the way . . ."

"The *ifs*?"

"Sure. *If* he forced this Russian hooker to sign with him, and *if* he had been able to get her actually to write the damn thing . . ."

"Write it? I thought it was all written."

Walter made a maybe-but-I-doubt-it shrug. "Have you actually seen a manuscript? Anybody you know actually physically *touched* a manuscript?"

I shook my head.

"So," Walter nodded, point proven. "Anyway, one more *if* . . . *if* Sirin Press had been able to promote the book, distribute it, get it reviewed, hype it, *sell* it . . . which I might add is an *if* about the size of maybe Texas, because the one thing you can say about Sirin's books is that there isn't a bookstore in the known universe that carries them . . ."

I waved my hands fast, to get Walter's attention, but maybe also to erase what he was saying. "Okay, okay, without the Sirin. The book was still his, even if Sirin didn't publish it. The rights I mean. He could sell them or something, and still make a lot of money, right?"

Walter thought for a moment, tapping the stem of his glasses against his teeth. "No, I'm sure I heard this right," he said after a moment. "Whatever money Brent-Waterhouse might have made off Volkova, all of it and more would have simply gone down the toilet."

"I've always hated that expression."

"Well, whatever you want to call it, but your publisher boyfriend was broke city. Tapped-out. Chapter-fucking-eleven down to his socks. In fact, guy who was telling me this said Sirin has like about a dozen judgments against it, with at least that many more suits pending."

"Come on, who would sue Brent-Waterhouse? Sirin Books is one of the premier publishers of modern Russian literature. Without him . . ."

"Who would sue him? How about . . ." And Walter with extravagant pleasure ticked off a dozen names. A regular Who's Who of modern Russian literature, emigré and domestic.

"Jesus . . . but *why?*" I asked, numb with surprise. "Simon *saved* a lot of those people. Nobody would even *know* about them as writers, if it hadn't been for him!"

Walter barked his mocking laugh again, then got up, walked to the corner office. I thought for a second he was simply abandoning me, too stupid even to be worth saying good-bye to. Instead though he spoke a few words to the fish-eyed man at the head of the table, then came back. "I've got a couple minutes yet, he says. They're still working on the front of the section . . . anyway, do you know what a Ponzi scheme is?"

I just stared at Walter.

"A pyramid scheme?"

I shook my head.

Walter sighed his disgust with the general ignorance of the universe he was forced to inhabit, then explained, "Brent-

Waterhouse spends his authors' royalties. Spent, I guess. He was publishing them on the promise that he was keeping their royalties in accounts over here . . ."

"Well, he'd have to! When he started publishing Soviets could go to jail for *years* for possession of hard currency, and even if they had it, there was no way any of those writers could have *used* dollars back then!"

"Precisely. 'Back then,' " Walter nodded. "Which is probably why Brent-Waterhouse decided there was no risk in using whatever came in to cover what was outgoing. Which if I remember right at one time included a used Rolls and an apartment in some fancy part of London. Mayfair or something."

"A flat," I corrected weakly. "In England they're called flats."

Walter lolled back in his chair, ignoring the interruption, knitting his fingers together behind his head. "Anyway, early 1970s, when he got Sirin started, it probably seemed like a good bet, the Soviet government would be pretty damn likely to make sure none of Simon's poor schmucks was ever going to get over here to ask for any royalties. In fact, likeliest of all back then was that one book would come out, and then the author is off to rot away in some gulag somewhere."

I strained to digest this portrait of a Brent-Waterhouse much uglier and far more mercenary than the icon I had been recently been painting for myself.

"Wait a second, though." I grabbed at what I hoped was more than a straw. "Some of those people Simon published, they've been out of the U.S.S.R. a decade or more! If he was doing what you say, wouldn't Sirin have been caught out long ago?"

"That's why I call it a Ponzi!" Walter sat forward triumphantly. "At first there was enough cash sloshing through Sirin that Brent-Waterhouse could handle three or four of his writers, giving 'em partials, like robbing Pyotr to pay Pavel," he chuckled at his own wit, then shrugged. "But then more and more and more of them started to come . . ."

"And all of the writers wanted their back royalties!" I finished for him, understanding in a flash.

Except I hadn't, completely. Walter gave me a for-that-you-get-a-B-plus smile. "Well, what actually kicked poor old Sirin down the chute was that Keystone Kops coup of theirs, because right after it Russia legalized private possession of dollars. So like last I heard, Sirin was on the short end of about seven or eight hundred thousand. Not to mention court costs, punitive damages, legal fees, accrued interest, and a few other goodies. Plus which the IRS was beginning to sniff around, wondering whether any of Simon's fancy bookkeeping had maybe slopped over into his tax work."

"Wow," was the best I could do.

Walter was not one to forego the pleasures of giving a downed opponent one more whack. "See, that's why I have trouble buying what you're telling me. Troubles like that guy had, it's no wonder he'd put himself out the window." Then, with an air of having won an argument, he shut off his computer screen and stood up.

"True," I stared up at him, then added, "but what you've told me, it sounds like if he didn't oblige by killing himself, there'd be plenty of volunteers, happy to do the job for him."

I had the satisfaction at least of watching Walter sit back down again, his eyes staring straight into mine. Waiting for me to say more, to justify my suspicions.

Which forced me to do some very fast thinking, because while I had lots of suspicions, they stubbornly refused to add up to anything sensible. For one thing, so Victor Pedlar was very probably also Vitya Korobeikin, who either hadn't recognized me or didn't wish to—but so what? It's a long way from *that* to Kim Philby.

Not to mention that Pedlar was a literary agent, not a nuclear scientist! What earthly good was it going to do the Kremlin to be "running" a midtown, big-deal author's representative? Actually though, on that one, I had a glimmer of an answer, even as I was wondering what use a secret agent-literary agent could possibly have been to the Kremlin.

There have always been two schools of thought about the KGB. One is that since the Soviet Union couldn't sweep its streets, harvest its potatoes, or make a paint that wouldn't wash off in the first rain, then the general efficiency of its KGB might reasonably have been expected to be somewhere between that of the Three Stooges and the infield for your average office softball team.

Then there is the other school, which sees the KGB behind every blemish on the face of modern life. *Roe v. Wade?* Secretly and personally planned by Feliks Dzherzhinsky in 1916, as a way to lower Western populations, and snip the moral fibers of America. Cocktail waitresses modeling lingerie at truck stops? Ditto on the moral fiber, plus it clogs up interstate commerce and distracts America from noticing the steady advance of socialism. The collapse of socialism in Poland, Czechoslovakia, Hungary, East Germany, Romania, Bulgaria, Mongolia, Ethiopia, Benin, Albania, and now even, God help us, Russia? That of course only shows the depths of KGB deviousness, their willingness to sacrifice half the globe in order to make the West complacent, while the spymasters pursue their program of world domination, which will proceed through the capture of the American college curriculum, particularly the social sciences and humanities.

Since there is a pretty close correlation between which school you subscribe to and the amount you know about the Soviet Union, I normally can be counted in the first (which of course those of the second persuasion would say is only to be expected of dupes like me). Today, though, I wondered . . .

Well, what if Pedlar *had* been a Kremlin plant? Wouldn't a

literary agent be perfectly placed for active disinformation? Vigorous intellectual fifth-columnry, flooding America with novelizations of movies, and psychic diet books, and *schtup*-and-tell exposes by the sons, daughters, and lawnboys of movie stars? Not to mention already all those 127-page "serious literary novels" where the characters do nothing but drink Diet Fresca and talk about life, until one of them nails the other one's ears to the floor, or somebody smothers a baby?

Crazy, correct?

Except that if it *were* true—and God knows the Soviets in their prime had had their filthy fingers in some spectacularly bizarre espionage stunts, such as killing Georgi Markov with a poisoned umbrella, or inducing a psychotic Turk to shoot at the Pope—then who stood immediately to suffer, if Polina did write her book?

Well, it was only a guess, but wouldn't an obviously sexy topic be an exposé of secret agents in America? Times maybe have changed, but there's still a lot of residual distrust of the Kremlin, out there in the Kmart heartland, that a photogenic Polina Volkova could help play to, in every tabloid in America. So let's say Vitya/Victor really is a deeply planted secret agent, and somehow—chance? design?—he ends up representing Volkova. For a moment that made no sense, until I realized that it made perfect sense—being her literary agent, Vitya would be in the best position for spin control. Tactfully, unobtrusively, he could push Volkova's book in the direction in which it would do the least harm to him, and to the Kremlin. Trivialize the whole issue into a silly, spacy sex confession, that would also make himself—and who knows, his masters as well?—a lot of money. While also keeping the nasty, more serious issues unraised.

Which he could do only if Simon Brent-Waterhouse's claim to Volkova's book were removed.

I could feel Walter staring at me, and I knew I had to say something. I also knew that all of this barely made any sense inside my head, and the minute I spoke any of it out loud, it would turn into nonsense, like in an old film comedy, whenever Joan Blondell tries to explain anything.

On the other hand, Simon Brent-Waterhouse *was* dead, in a suspicious but very clever way, and someone *had* been in my apartment, also in a very clever way, looking for a letter I didn't have. And then Vitya. Whom I knew, who I couldn't believe didn't know me, who I hoped to God believed maybe I had forgotten him.

And who knew my phone number, which I hadn't given him. Okay, maybe he had dialed every M. Cohen in the five boroughs and Jersey, but somehow I doubted it.

All these ghosts flitting about made me shiver, but they also gave me the spine to glare right back at Walter.

"You've got to help me ask Volkova some questions."

"How the hell do I know where Volkova is?" Walter was getting jumpy again, because the chairs were screeching and scuffing in the next room, indicating that work was switching into higher gear without him. "You want to know where Volkova is, you call her agent."

"Walter, it's her agent I want to ask her questions about!"

He shrugged, then eyed me coldly. "You want to finally tell me what any of this has got to do with national security?"

"Suppose just for a minute," I said gently, "that her agent is who I think maybe he is. A KGB agent."

Walter said nothing, waiting. Almost whispering, I sketched as believable a version of my paranoia as I could put together. It maybe drew a little heavily on Len Deighton and John Le Carré, but it seemed a reasonable guess that Walter and the people he worked around would be inclined to like obscure, wheels-within-wheels explanations. I was just beginning to feel panicky sweat beading my upper lip when Walter nodded abruptly, ran his thumb along the edge of his keyboard, then unhooked his dark glasses from his ear, folded them, and put them in his desk drawer. "Look, Midge . . ."

"Walter, I know what you're going to say, that this is all crazy. I agree with you, you put it together, it seems nuts. But all the parts are *true*. Somebody broke into my apartment, Simon's dead, Pedlar is Korobeikin, I swear to God he is, and the cops aren't buying suicide. And *all* of this has something to do with Volkova's book! So that's why I want to talk to her, to see what it is that she's got that's such dynamite!"

"Some of the guys who were at a lunch Piper-Wilkey gave for her say that's all you got to do. See her . . ."

"Walter, the *book*! Whatever it is that's in that book, somebody *died* because of it!"

Walter made throat-clearing noises, which I knew from experience meant he was thinking. He glanced at the inner office again, where Madison gave him a quizzical look, then at me again. "Midge, Pedlar's the one you claim is the Russian agent, right? If he is, then what's the sense in killing Brent-Waterhouse? To get a bigger ad budget for his client?" He shook his head, condescendingly. "Look, kid, you're right, this is weird, but *publishing* is weird, all right? What do you expect, from an entire *industry* based on going out to lunch? An industry in which, if you don't mind my pointing this out, I've really got to go do my little bit now, or else 'Children's,' 'sci-fi,' and 'Also of interest' don't get edited, and then maybe the book review folds, then the book industry shuts down, and suddenly half the waiters in Manhattan have got to become out-of-work actors, instead of aspiring writers. I could sleep with that on my conscience?"

"Jesus Christ, Wally," I snapped, my face flush with disappointed anger, "they give you humility lessons here, or is it like a continuing ed. class you take at the Y, on weekends?"

"Joke, Midge, joke. You remember what those are?"

"You want to laugh, laugh. But do it while you're finding Volkova for me, would you, please?"

"What do you think, I'm just going to call up that agent of hers, say I'm from the *Times,* and can I please have your client's number?"

"Well, actually, yes," I said, confused that he found the obvious so unthinkable.

"That's *fraud!*" he whispered, his face red with the strain of not shouting. "I can't misrepresent the paper like that, I mean *Christ,* the paper finds out I've done a bone-head stunt like that and I'm back with the goddamned graduate students again!"

I kept quiet then, because I knew what Walter said was true. It *was* fraud, but even worse, if the *Times* ever found out, he *would* be fired, and it would be my fault.

Well, sort of my fault. I couldn't actually *make* Walter agree to do something sneaky, correct? I mean, Walter could have said no, even after I told him that the whole reason I had to meet Polina was to see if I could figure out whether Pedlar really was a spy, which if he was clearly made Simon's death of vital importance to national security, and raised the obvious possibility that Walter might *single-handedly* unmask a dangerous KGB agent. He certainly *could* have said no . . . but then he wouldn't have been Walter. Which I had known, when I laid out my suspicions in the way I did.

Walter sat silent for a moment, tapping the space bar of his switched-off keyboard and staring vacantly at the water cooler. Then he grinned. "On one condition."

I looked quizzically at him.

"You set up an interview for me."

I gaped, as he stood, smoothed his shirt.

He laughed, patted me on the shoulder. "I mean, Jesus, if half of what they're saying about this broad is true . . . well, it seems like my solemn duty as a reporter to check her out myself, right?"

8

EXCEPT that it turned out that I didn't need to find Volkova, at least not to ask her questions about Pedlar, because when I got home he was waiting outside my building for me.

"Miss Cohen?" he stepped out of a car parked in front of my building.

"CHRIST! Don't *do* that!" I leaped around, my keys raised high to jab them in the attacker's eyes.

"Please, please! I didn't mean to startle you!" What I had thought was a stranger stepped away from the light of the door, hands raised, face radiating genial jovial harmlessness.

Heart hammering, I dropped my raised hand, stunned to see it was Pedlar, and relieved that this wasn't a stranger, so I wasn't about to be mugged. Then I remembered that I had spent the afternoon convincing Walter—and myself—that Pedlar was a murderous KGB agent. I raised the keys again, nauseously aware of how ineffective they would be against anybody with real training, praying only that at least one of the deaf old biddies in my building would have grandchildren visiting, so someone would hear my death screams.

"What do *you* want?" I growled, in my best big-city voice.

"Vic Pedlar, remember?" he still had his hands up, framing an Aquascutum raincoat, the sulfur of the street lights on Ocean Parkway bouncing off the gold of what I suspect was a Rolex. "We met the other night? Dinner, with Simon Brent-Water-house? And I left you a message, on your telephone?"

It had turned into a drizzly night, but it never really gets dark in Brooklyn, and there was a lot of light coming out of the building, so I could see Pedlar quite plainly. Well enough to wonder—*could* this be Korobeikin? Had Korobeikin's cheeks been that round? And his chin, surely that had been pointed, not double?

But just then Pedlar twitched his head nervously, to cast a lock of hair further back up his sloping forehead, Korobeikin's most characteristic gesture.

"How did you get my address?"

Pedlar apparently took that as invitation. He came a step closer, dropped his hands. I raised mine again, car key clutched like a miniature knife.

"Hey, what is this, don't you recognize me?" he stopped again, no longer smiling.

You bet I do, I thought, my mouth dry, wondering whether he recognized me, as someone he had known more than a decade ago. The light was on his face, which I hoped meant it *wasn't* on mine.

"Answer the question."

"How I got your address? I don't know, one of the girls does that. In the office."

"Gets the addresses of perfect strangers, so you can follow them across the five boroughs?"

"You didn't return my call!"

"There're a lot of calls I don't return. You're the first one that ever followed me home."

Pedlar straightened his tie—yellow paisley, of course—then gave a credible imitation of a Gerard Départieu smile, with a conciliatory chuckle. "I find *that* hard to believe, but . . . anyway, look, I've been waiting out there . . ." he pointed out to the curb, where a gray Volvo sat in the loading zone in front of the entrance, "for almost two hours."

"You have nothing better to do?"

"Actually, I have a *lot* better to do, which is why I'd really appreciate it if we could talk."

"So talk."

"Here? I was thinking that maybe we could go someplace for a drink, or a cup of coffee," he looked up at the building, "or even up to your place. This is business," he added hastily.

"You want to talk, I'm listening. Otherwise, I'm going through that door," I pointed over my shoulder, but still kept my face in the shadow. I hoped.

"Actually, it's about Miss Volkova's book, and is kind of, well, ticklish. . . ." He dropped his voice and looked from side to side, as though people might be standing in the junipers by the door. "That letter, if you know the one I mean . . ."

There are those among you who will notice that this is the moment when I *should* have said, "The letter? Ha, I lied, nothing to do with me, and I have no idea where it is!" Remember, though, you hadn't just spent all day bouncing around Manhattan, in terror of precisely this conversation, which had been sprung on me out of the dark.

On the other hand, even *I* can't figure out why I said what I actually replied.

"The letter that gives Simon representation rights for Miss

Volkova? Better you go talk to a probate judge on that one, Mr. Pedlar."

"*Probate* judge?" Pedlar looked as though I had punched him in the chest; he actually took a step backward, then forward again. "What's a *probate* judge got to do with this issue?"

I lied some glib mishmash made up out of *The Defenders* and Scott Turow's books, about how Simon's corporate and personal assets were hopelessly intertangled, and the executors of the estate were battling with the Sirin stockholders over the mess his affairs were in.

"He did die rather unexpectedly, you know," I concluded tartly, wishing I could disappear through the abyss of my own stupid mouth.

"There *are* no stockholders of Sirin Press!" Pedlar brushed aside everything I had said, like so many blackflies.

"Or whatever!" I shouted. "I don't know exactly, but I know that it isn't fair that you should just come in and snatch this book from under Simon, sell it for the money he worked so hard for and took so many risks for and then . . ."

"But Simon's *dead*," Pedlar said reasonably, apparently having expected my outburst, which was even odder, because I *hadn't*. I hadn't even known until that moment that I *didn't* think it fair. But it wasn't really, all the effort Brent-Waterhouse had put into helping those wonderful crazy talented Russians break through the stifling oppression of Pedlar and the other KGB goons he worked for, even if he did steal most of their money afterwards. And now Pedlar would sell Volkova's book for lots of money, and the authors Simon stole it from wouldn't get any of it now ever, and Simon was dead.

"Anyway, that's why I came out here to talk to you about that letter. Because it isn't the money . . ."

"Oh, it's not because of money you wait two hours outside my door?"

Pedlar gave a weary toss of his head, shrugged. "Now that the

Piper-Wilkey deal seems dead, we're hoping to have enough manuscript to take the book out to auction early next month, with a six-figure floor, and that letter complicates the situation enormously, but. . . ." He waved the back of his hand at the Volvo again, indicating that such paltry sums were scarcely enough to keep *him* hanging around darkest Brooklyn at all hours. "You're sure that we can't talk someplace more . . . private?"

"This is plenty private, there's no one around." Which was true, but why had I pointed that out? I readjusted my hold on the keys.

Pedlar thought for a moment longer, then seemed to reach a decision. "All right, if it has to be here, it has to be here. Look, Miss Cohen, the issue with Polina's book isn't money, it's something larger."

"Polina?" I muttered.

He looked discomfited, but only for a second. "Miss Volkova. Sure, her book is going to be lucrative, but the way I look at it, that's the frosting, the *gimmick*. You can't get anybody's attention anymore, can't get anybody to think! And that's what this book is supposed to do! *Has* to do! Miss Volkova was very close to Yuri Andropov, Miss Cohen. I don't know how much you know about Andropov . . ."

"I know my history," I interrupted, not wanting to find out how much Pedlar knew about him. The former head of the KGB, the patron of Gorbachev . . .

"You see," Pedlar went onward, in a rush, "Andropov was a very dangerous, devious man, which Polina knows better than anyone. Even a child would know to fear a thug like Khrushchev or Brezhnev, but Andropov? He was smooth, he was skilled. He let it about that he knew English, that he collected Ella Fitzgerald records, read Agatha Christie, drank Scotch. . . . People *liked* Andropov, Miss Cohen, especially your journalists and leaders. Which makes it all the harder to make people understand that what Andropov set up is a time-bomb, and pretty soon, one of these days, it's going to go off!"

I smiled a second at that "your," then scowled again. "So what? He's dead."

Pedlar nodded, checked the bushes for spies again, then said softly. "That's just it. His protégés aren't, and neither are the plans Andropov made for them."

"Protégés? Like Gorbachev, you mean? Lord, the only difference between him and Andropov is that Andropov is *literally* dead. There isn't even a Soviet Union any more! So what possible damage could this Polina's book do the place, anyway?"

"Not *do* damage. *Prevent* damage. And it's not Russia that I'm interested in helping, it's America."

"America?" I said, my brain working a lot slower than my mouth. "But you're Russian!"

Pedlar shimmered for a second, as if I had slapped him; a flash of anger glinted, but then quickly was smothered by a theatrical grin. "All that money I pay for voice lessons, and still it shows, eh? Oh well . . . at least being Russian comes in handy, when a project like Miss Volkova's comes along."

"Polina," I reminded him, studying his face as I tried to figure out whether this meant he really hadn't recognized me, from my Moscow year.

"Polina," he acceded. "But I'm American now, and my kids are American. My wife . . . she's a Connecticut swamp Yankee, her people are here . . . pfff, who knows how long?"

"And that's why Sirin should give up its claim on Polina's book?"

"You haven't read the book."

"*Nobody* has, as far as I know!"

Pedlar shrugged that off his expensive raincoat, smoothed mist from his expensive hair, the expensive signet ring on his pinkie shining. "The manuscript is incomplete, sure, but the point is, it's crucial that this book get the very widest possible distribution, the most attention. Crucial for *us*, for America. I'm sure Sirin would have done a perfectly credible job of actually *publishing* it, but. . . . These issues need *attention*, need somebody who can cut through all the Russian *bullshit*, and make this country understand."

Just then the front door opened, and Sasha emerged, grinning like something a stone mason puts high up in the corner of a cathedral. Sasha was the janitor of the building, an emigré, a painter. And, until fairly recently . . .

A very close friend.

In the way that he had of doing, Sasha grinned blindly at both of us, then did a double-take. Actually about a quadruple-take, where first he recognized it was me, then wondered why I was standing in front of the building, then noticed Pedlar, and smirked, like he had caught me out. Only then, finally, did he seem to pick up my agitation.

"Midge? Everything is all right?"

"Yeah," I smiled overjoyed that he should have turned up just then, "everything is just . . ."

"Hey, Alix! Wait up!" someone shouted from inside the building. Then Karla Braverman bounced out, the aerobics instructor who lives on the top floor back. One of the reasons why Sasha and I aren't such close friends anymore, ever since I discovered among his canvases a half-completed study of Karla in the buff. "Wait up, you cute little furry beast! Oh . . . Midge. Hi." After a second's hesitation, she took Sasha's arm. Sasha at least had the decency to look uncomfortable, and then glanced again at Pedlar. "You're sure everything's okay?" he repeated, this time in Russian.

"He's Russian," I said, nodding my head at Pedlar, who stuck out a hand, automatically. Sasha shook as automatically, while they eyed one another. Finally, another uncertain glance at me, and Sasha said, "Well, in that case . . . good night. We're going to get some pizza."

I looked at Pedlar, and something within me shivered, certain I didn't want to be left alone with him.

"Pizza! Good lord, what a great idea! Come on, Vic, you want to go get a slice or two? It's okay, isn't it Sasha, we come get a slice with you guys?"

I strode smartly forward and took Sasha's other arm. His eyes opened wide, then he glanced uncertainly from me to Karla to Pedlar.

"Pizza?" he asked Pedlar.

Pedlar glowered, his face sour and predatory. Then he shook his head, pulled his raincoat collar up. "I can't stand that glop, it sits coiled up in your stomach like a rope."

"Well, then . . ." I grinned, almost manic with relief. "I guess it's good night?" Then I elbowed Sasha, that we should move on.

Just as we did though, Sasha uncertain and Karla glaring daggers at me, Pedlar caught my outside arm, and leaned over to whisper in my ear, in Russian, "If you don't want those Moscow wolves-in-democrat's-clothing hanging noodles on our Uncle Sam's ears, then you better find that letter, so Polina's book sells *millions.*"

I snorted, tossed my head, and jerked on Sasha's arm, striding off down Ocean Parkway, so briskly that Karla, on three-inch heels, had to break into some sort of trot that made most of her wobble like a waterbed.

"Midge, Midge," Sasha panted at my side. I paid no attention until I was around the corner, out of sight of Pedlar. Then I let go of Sasha and collapsed against the building, trembling.

"Tears?" Karla asked me after a minute, even reaching up her red fingernailed-hand to touch my face. "Ah, come on, honey. . . . He can't be *that* . . ."

I pushed her hand away, straightened up, wiped my nose defiantly. "No, no, Jesus, he's nobody, it's a cold, or hay fever . . . just, would you look, make sure he's gone?" I smiled, pleading, watery at Karla.

Snapping her gum, her hair processed to look as wild and stringy as the strands of her pink fake Karakul, her eyes brown and enormous, Karla nodded, and let go of Sasha's arm.

Then I squeezed his fingers so tight he yelped, tried to jerk away.

"Sasha, you son of a bitch," I was fierce now, snarling at him in Russian. "You let that bastard into my apartment, didn't you?"

Sasha's right ear was deafened in military training, so often, when he is uncertain whether he has understood, he turns his left ear toward you; he did that now, his ripe-olive eyes confused and—I was pretty sure—a little guilty.

"Him? I never!" he swore stoutly. "That guy I see for the first time in my life!"

"Sasha, goddamn it, you let *someone* into my apartment, didn't you?"

"Yes, of course!" he shouted back, exasperated.

"What do you mean, 'yes of course!?' " I let go of his hand. "You let somebody into my apartment when I wasn't even there?"

Sasha looked confused, puzzled. Then, slightly worried. "Yes . . . this is wrong?"

"What do you mean, this is wrong? This is *America,* for crying out loud! You don't just let people into other people's . . ."

"Not people," he interrupted me, then, after glancing at Karla, who was still leaning around the edge of the building, he dropped his voice. "A cleaner."

"A cleaner?"

"Yeah, sure, a cleaner. A woman . . . she gave me a card, and a work order. With your signature, I was certain," he said, defensively.

I said nothing, so he relaxed a little, went on with the story. "She said you had wanted everything cleaned, and you didn't want to be there, because of the dust . . ."

"*So you just let her into my place!?*"

"You didn't hire this woman?" Sasha's fierce Maccabee face sagged forlornly. "But I was sure, I mean, your apartment is always such . . ."

I shot him a glare, to remind him that at least my place wasn't covered everywhere with paint flecks, and that unlike him I changed the bedsheets more than once a decade.

"Sasha, I mean, my God, I could have your *job,* I could even *sue* you, letting someone . . ."

Sasha drew himself up, fierce again. "It was a mistake, maybe, but I can swear . . . that woman took *nothing.*"

I was still feeling numb and trembly, so I just looked at him blankly, wondering how he could be so sure.

Which Sasha understood. He grinned, pleased with himself. "I maybe made a mistake, but I am not *stupid.* The lady seemed strange to me, like not really a cleaner. So just to be safe, I stayed and watched her the whole time. To make sure she was actually cleaning, doing her work."

"He finally left!" Karla bounded over, smiling four-inch teeth the smooth hard white of Chiclets. "What a *weirdo!* He stands there, jangles his keys, starts the car and *still* sits there! What is he, some sort of pervert?"

I ignored her, though what she had said made me feel a little more calm. "Strange?" I repeated to Sasha.

He smiled. "Actually, not strange." He flicked his middle finger against his throat, the Russian handsign for a drunk. "Alcoholic. I saw enough of them back in Leningrad to know what kind of house cleaner she was going to make, and I didn't want you paying for work she didn't actually do."

I smiled. A pale, scarcely visible smile, but real for all that. Because whoever it was that had gone through all the effort of that elaborate and risky hoax, in order to be able to search unimpeded through my possessions, the plan had been foiled by an alcoholic scrubwoman and an emigré janitor concerned that I wouldn't get good value for my cleaning dollar.

Hand still trembling I patted Sasha on the shoulder, hesitantly, said goodnight to Karla, and then headed back to my apartment.

9

"GOD! How I envy you! What wouldn't I *give* to live in this city!"

"Will you get down off the lamppost and *listen* to me?" I shouted, the shrillness of my voice giving even me a headache. "You keep dancing around up there and somebody's going to drive his cab right into you, and then you won't be living anywhere!"

Polina gave me a look that the only word I could think of to describe it was "winsome," then, after a final hug and a parting pat on the pole's green flanks, she did as I asked.

"All right," I said vaguely, and gripped her arm, feeling sort of like wicked Baba Yaga, leading Yelena the Beautiful to the oven of my chicken-footed magic hut.

To say I hadn't slept well would be to imply I had slept at all. But who could sleep, in an apartment that half of Manhattan now seemed to know where it was, coming and going as they pleased? I had locked and bolted every piece of hardware the door possessed, and then stuck a chair under the doorknob besides.

And *then* the phone had rung. Pearl, I was sure, trying to decide how much, and of what, I would tell her as I reached for the receiver.

Except it wasn't Pearl.

"Hi, Margaret Cohen? This is Susan Griswold. You don't know me, I think, but I was working with Simon Brent-Waterhouse, until I had a little accident. Anyway, I'm trying to clear up his affairs, and what I understand, you may have some important business documents, that I was wondering whether I could get them back?"

Susan Griswold?

"Oh, my God!" I guessed, "You're the woman who broke the tooth!"

Although it lasted several minutes, and was considerably more profane than even I am generally capable of, the explosion that comment set off at least clarified a few things. For one, this Griswold woman had paid for the pizza that crippled her, meaning Simon Brent-Waterhouse had been just as broke at midday as he had been that evening.

For two, she was still in considerable pain, and for three, in spite of that pain, she was bound and determined to get hold of Volkova's letter.

Which, despite repeated protestation to the contrary, she was still convinced I had.

"Well, if you haven't got that cursed woman's letter, who has? Simon definitely had it with him when we were at lunch!"

"I told you, the only letter I know anything about was a photocopy. Maybe that's what he showed you?"

"Damnit, I *touched* it, it was the *original!*"

"All I know is, I haven't got it, and I don't have the faintest idea where it is!"

"That had better be the truth, you know, because I have eighty thousand bucks sunk in Volkova's book . . . and I don't intend to lose it to you!"

"Well, stay away from the olives then," I had finally said, then hung up, pretty certain Susan Griswold and I would never be friends.

I probably wouldn't have slept anyway, but the question I had forgotten to ask before I slammed the receiver down at least gave me something to think about while I stared at my paint-peeling ceiling—namely, where had *she* gotten my number from?

By the next morning though, when insomnia had turned my mouth ashen and left my head "pinging" like an overheated radiator, strange cold and hot flashes coursing through my exhausted body, I was mad.

Because, goddamn it, I was starting to feel messed with.

After an icy shower, two cups of black coffee that would dissolve a spoon, and a pair of jeans that even with the weight I had lost still bit into my stomach brought me to a vengeful, intent simmer, I finally achieved precisely the mood I needed to be in, if someone was going to be made to *pay*.

The sort of mood that made me feel sorry for anyone who got in my way. *Even* Walter Goldberg.

"How'd you get this number?" he snapped, when I called him at the paper, so early that even I was surprised he was there.

"Read it off the phone yesterday," I snapped right back. "What do you think? Anyway, did you find Volkova?"

He started a grouchy explanation of what a terrible person I was, which I interrupted with a very brief description, much less profane than Susan Griswold would have given, of how my day had ended yesterday, and my by-now absolute certainty that Pedlar and Korobeikin were one and the same.

Which at least silenced Walter for a moment. Then he said, "Still, Midge, if you think this guy killed your publisher, the police is who you should call. I can't help you right now anyway, I've got a newspaper to get out!"

"Walter, for chrissakes, you aren't Ben Franklin, peeling broadsheets off a handcrank press! If you don't want to call from your desk, you must take *lunch*, at least! Call her then!"

"New rule, can't leave the building while they're running the section! Sandwiches, at the desk. Anyway, that's broadsides, not broadsheets."

I didn't believe Walter for a minute. "Do they make you sleep there, too? Bring your teddy and toothbrush, just in case a last-minute punctuation crisis breaks out?"

"Midge . . ." Walter had said in a voice that warned I had about two seconds before his thumb hit the button.

"I'll bring her to the paper!" I promised, made a genius—or a panderer—by necessity.

Whichever—at least it had worked, and Walter got me the number. I was able to call Volkova up and offer "to show her a little of the city," the only pretext I could dream up that would give me time to question her alone before delivering Polina to Walter's slavering attentions.

I was a little taken aback that Polina recalled me so immediately, and responded so enthusiastically, but when I met her in the lobby of her dumpy midtown hotel, I understood why. The hotel was better than Simon's, but only just. She had plonked a cloche hat onto her steel-wool hair, then shaken her candy-cane–striped tights, fake-fur coat, and off-the-shoulder electric green Danskin top like a cockatoo who has just found the clasp on its cage undone. That every male in the hotel was watching, open-mouthed, should have warned me what the rest of this excursion was going to be like.

Now Polina threw her arm, bracelets clinking, over my shoulder, and loped along, her hair bouncing like a stiff purple-red triangle as she bellowed in Russian, "To think, this pole is on the corner of Broadway and Wall Street! In *America!* This is like one of the nails that holds down the map of the world, isn't it?" Then she halted, as abruptly as she had loped. "You know, when I was a little girl, I dreamed, maybe I could become a cosmonaut. The boys made fun. 'They don't send *girls* into space!' But then came Tereshkova, and I think, maybe maybe there is hope after all! They will send me into space, and at least I can look down on America from up above. Because I *know* . . ."

Here she fell dramatically silent, as we were almost trampled in the Wall Street crowds. I had a strange suspicion that some of the men at least were jostling us deliberately, to be able to bump into Polina, but if they were, she was totally indifferent to it.

". . . because I *know* that Polina Volkova they might send to the moon, but they would never ever *ever* let her go to America! And now here I am!"

And off we loped again. "Even with Andropov?" I panted, finding it hard to keep up, let alone ask cunning questions.

"Feh, Yurochka," she said, with an indefinite noise, that I took to be disgust. Then, the abrupt stop again. "You know what he thought of all this?" Her arms were spread wide and she circled, like she was auditioning for a Melina Mercouri part. People ducked, but this being New York, they went on, most not even bothering to look back.

"He hated it?" I ventured.

"He *loved* it! And that's why he wanted to own it." Suddenly she dropped the dingbat act, and studied me shrewdly. "That's what you Americans never seem to get about those guys. You thought it was about ideology, when all it's *ever* been about is shopping. Goodies. *Money.*"

"This is what your book is about?"

"Pah, the book. . . ." She made another dismissive noise, and walked ahead again, but slower. "Stupid Victor wants me twenty hours a day in that stupid hotel room, spilling my guts into his cassettes. In *New York*. But," she shrugged, after a moment, "he's probably right. The sooner I get my story finished, the sooner I can get my money. Where to now? The theaters are near here?"

That's the thing you always forget about Wall Street—how short it is. Broadway, on the other hand, isn't. "No, they're . . ." I waved my left hand, toward uptown. "We'd have to take a cab. Maybe later, after our appointment at the *Times*. Want to head down toward the water instead, Battery City? We can find someplace there's a view of the Statue of Liberty?" Polina shrugged, so I pointed her in the right direction, then asked, as casually as I could, "You're saying it's really Victor that's pushing this book forward? It wasn't your project?"

"Of *course*," Polina answered, off-handed and ambiguously. Then, after studying me for a moment, she asked. "You are divorced?"

The change of topic caught me off balance.

"What?"

"You are divorced? You are too pretty never to have been married."

Have you ever noticed that, how we'll take compliments from *anywhere*? I forgot about the black circles under my eyes, the pallid complexion that I hadn't bothered to hide under makeup, and smiled, self-consciously smoothing my hair. "Thanks, but . . . yes, I'm divorced."

"Is it difficult?" Polina's smoky green eyes seemed almost to embrace me, giving me a whiff of the intoxicating heat of Slavic friendship, which can come—and go—as swiftly as a Russian summer.

"Well, yes, sometimes . . . but I have . . . other friends, and . . ."

Polina hugged my arm. "I'm sure you do! But what I meant, is it hard to *get*? A divorce?"

I was mystified. "But you're single, aren't you? And anyway, a divorce isn't something you can take home from a trip to the States, like a VCR or a sweat shirt."

Polina gave her elflike glance about, a sly amused twinkle in her eye making it easy to understand why she might have come to romp the sheets she had. She was like a six-foot Tinkerbell, and even for me, being around her was fun.

"Not for me. For Vitya."

"Vitya?"

"Victor. My agent. I think I want to marry him."

But for Polina's tug on my arm, I would have gone straight off the curb and into the traffic of Water Street.

"WHAT?"

"I am going to marry him, Midge."

"Does *he* know this?"

"Maybe he suspects, a little. Maybe he just thinks I like him a lot." She laughed. "You know, in almost thirty years that I am a whore, I never once met a man who didn't think it made perfect sense that I would go to bed with him! Even when it was for money, they think I take that to keep my self-respect."

"Listen," I started cautiously, unsure how to broach the worries that I had wanted her to confirm. "How much do you know about Pedlar? I mean . . ."

"Vitya?" Polina pouted. "He is young, he is handsome, he is rich. . . ." Then her voice changed, to become absolutely flat and businesslike. "And he is an American citizen."

"Ah . . ." I nodded. At least *that* motive made sense.

"I am not going back to that place, Margaret, I simply am not. It is hell." She repeated that hoary cliché with a flat despair that made it seem literally, terribly true. Polina's face suddenly was haggard, tired, and intensely determined, like that of an actor in the dressing room, after a sweat-soaked performance. That glimpse—of struggles the fate of my birth had spared me, of a desperation to survive in an environment that did worse than kill, because it made you ugly—made me feel sober, grateful I had been born where I had, and very tender toward Polina.

Instead of speech, I squeezed her arm, then, because I understood her intensity, I said, "But you know . . . he isn't *born* an American."

"Of course not, he is from Grozny," she looked at me about the same as she would have if I'd just pointed out that Pedlar had two legs. Then she smiled, a dazzling thing that might almost have tumbled winging pigeons from the sky. "But now he is a citizen, and that means his wife can stay. *Here!*"

I stood there, mouth gaping so wide I must have looked like a mailbox that someone was about to dump a letter into.

"COME, dear Midge, the statue!" Polina took my arm again, dragging me along. "I want to see for myself, is it true, that she looks just like Elvis Presley?"

Eventually the Novocain in my brain wore off. "You knew Victor in Russia then?"

"Of course I knew him. How do you think I got to America? Maybe the borders are open now . . . hell, since the collapse, *everything's* open. No point in keeping it closed, if there's nothing inside. But *tickets,* that's a problem, if you don't have dollars, and have someplace to *go,* that's even worse! What good does it do me to go *out* if I can't come *in?* To get a visa into America now, it's *terrible. Everybody* your embassy accuses of wanting to stay here." She smiled. "Of course, they are right, so. . . . To come I needed an invitation, a guarantee I had someone to stay with and support me. I needed a ticket. So, I called Vitya . . ."

"And, just like that, he flew you to America?"

"Not me, Midge! It is my *book* he flew here! My book that

I am very very careful to keep only in my head! I only told him a little bit, of course, because it was on the telephone. People say there's no KGB, nobody is bugging the phones anymore, but . . ." She shrugged scornfully. "All I can say is, the guys *I* knew, they are still working." Then, with a yelp of enthusiasm, she raced off in the direction of a shivering clutch of Ghanian jewelery, watch, and bauble vendors, who were happy to begin spirited exchanges in mutually fractured English while she tried on their wares.

Watching her flirting with those Ghanians, whom within five minutes flat she had bounding about like poodles hopping through circus hoops, I tried to puzzle out a growing suspicion that I might have hooked my carts and horses backward. I mean, here I had assumed all along that it was Korobeikin who was guiding Polina's book, and destiny. And now Polina all but tells me that the memoirs were her idea from beginning to end.

It is a testament to her ability to seem guileless, that once I thought about it I knew it made perfect sense. Even a great whore gets old eventually, and then she's out of business, no matter who she once had for customers.

And in Russia right now retirement even from regular jobs means a pension worth eleven cents a month, on which you survive by peddling your miserable possessions in some filthy pedestrian underpass.

Hardly Polina's style.

A trip to America, *that* was Polina's style.

Social security, of course, Polina wasn't going to get, but her knowledge of the inner doings of the Kremlin, properly played, would sustain her old age no worse.

"This is only twenty dollars. Do you like it?" Polina held out her right wrist, which was clutched by what looked like two wart hog tusks set in old silver.

"Twenty dollars? The ivory's real?"

"I bargained a bit . . ." she nodded toward the dealers, who were crowded around, commiserating with one of their numbers as if he had just been in a traffic accident. "But I'm sure it's real, and the silver's good. I have a good eye."

Of that I was confident, though I didn't say so. I stifled a spasm of jealousy at this unearthly bargain, to say simply, "Twenty dollars. Wow . . ."

"Midge . . . I am sorry, but . . . well, you know how it is with us poor Russians and hard currency? Maybe you could make this a present to me? A souvenir of our walk, just until my book is finished?"

A little numb, I walked over to the vendors, who made sympathetic faces while I fished out my two tens; we nodded knowingly at one another for a little, commiserating at being the meek of the Earth.

However, it was actually probably worth twenty bucks, to have had this first-hand demonstration of how good Polina was at manipulating, even when you don't want to go to bed with her.

Twenty bucks also gave me the right to make my questions more pointed.

"Polina, why exactly did Victor invite you over here?"

"I told you, we are old friends!"

"Old friends, eh? Old enough that he would have known, once you were here you weren't likely to go back?"

"Midge! That is unkind!" she eyed me merrily.

"Kind or unkind, I'm beginning to think maybe you should tell me a little more precisely what's in your book."

"You know, everyone has talked about it! Sex, sex, and more sex, with a little politics thrown in to keep the reader interested!"

"Sex I know about," I started, in a loud exasperated voice that made most of the heads within half a block turn my way. Blushing furiously, I continued more quietly, "what I want to know is the politics. Whatever's in this book, it has to be something that would make Vitya think it's worth bringing you over here, even though he had to have known that . . . well, that you're a very persuasive person."

Polina studied me enigmatically, toying with a coil of her hair. Finally, the flatness of her voice suggesting this was true, she admitted, "Vitya and I worked together, in the Komsomol. You know, the Young Communists?"

For a moment I was shocked, because "Vitya" to me was that impassioned youth who had raged away in my shower, damning communism to seven hells. Certainly not the type to have been a *member* of the Young Communists. But then I remembered "Victor," the Russian who wasn't, the man who last night I was not only convinced had pushed Brent-Waterhouse out a window, but maybe was about to push *me*. That person made much more sense as a Young Communist.

"Christ, you mean Vitya was a *stookach?* An informer!" I blurted.

Polina's slightly surprised glance made me wish I had been cleverer still, clever enough to keep my mouth shut. But I hadn't. "More a provocateur, actually, but . . . you knew him?"

I said no, my blush said yes. I was wrenched between a retroactive horror, that a memory which had in some way defined what I had loved about Russia ("Vitya's" faint yelp for freedom, all the more precious for being so dangerous he had to restrict it to that shower) had in fact been political provocation, and an equally retroactive self-congratulation, that even at the time I had been smart enough to avoid getting hooked by so elementary a piece of political make-believe.

Polina said nothing, just waiting. After a bit I found a lie close enough to the truth that I would probably not turn pink as I said it.

"There was something familiar when I met him, at that dinner. I couldn't place him then, but I must have run across him at some point. When I was there. In Moscow. A long time ago."

Still Polina said nothing, studying me intently and somehow professionally. It made me very uncomfortable, almost as though I were a commodity. Finally she completed whatever calculations she had been running, and set off again, my arm tucked to her ribs. I walked too, fighting down an urge to pull my hand free.

When she finally began to talk again, it was without theatrics. "Well, so you understand then, how Vitya got himself over here. You were a, what's the word? Black copy?"

"Black copy" is Russian, and sounds marginally better than "rough draft."

The rush of memory at that moment was literally nauseating. Memory explained, a past I had cherished suddenly revealed to have been something else entirely. The sort of shock you get when you suddenly learn you are adopted, or that your husband has been *shtupping* your girlfriends.

Those long, cold nights in those tiny university dormitory rooms, high up in a tower Dracula might have built, above an enormous, alien, mysterious city. Those of us who had left loved ones behind, we got letters twice a week, in the American Embassy, forwarded through Finland, and we sent them out the same way—unsealed, so that the consular officials could make sure we were smuggling nothing our falsely smiling hosts did not wish us to. Letters—to a husband who had not wished to postpone a veterinary residency in order to accompany me, and his replies to a wife who missed him ever more desperately as she began to understand she really didn't need him at all—could take as much as a month, question to answer. In between lay gnawing, aching loneliness, embroidered round with a barbed-wire lace of fear.

And lit, at far too infrequent intervals, by the excitement of Vitya's midnight descents, and our steamy clandestine conversations. I was married, I had many other friends in Moscow, I am about ten years older (well, let's make that about seven years), and I am clumsy at amorous signals besides . . . yet I had always been happy to see Vitya. Even then I guess I was aware of how little it might have taken to move our conversation from the shower to my narrow divan-*cum*-bed.

Had I ever been tempted? A decade later, in another country, I can't remember. But that did nothing to lessen my sense of horrified loathing, that *had* I made that move, *had* I taken him into my bed . . .

It would have been at Komsomol headquarters he was scoring, and not with me.

The cynicism, the *insult* of it all took my breath away, even if I had never succumbed.

And then I remembered that, my year in Moscow alone, eight Americans had married Russians. As had two Brits, one of the two West Germans, a Dutchman, a Fulbright professor, and something like fourteen Italians.

Twenty-seven Soviets, who had come to live in the West. Like Vitya had, some other year. Vitya, who had been in the Young Communists. With Polina, who had become Andropov's mistress.

The implications were multiplying like the images in mirrors placed face to face, bending off into an obscure infinity that made me shiver.

"But Christ, what for, Polina? It wasn't like the government wouldn't *know* they were Russians. What were they supposed to *do?*"

"They?"

"Well . . . it wasn't just Victor, was it? Who got married, to come here as agents." After all, in every case, it was the Russian spouse who had left, to live abroad. God, I thought bitterly, how *easy*. "Arranging" those marriages must have been less challenge than shooting fish in a barrel. Poor, unsuspecting, lonely little fish, swimming about in their Moscow State University barrel.

"Agents? That's awfully grand, isn't it?" Polina looked amused and weary, that special European grimace that somehow mocks us Americans for our naiveté even as they are admitting to us that they have lied and cheated and borne false witness.

"Call it whatever you want," I snapped, with a viciousness I hadn't expected myself. "Abusers of affection? Hypocrites and scoundrels?"

Polina's face for a moment glinted some of the ice, which must lie at the center of her heart. "Of course Vitya wasn't the only one. We all had our . . . functions?" She laughed, but we both knew it wasn't funny.

"And you? Why didn't *you* snare yourself an American?" I was still blazing with anger, at her, at Vitya, at the Soviet Union.

"Orders," she said, in a flat, definite way that made clear she wouldn't say more. "One whores as one is told."

"All right, orders . . . but still, why? What are they supposed to *do?*" I had confused notions of academics' wives as fifth columnists, blowing up the bike paths around their campuses.

"Do? Nothing. Be there. *Here,* I mean. Learn. Watch." The way Polina said them, each of these activities sounded more sinister than the one before.

"And this is what your book is going to be about?" The warren of old Dutch streets at the tip of Manhattan was finally bringing us out toward Battery Park. The prongs of Miss Liberty's torch were visible between the slabs of buildings. I could imagine the dinner tables around America, once Polina's book was published. American spouses studying their Russian spouses and wondering . . .

"In part," Polina sounded evasive, dismissive again, and I didn't pursue her, because I had only just understood that of course there had to be more to her book than that. Something considerably more.

In fact, a lot of things about Polina and her book now made sense.

Except maybe one.

"Listen, Polina . . . that letter. You signed that thing clear back in 1978, it seems like Simon would have forgotten it *years* ago. How was it that he got wind of you and your book almost as soon as you set foot in America?"

Polina was eyeing Trinity Street, preparing herself to dash across.

"Simon? You must not have known him, he was an elephant. The man forgot nothing. *Nothing!* That's why I called him as soon as I arrived, to make sure that he wouldn't make trouble for me with that letter. Shows you what kind of stupid whore I am, eh? To have given a man like *that* such a letter. Wouldn't I love to know where that cursed letter is now!" She more barked than laughed.

"Wouldn't about half of damn Manhattan!" I laughed, starting to add that most people were assuming that I had it, but then I remembered something, which shut my jaw so fast I almost bit my own tongue.

Why would Susan Griswold have thought I had that letter? She wasn't at the dinner!

But Polina had just noticed Miss Liberty's crown showing between the buildings up ahead; gaping upward, she didn't see me stalled dumbstruck in the middle of the sidewalk behind her.

There was only one explanation for Griswold's assumption, that someone who had been at the dinner had told her I had claimed to have the letter. The problem was, the only person present who I *knew* had had a connection with Susan Griswold was Simon Brent-Waterhouse. Who was dead.

Which *had* to mean that someone else who was there that night had told her.

"But she has her back to us!" Polina whirled about, eyes

shining. "Midge, this statue, I have heard that it is possible to go up the inside, to the top. Can we do that?"

"Not on Tuesdays, Polina, and anyway, they're waiting for us at the *Times,*" I said very firmly, with an eerie sudden certainty that I didn't want to go anywhere above the second floor with this woman.

10

"MARGARET," Pearl's surprise at seeing me wore off quickly, letting her launch into scolding before I even finished my demand to see Susan Griswold's file. "I'm afraid I really must say a thing or two to you about this mystery mania of yours. After all, I'm your mother, and, well . . ."

"I *know* you're my mother," I tried not to shout back, "and it's a damn lucky thing for you, because if you weren't, God, I don't know, I'd probably punch you in the nose or something!" I slapped the counter, sending dental files scudding in several directions. I don't think I was being unreasonably impatient for a person who not only had probably been shoved by her meddling mother into the middle of some obscure KGB kind of murkiness, but who also had a New York cab double-parked out on Fifth Avenue, at 4:45 on a weekday afternoon. On the plus side, I had also left Polina out there, so whatever else happened, the cabbie at least wouldn't be complaining.

Still, if we were going to meet Walter anywhere even close to five, I didn't have time to fight with Pearl. "You know you can't get fired for just looking through the records," I dropped my voice, to a hoarse whisper, "that's what you're *paid* for, looking through the records."

"This your daughter, Pearl?" A blonde in a tight nurse's dress looked around the corner into my mother's receptionist cubicle, snapped her gum at us, and eyed me curiously.

My mother was so flustered she dropped the files she had just picked up, then introduced us, as red-faced as if we had just been kissing. I said "Hi," coldly and indifferently.

The hygienist said hi back, then completed her business with my mother, while I drummed my finger impatiently and looked around. The offices of Kornbluth, Katzenbaum, and Singh, D.D.S. were about what you'd expect for a dental practice a block north of Washington Square. Wood paneling, old framed prints of horses flying like Superman, legs extended fore and aft, brass lamps and leather chairs, and a selection of magazines chosen for the sort of patients who like to while away the minutes until root canal work by rethinking their investment strategies.

The hygienist left; for a moment my mother listened to high heels clicking away down the hall, then, a wicked twinkle in her eye, she whispered, "Dr. Kornbluth *shtups* her in the flossing chair Tuesdays and Fridays. But *he* doesn't know about the 'oral hygiene sessions' with Katzenbaum on Wednesdays, when Kornbluth stays out on the Island with the golf. And *she* doesn't know that Singh has already put an ad with the agencies for a replacement, because he can't figure why the practice is paying forty dollars an hour for a hygienist. Plus benefits."

I waved this away. I had had enough of the human comedy

this week. "Never mind that. Mother, *did you give Susan Gris-wold my phone number?*"

Pearl sat back indignant. "I did not!" Her gray-and-black hair quivered beneath her nurselike tiara for a second, before Pearl slumped, huddling in the white cardigan she wore over the shoulders of her blue pinstripe receptionist's dress. "But I talked about you. Not to her, to that Mr. Brent-Waterhouse. Simon. While she was in the chair. What you do, your ex, Paul, the novels . . ."

"And where I live?" I guessed.

"Well, not exactly, but the neighborhood, maybe," Pearl admitted; she looked miserable for a moment, until she thought of a counterattack. "I've *told* you to take your name out of the phone book, haven't I? You see what can happen, some total stranger finds out your name and your neighborhood, it's *nothing* to get hold of your number!"

Especially when the total stranger is given that information by your mother, I didn't add. Instead, I just held out my hand.

"Mother, the file?"

My mother cocked her head. "Margaret . . ." she dropped her voice half an octave, "I'm not supposed to give out information about patients."

"You're not supposed to give out information about your *daughter,* Mother!" I snapped back. "If it weren't for you, I wouldn't even *be* in this mess!"

"For *me?* I didn't *make* you go out with him," Pearl defended herself, but a shade uncertainly; she wouldn't meet my eye. "Besides, it wasn't really a date. It was simply, well, I thought maybe it would be interesting for you."

Pearl struggled with her conscience for another moment, then took a deep breath, looked at the door that protected us from having to learn even more about Kornbluth and his hygienist. Then, almost faster than the eye could follow, my mother scut-tled her receptionist's chair to a bank of shelves, where manila files stood in color-coded ranks. She counted rapidly on her fingertips, then checked against a calendar, before sliding along to a bank of yellow-ribbed folders. Grunting, she bent almost to the floor, found the file she wanted, then gestured me urgently over.

Infected by her nervousness, I looked about the deserted waiting room, then scurried around the receptionist's barrier.

Pearl held up the file for me to read, but did not let go of it, any more than she took her eye off the inner office door.

It was a standard new patient's information form, stapled inside the left-hand cover of the manila folder. Name, address (a town near Port Jefferson, out on the Island), social security number, height, weight, age (all more than mine, I was pleased to note in passing), boxes to be checked about allergies and past medical history. Method of payment, cash.

I read the form twice more, quickly. It told me nothing.

Pearl turned around and looked at me. *"Nu?"* she whispered.

I was so dispirited I just shook my head. My eyes got blurry, the not-quite tears stinging the back of my nose.

Then Pearl turned the manila folder inside out, and flopped the sheet over, so I could read the back. She said nothing, simply looking questioningly at me as she held it up, then once more looking over her shoulder.

I read it once, then twice. Then, to make sure it wasn't going to shimmer and disappear, I read the "To Be Notified In Case of Emergency" box one more time.

The same round, girls'-prep-school hand as had filled in the front of the form had printed there, in bright blue, "Victor Pedlar." And, in the next box, "Relationship to Patient," also in blue . . .

"Susan Griswold is Victor Pedlar's wife?" I stammered, staring at my mother.

* * *

EXCEPT I had no time to process that fact. As we had agreed he would be, Walter was waiting for us outside the *Times*, bouncing with impatience when we finally pulled up. What we had not agreed though was that he would be dressed like Indiana Jones. Bomber jacket, dark glasses, and—the telling detail—tasseled loafers. The surprise though was that instead of helping us get out of the cab, he got into the front.

"The St. Regis," he barked at the driver, then turned about, a huge dazzling smile, above which I got a glare, and Polina got eyes widened in appreciation. His cheeks were fresh-shaven and his mustache trimmed to military precision, and I'm pretty sure had recently been slapped with something that had a musk base. He held his hand out to Polina.

"Hi, Walter Goldberg, of the *Times*."

The driver scowled viciously at Walter, probably because the trip from the World Trade Towers to Times Square had given him enough time to fall hopelessly in love with Polina, or at least her legs, which he had ogled in the rearview mirror all the way uptown, but he threw the cab into gear and pulled away with a jerk.

The St. Regis? I was in jeans, my face looked like I was an extra in the Addams Family, I was with a freak of Russian fashion—and *today* is the day Walter decides to branch out from Hyman's Deli?

"Oh, Christ, Walter," I couldn't help growling, "I'm not dressed for this. Can't you just talk to her at your desk, like I thought you were going to?"

"Midge-sweetie-who-made-me-*do*-this?" Walter spoke fast and high, right through his still-clenched smile, so Polina wouldn't understand. "Anybody-from-the-paper-finds-out-I'm-doing-this, it's-my-*ass*." Then, slower and in considerably more plummy a voice, he said, "I'm sure Miss Volkova would like a chance to see something of the Big Apple, wouldn't you?

And no writer should miss a chance to visit a famous landmark like the King Cole Room, eh?"

"Walter, they *closed* that, for renovations!" Actually, they had reopened it, but I was damned if I was going to go there in old jeans and a faded turtle neck.

"Oh," he said, for a fraction of a moment looking crestfallen, even embarrassed. Then he recovered. "Well, name some other trendy place in midtown then, all right?"

"Trendy"? I grimaced, cursing my luck. For once in my life I stumble into an occasion when a man wants to throw a chunk of money around New York, to really impress a girl . . . and not only am I not the girl he wants to impress, but the man is somebody whose idea of a really great New York hotspot is the Gotham Book Mart.

Which is why I told the driver to let us off at Top of the Sixes; the view would impress the socks off any Soviet, and dinner would cost Walter a bundle.

We were shown to a drinks table, after the usual oohing and aahing over the vertiginous views. Walter sat, perched his sunglasses in his curly black hair, and unzipped his jacket to bare an expensive oxford cloth shirt. He leaned forward intently, doing his best to suggest he was maybe an Israeli pilot, just returned from bombing an Iraqi reactor; the image was undercut a bit because of his little-boy habit of fiddling with the tassel of his right loafer. Polina sat across the low cocktail table from him, her arms and legs folded at endearingly gawky, clumsy angles, a sober, slightly awed expression on her face as she studied the twinkling Manhattan around her.

And I sat as near to the middle of the room as I could, well away from the windows while I mulled over why it was that the more suspects I had for who had chucked Simon Brent-Waterhouse out the window of the Van Horn Hotel, the less motive any of them seemed to have for doing it?

Polina was slight, but far from weak, and obviously plenty

resourceful; the day I had spent with her made me certain that if she had wanted to stuff Simon overboard she could have engineered it, somehow or other. And coltish as she affected to be, Polina had shown me enough of her inner steel to leave me little doubt that if Brent-Waterhouse was all that stood between her and something she wanted, then it would be *do svidania* Simon. But what did she gain by his death? It was a green card she wanted, not a bestseller.

So maybe she had to have the rights to her book in order to keep Pedlar interested in her?

The memory of Pedlar's parting words was vivid—"hang noodles on Uncle Sam's ears." Russian for "make an ass of." Meaning Pedlar wanted the book out for patriotic reasons, to expose some truth, to protect America from harm.

Which seemed awfully idealistic for a man who had married on Komsomol orders, in order to become an agent in place in America.

So maybe now that the Komsomol and the Party and the Kremlin are all dead, Pedlar wants to settle a few old scores, like all those KGB generals who troop through the States, decrying atrocities they had helped engineer in the first place? Any old scores Polina would settle with her former whoremasters in her book, presumably as many scores would be settled for Vitya Korobeikin, Toy Boy for the Cause.

And that's why he had his wife passing herself off as Simon Brent-Waterhouse's secretary, "investing" in Polina's book in order to get control of it? But one of the things that the book would reveal, presumably, was that if Vitya Korobeikin had married out of love, it was love for Lenin, not for Susan Griswold?

So perhaps he was only *pretending* to want the book published? So then the best course would be to *let* Sirin Press bring Polina's confessions out, and they would sink into obscurity?

But they would still be out, and Susan Griswold could learn of the real nature of her husband's affections?

Well, at least one thing was certain, I decided when the whole thing had begun to make me dizzy—whoever did throw Simon out the window, it couldn't have been Susan Griswold, because she was home with a fractured tooth and a big prescription for Demerol.

Then I realized that that didn't mean Susan Griswold had *taken* the Demerol. Insomnia, the glass of Rhine wine I was nursing, and the waves of raw sexual nervousness that were wafting from Walter all made me feel as if my brain were breaking up into little granules. I choked down a fistful of salted almonds, then gripped the sides of the chair, which seemed to want to dump me on the floor.

"You see, Miss Volkova," Walter was chattering nervously, oblivious to anything but Polina, "it isn't the usual practice of the newspaper to, in effect, assist the commercial success of a book. We review, after all, not sell. But in circumstances of compelling public interest, as say in the case of the Pentagon Papers. . . ." He swigged from his Corona long-neck beer bottle then, à la John Wayne, bit into the lime that had come with it.

Polina smiled for a second at Walter's grimace, touched her own drink—Sex on the Beach, ordered at Walter's giggling insistence—and glanced at me, for explanation. I signed that it didn't matter. Walter, scarcely noticing, went on.

"Any rate, there have been rumors to the effect that you make some extravagant charges in your book . . ."

"Excuse please. Extravagant?" Again she looked at me, and I translated.

She nodded, a little surer. "Means false, yes?"

"Big, and maybe false." I concurred.

"Then is not extravagant," Polina repeated the word with care. "Is not false to say that Russian coup is fake. Is not false to say that so-call democrats no different from communist. Is not false to say that whole thing is game." She nodded in punctuation to each claim. "So, is not extravagant."

Even from where I sat I could feel Walter throbbing, engorging with the excitement that he had a *scoop*.

"Those reports were heard, of course," he finally said, with that stiff uncertain caution of a date probing whether your doorstep kiss is a full stop or a comma for his evening's activities. "But our State Department and the White House seem reasonably convinced that the August events were spontaneous, and the changes appear to be moving in the direction of genuine and constructive transformation of Soviet society."

"Of course," Polina shrugged and then, because Walter looked nonplussed by her answer, she added, with a smile, "such was plan. To seem like that."

"Plan?" Walter said, chorused now by me.

Polina stretched, rubbed her hands nervously along her thighs, looked around the room. Walter examined her neckline. I took more almonds.

"You will not tell?" Polina's voice was terse, as if she had made a difficult and dangerous decision. "This information is middle of book, what Victor calls meat."

"We won't tell," Walter agreed hastily; then, forcing himself to remain dispassionate, added, "if it's true, of course."

"True?" Polina laughed, but looking infinitely sad and wise, in the way that only European women can. "If I am true, then this is true. August 1981, I am working at Pitsunda. Black Sea. Horrible place, very hot, beach all pebbles, many medusa in water. And 1981, maybe you remember, our clients . . ." She made a comical gag, crossing her eyes and sticking out her tongue. "Old, sweaty, so fat. Only good thing, they all fall asleep quick. Much time for us girls watch television. And good thing. You don't know maybe, but August 1981 happens extraordinary extraordinary thing in Russian television. Polish Party congress . . ."

Gawd, I thought, disappointment intensifying my weary dizziness. The meat in Polina's book was going to come from Polish Party congresses?

Walter, though, had sat bolt upright. "The Solidarity congress!"

Polina nodded, appreciating his knowledge. "Yes. All summer, everybody is sure is 1968 once more, Prague then, Warsaw now. But no invasion, no invasion. Instead, in August, this congress. On our television. So? everybody thinks, brotherly Party congresses always on television. But this time . . ."

"My God," Walter put in, "they *broadcast* that congress? That was the first time the Party took any hits! The Party did this wrong, the Party did that wrong! And they showed it on Soviet television?"

Polina nodded, tried to force her hair behind her ears. "And the Polish Party bosses just sit there, like fat old fools. Like *our* fat old fools! It was beginning of end, of course."

It was a pity Polina added that final bit, because until then she had Walter hooked like a trout. "What, you're saying just because people saw that on television, ten years later they're waving flags in front of the Russian parliament building, trying to stop tanks with bare hands? Okay, maybe it had something to do with beginning to create a *climate,* but it took another ten years, of Brezhnev's death, and Andropov and Chernenko and . . ."

Polina stopped him very neatly, by leaning across the cocktail table and putting her long, scarlet-tipped index finger across Walter's lips. Surprised, Walter jerked his head back, then looked regretful that he had flinched.

"You did not listen me. That was beginning of end. I know, because same night, next night, I don't remember exactly, there was a call. Girls were needed at dacha near Min-vody. Caucasus. Such a one, such a one, and me. Very exciting, helicopter right down to the beach, and off we go, over the tops of the mountains."

"Those guys lived all right, didn't they?" Walter grinned at me. "There's days I wouldn't mind just dialing up a chopper full of hookers."

I glared, to remind him that this wasn't the locker room, and I wasn't his buddy, but Polina laughed, tapped him on his knee. "Not hooker. People's Master of Recreation. And not easy job to get."

Walter and she eyed one another for a moment, his thoughts at least beginning to steam the mirrors up, so I nudged Polina. "The resort?"

"Oh, yes . . . very pretty place, meadow in mountains. I think you see this place since, on news, that is where German Kohl signed papers after we give him our Germany. Top secret then, naturally. Anyway, it is small meeting, called by Yurochka. That is when we met, actually." Surprisingly, Polina dimpled, as if treasuring a memory.

"Andropov," I whispered. Walter nodded, eyebrows raised.

Then Polina straightened. "That is when they planned it. Three, four days in Caucasus. And I heard them."

"It?"

"Timetable. Berlin Wall, troops out of East Europe, all that stuff," she waved her hand, as if what she had said was so much smoke. "What you think is end of communism."

Walter crossed his legs the other way, then crossed them back. Finally he leaned forward. "What you're saying, all of that, everything that has happened this last decade . . . *it was all planned that weekend?*"

"In truth, I think Yurochka already had his plan for a long time. But that was when he tell them. Because of television."

Both of us sat in stunned silence, grappling with the idea that the most tumultuous historical events of at least the second half of the century had been put together on a summer weekend, kind of like you or I might do the shops in East Hampton.

"It was money," Polina went on, in our silence. "Like I told you, Midge. Yurochka showed them how much costs the Afghan war, what costs troops in Poland, Czechoslovakia, Cuba. Rotting harvests, alcohol, high death, low birth . . . you know all these things too, now."

Walter was doing what he could to rally. "So you're saying that in 1981 Yuri Andropov predicted that the U.S.S.R. was going to go bankrupt, and he proposed a plan to try to prevent it?"

But Polina shook her head. "No. What Yurochka said, U.S.S.R. is already bankrupt. He said Russia is like Brezhnev, a corpse too stupid to lie down. So what he propose was different. Look for buyer before everybody understand that horse is dead."

"A *buyer?*" Walter shouted and slapped his foot, then glared at me, because I had obviously tricked him into a demented prank of some sort. In fact, I think the only thing that kept him from punching me right then was that I was goggling at Polina, stupefied. He turned back to Polina, to give her his famous derisive laugh. "My *God,* Miss Volkova, I'm sorry, but I really can't sit here and have you expect me to believe that this bunch of Soviet leaders sat down and seriously discussed *selling* the largest country on Earth!"

Polina made Bambi eyes at him. "I am sorry, perhaps the word is not quite right. What do you call West Germany, when they must send millions and millions of marks to East Germany. Donor is better word? Sponsor?"

Actually, from what I knew of the costs of reunification, and especially in light of what Polina was saying here, the best word of all might be "sucker." East Germany and the U.S.S.R. had forced Bonn to pay untold billions for a blind parcel, which when Kohl and Company opened it proved to be full of roads that had been crumbling since the thirties, houses that had needed roofing since the forties, rivers so polluted they were fire hazards, air so foul that no birds flew through it, and the trees shriveled and turned black, and a population that had not only forgotten how to work four decades before, but had also grown up in the firm conviction that it was entitled to free or cheap housing, day care, education, medicine, and food. Bad, maybe, but free, certainly.

By comparison with that deal putting your life-savings into an offer for the Brooklyn Bridge seemed like sober, conservative fiscal management.

Walter, for the moment at least, agreed. "What you're implying then is that German reunification was nothing more than a run-through? Andropov and a bunch of his men actually sat down and planned this whole thing, like a bunch of punks who want to knock over a candy store?"

Polina paused, puzzled by the idiom, then shrugged. "What Yurochka actually say is that next task is create conditions for secure the favorable financial assistance from the enemy."

"I think I like my image better," Walter said, his eyes shining, so excited by Polina's version of the 1980s that he could scarcely keep himself from fidgeting off the chair. "But hang on a second, all the same, even if Andropov was a god, he *died* in 1984, so how could all the rest of this be part of his plan?"

Polina gave another of her Simone Signoret smiles. "You would not remember, but Min-Vody is in Stavropol district . . ."

"Gorbachev's district!" Walter understood immediately.

Polina nodded, pleased with his quickness. "That's why meeting was in Min-Vody camp, and Mikhail Sergeich was there, of course . . ."

Walter continued to squeeze Polina for details, which she gave, with a seemly reluctance. I gradually stopped listening though, my attention usurped by burgeoning, enormous dread. Kind of like what you might feel three sleepless days and nights after you first agreed to a friendly game of cards, and just now discovered yourself, unwashed, red-eyed, and dim-witted with fatigue, on the verge of gambling away house, car, and the shirt on your back.

Or, I remembered, thinking of Simon, Pedlar in the bushes outside my house, Susan Griswold's phone call . . .

Maybe it's my life I'm gambling?

"Polina! Polina!"

My cry was so loud even I jumped, startled, and the other two leapt up, expecting at least fire.

"What? What?" Walter looked around, frantic.

I smiled brilliantly. "I'm sorry, I didn't mean . . . but I wanted . . . Polina, the book, the one thing I haven't heard you talk about yet. Tell Mr. Goldberg . . ."

"Walter, Walter," he assured Polina, not quite winking at her.

"Tell Walter about how they got their agents into America." I grinned at her.

She looked at me as if I were off my head.

"Agents into America?"

Sensing there was some problem, I switched to Russian. "Tell him about Vitya, and the others. That married Americans, but . . . Vitya's in the book, isn't he?"

"Not so far," Polina's answer was noncommittal, but her glance might have been doing thoracic surgery on me.

"But the others? That married to come over? You said that . . ."

"Agents?" Walter asked, something in his voice so delighted you might have thought I had just proposed the three of us play strip poker. And cheat.

I answered Walter, but kept my eyes on Polina. "What Polina was telling me," I said very slowly, to be absolutely certain that she understood me, "was how part of this policy was to send as many Russians here as possible. By marriage, at first, and then . . ."

"The emigrés?!" Walter was a quick study. "She's claiming that letting the *emigrés* out was part of Andropov's plan?"

Polina was no dummy either. With an opaque but forbidding glare at me, she addressed herself to Walter, controlling whatever damage it was that I had unwittingly done. That I had spoiled some part of her plan was clear, but I had no idea what.

"Not all, of course. And not all marriages, either. But yes, it is true, Yurochka saw merit of putting many Russians in your country."

"Like sleepers, you mean? Agents who could be activated, fifth columnists and so forth?" Walter was squirming about in his chair, face ruddy with excitement.

Polina looked at me, uncertain of the terms; I did what I could with translations, trying at the same time to understand why she was seething at me. When I was through, she nodded, then crossed her legs, examining Walter coolly. "There are some, but it is not so easy. Only one, two people out from millions can *become* other person. Speak English like American, become American. Easier to use foreigner, then it is okay he sound foreign. But that was not what Margaret speaks of. After all, how many such . . . sleeper, you call them? How many sleeper you need? No, what Yurochka spoke of, Russian is the mystery to Americans, Russian is superman, very very frightening. So let many Russians come, let Americans know Russians . . ." Polina smiled, hugely now, lips peeled to teeth the size—and color—of elephant's toenails. "Then, who can be afraid of Russia?"

I laughed too, thinking of the emigrés I knew. Bumbling and pathetic at their worst, rarely more than passably competent at their best, able to argue all night about the relative superiority of Soviet education over American, but unable to fathom the use and purpose of a checking account, content to invest countless time and energy into perfecting ways to cheat Medicaid, ADC, and welfare, but far too proud to take a job, at least for anything less than Bill Clinton's salary.

My laugh faded, though, as I realized what Polina meant. As long as America pictured Russians to be like something out of *From Russia with Love*, the chances of getting so much as a nickel of outside aid were nonexistent. Turn the Soviets into a nation of inept, daft, and loveable goofs, though, who just happen to possess a couple thousand nuclear weapons that in their bumbling might accidentally be set off, and the money would torrent in, like the Mississippi rolling down to New Orleans.

I was just starting to wonder where such money would go, when Polina put her long, lacquered, and slightly bony index fingers together in front of her nose, her sparkling feline eyes closing not quite to a wink, so that she looked like one of Santa's elves about to give you an illicit peek into the workshop. "But enough of this! Victor will kill me, I tell you whole book! Instead, Mr. Goldberg, your advice please. As *professional.*"

Polina grabbed up her duffel-sized handbag and began to rummage intently. Walter watched for a little longer than was polite, then turned to me. He raised his eyebrows in comic question, then took another big swig from his beer. This time, I noticed, he did without the lime.

"Ah-ha!" Triumphantly Polina pulled a sheet of photo paper from her bag, and held it up, first to Walter, then to me. "What do you think? Would this make good cover for on my book?"

The photo was amateurishly developed, the print size somewhere between postcard and napkin, its edges fuzzy and indistinct. The image itself could also have been sharper; obviously a Soviet camera and Soviet film, shooting in a Soviet basement.

Still, it was clear enough.

Walter reached for the photo, pulled back, then, purple, reached again, leaning down to study the image under the low table lamp. "This is supposed to be like that statue, right? From the 1939 World's Fair?"

A man and a woman striding forward, shoulder to shoulder, he holding aloft a hammer, and she a sickle.

Polina and Vitya Korobeikin, both much younger.

It wasn't hard to tell that Vitya at least had found the whole thing very exciting.

Neither one of them was wearing a stitch of clothing.

11

"GOD, that Polina is some number, eh?" Walter said, for about the fourth time in as many minutes.

"Look, Walter, you want the picture, just let me make a copy, then you can have it, all right? You can take it back to Polina. More coffee?" I glanced over at the clock, hoping he'd say no. Today was already yesterday, and we were half an hour into tomorrow.

"Yeah, sure, 'nother cup," he pushed his cup toward me, then stretched back out; he was somehow occupying most of Aunt Dora's couch, legs akimbo, heel on knee, arms spread along the back, leather jacket gaping. The knee-suspended foot was bouncing up and down, metronome of Walter's excitement. "But the picture, naw . . . or maybe, sure, yeah. For laughs. But what I meant, the *story* she tells! You sit and talk with Polina, it's like A leads to B and that means C, everything makes sense. But then five minutes later its like *Whaaat?!* Gorbachev and Andropov and a bunch of the Politburo sat down and planned how they were going to get top dollar from liquidating the Soviet Union? Makes the damn Nabisco buy out seem like a pile of Oreo crumbs, if it's true . . ." He shook his head, still grinning, foot tapping. "And so what you're figuring then, this is the news that somebody chucked old Simon down the airshaft for, because he was going to go public with it?"

We hadn't had dinner after all—no doubt because Walter had figured, correctly, that I was trying to stick him with a big bill—but instead had continued to pay for our seats by ordering drinks, plus which I hadn't slept in so long my pillow must have thought I was away at summer camp, so all I really could have answered him was that I *think* that was what I thought. Because by now I wanted to sleep so badly that I decided it prudent to say nothing at all, hoping Walter would get the hint and go home.

Not that I had been displeased when Walter insisted on sharing my cab back to Brooklyn, after we dropped Polina off. Even without having discovered today that the nice friendly case of fraud and murder that I had *thought* I had inadvertently blundered into was really something far worse—nasty, confusing, and very dangerous—I was not so happy anymore going back to my apartment alone, what with the number of protagonists in this tangled little tale who seemed to know where I lived. I didn't even mind when Walter paid off the cabbie and came up, paying no attention to my warning that not only would he never find another cab, but I was pretty sure even the livery companies wouldn't pick him up. Not at that hour, anyway.

"I'll get a cab, I'll get a cab," Walter had dismissed me, still pulsing adrenalin from what Polina had told us during the evening.

When I started to mind Walter was when we were standing at my door, me fumbling in my bag for keys, and him staring at my peephole and humming. Still, what was I going to do? I asked Walter in, made him coffee. Bad coffee, stale instant that I had to scrape out of the jar with a grapefruit spoon. And, after the second cup, I quit waiting until the water boiled.

But Walter *still* wouldn't go home. And as long as he stayed there talking at me and looking around my apartment, the evening was going to chase itself around inside my head like a Pekinese after its own tail.

I clearly had done *something* wrong when I started to bring Victor Pedlar into the conversation at Top of the Sixes; the question was *what*? This morning Polina had *told* me that she and Victor had worked together, that both were under similar orders—"One whores as one is ordered."

So maybe Polina was using her knowledge about Pedlar's past as a club? Blackmailing him, in a word?

For a moment the explanation made sense, but only for a moment. If Polina's book was going to detail a secret Kremlin program to export thousands and thousands of Russians to the U.S., then all the Russians in the States were going to look suspicious, even if they had no connection to Andropov's cynical scheme. And as for a Russian who had changed his name, and was passing himself off as American, betrayed only by an occasional vowel sound . . . I mean, if Victor Pedlar *wasn't* going to look fishy after Polina's book, I don't know who *would!*

Assuming that Polina's book was written, distributed, and bought. So if Polina didn't want people looking askance at her husband-to-be, then wasn't the most sensible thing of all not to write the book?

Put it another way. The book that Polina proposed to write would show that a small group of Soviet leaders were nothing better than a clutch of sleazy salesmen, who if they weren't heads of state would have been peddling home improvements to credulous widows, but who because they were, were deliberately manipulating Soviet events and Western opinion for their own material benefit. Simon Brent-Waterhouse proposed to publish that book. Insisted on it, even. So, given you were a Soviet agent, which Polina had told me Victor Pedlar was, it made perfect sense to push Simon Brent-Waterhouse out a window.

Except that removing Brent-Waterhouse from the picture opened the way for *bigger* publishers to handle the Volkova book, who could guarantee it much greater attention. And besides, faking suicides to prevent publication of manuscripts *has* to be a lot more work than it would have been simply never to have invited Volkova in the first place. Which Pedlar had done.

"What did you say?" I tuned in late to what Walter was saying, with a sinking feeling that I was going to be sorry I had.

"I was just asking, your divorce and all, how long it took?" Walter had his head canted to the right, his expression radiating irritation at my inattention, thinly disguised as friendly interest.

"What took? The divorce? Six months maybe, it wasn't contested, and the community property . . ."

"No, no, I meant the . . . well, getting used to it." Walter glanced at his own ring finger; he had been single long enough at least that the ring mark was gone. "You know, not feeling guilty when you talk to somebody of the other sex, like you're cheating. Or Sunday mornings, nobody to talk to, it doesn't matter what time you get out of bed, but there's nobody to linger in there with either!" He laughed, a little forced.

"Working at home, the days of the week are pretty much the same to me," I lied, pretending this was still just information, and definitely not wishing to admit to Walter that yes, many Sundays, I would be willing to become the Bride even of Frankenstein rather than catch myself poring through the Business and Real Estate sections of the *Times,* pretending I was enjoying my leisurely Sunday alone. Even through all my exhaustion and raw-edged nerves I was beginning to wonder—was Walter not going home because he was going to put a *move* on me?

"Work? Oh, your writing, you mean?" he smiled. "So, how's that going? I mean, you think it's going to . . . well, pan out? Turn into anything?"

"I've *published* three novels!" I shot back, bitterly, then glared, daring him to mock me with the truth, that mysteries for Girl Scouts ages eight to eleven are not *Moby-Dick*.

Mockery, though, seemed not to have crossed his mind. "Wow, so many? I guess I didn't realize. And you're working on something now?"

I glanced at him sharply, thinking maybe this was a dig about the book review I owed him. When I decided it wasn't, I nodded, shrugged, and then, almost as stiffly as if I were undressing in front of him, I told Walter a little about my adult novel. A bright executive in New York, driven by the demon of her ambition, unstrung suddenly by her inexplicable attraction to the man who comes to install her stair-tread exerciser. Their cautious dates, the fun she has on them, the laughter she thought she had forgotten. His mother's rejection of her, because she is Jewish and he is Italian.

"I won't say I've never heard the plot before." Walter pushed his glasses further back up his forehead, with a chuckle. "But you know what they say, there's only seven plots anyway. Tell you the truth, working at the paper, I sometimes wonder if there's that many, even. Trick is how the book works, right? What you do with it. And I guess you're feeling good on that score?"

Torn between the desire to have Walter go home so I could sleep, and a sudden desperation, to have somebody, *anybody*, say something encouraging about my writing, I nodded, then shrugged, then shook my head. Then I got up, stretched ostentatiously.

"Walter, I've got things I've got to do tomorrow."

He didn't get up. "Yeah, me too. . . ." He drummed his fingers on his ankle bone, then cocked his head at me again. "That's what I was wondering, why I'm asking you. . . . All this cloak-and-dagger stuff, amateur detecting, you just using it to spice up your life or something? Because the writing, that's your work, right? And yet here you are spending all this time, running around New York, chasing after things that really have nothing to do with you. So it's for the thrill of it, right?"

"*Walter,*" I growled, seriously angry.

He held up his hands, then put both feet on the floor, ready to stand up. "I'm going, I'm going. I just wanted to inquire, that's all. Curiosity. Because maybe if like a hobby or something works for you, I mean puts some zest back in life, well, maybe it would work for me too, you know?"

"*A hobby?!*" I shouted, even picking up a book, to fling it at him.

Walter stood, zipped his jacket, pulled his collar up, then held his hands up in mock surrender. "Or whatever you call it. A distraction, something to take your mind off work. I'm wondering, maybe I need something like that too. So what I'm asking you . . . what I'm wondering. . . . This Polina, you think maybe she'd go out with me?"

WHETHER it was exhaustion or the wine, I don't know, but *something* let me sleep that night, so when I tested my brainflash of last night over the morning's branflakes and still thought that it made a pretty good idea, I decided that, well . . . it must be a pretty good idea.

It was not until I saw Polina's photo last night that I realized *one* way, at least, of checking who might have gone back to Simon Brent-Waterhouse's hotel room that night was to see whether any of the other clients at the Van Horn recognized Victor.

"You want to show this photo to your *mother?*" Walter and Polina had both shouted, when I explained why I had snatched it up from the table, and stuffed it into my own purse.

"Well, yeah," I had blushed, confused by the wine and my own excitement. "Like I told you, Polina . . . I knew . . . well, I wanted to . . . I've been talking about you, and . . . please? I *did* buy you the bracelet, right?"

After a long look at me, Polina had conceded the point, and then begun to show her new warthog tusk bangle to Walter, who had been extremely interested. In fact, he had been extremely interested in all of Polina's jewelry, holding each piece while the woman described, in *Ninotchka* English, where each had come from and how. Then there was another round of drinks, and the photo was forgotten. At least until Polina's parting admonition, that I should return it to her today.

Which I was going to be perfectly happy to do. *After* the police showed it around the Van Horn.

When I called, Detective Inderlund, after some coaxing and maybe a little whining, agreed to meet me at a café that proved to be about three blocks from the Van Horn Hotel, one of those tattered New Agey vegetarian places you sometimes find on the edge of the ghetto. I suppose they cluster like that because the rents are cheap, but cafés like The Dragon's Egg generally don't last too long, because Morningside and 119th isn't really a tofu-and-black-bean kind of neighborhood. Not that many people could have kept an appetite with our waitress anyway, who had eight ear studs and a ring through her red, runny nose. Ferns, rough-cut redwood, and a staff that seemed mostly to be floating, camouflaged in tie-dyed Ben and Jerry's Rainforest Crunch T-shirts.

Inderlund could have been sixteen, with her pink satin warm-up jacket, her short, blond french-braided hair, her square shoulders, and blocky chest. Her face was pretty, though my mother would have said there was more flesh about the dimpled chin and apple cheeks than the woman should have been carrying. Her eyes, the color of a summer sky and the size of half dollars, made it even harder to believe her response, when I handed the photo to her across the steam of our lemon zinger tea.

"Judas," she whistled, "the guy's got a dong like a donkey!"

I reached for the photo, then snatched my hand back, blushing. "Yeah, well . . ." I slurped at my tea, which was like a swig of hot furniture polish. "Anyway, it's the face I want you to show people, not his. . . . It's the only photo I've got. You think it will work, to show it around the Van Horn?"

"Even a place like the Van Horn, people would probably recall a guy who runs around waving his Oscar Mayer, if your friend always dresses like that. Which I suppose he didn't. So maybe we should crop the picture down a bit, because as it is, the pair of them here could have heads like Bullwinkle Moose and Rocky the Flying Squirrel, and nobody would even notice."

"I can't do that, it's not my picture, it's borrowed and I've got to return it. Today."

Inderlund shrugged, then slid the photo into some inner pocket, past the shiny snaps of her jacket. "Okay, so we'll give the crowd at the Van Horn a little thrill. We'll just keep the thumb over the PG-thirteen parts, so nobody can accuse New York's finest of peddling smut. You ready to go?"

"Go?"

"To the Van Horn. To show the photo around." She patted her breast, where Polina's picture lay.

"I'm going with you? I thought it was . . . you know, police stuff. No civilians allowed."

Inderlund sat there a moment, curling and uncurling her right bicep, which she monitored with her left hand. "Police work?

This is your show, sweetie. Russo didn't want you getting hurt, so that's why I agreed to back you up, as a favor."

"My show? Catching a murderer is my show? This is part of New York's cost-cutting program, citizens will now do their own police work?" I snapped, wondering exactly *why* it was that Russo had asked this woman for a favor, and why she had agreed to do it for him.

Inderlund's expression gave away nothing. "The way I got what Russo told me, for you this is like 'America's Most Wanted' or something, sort of a hobby, playing detective. Like maybe if I wrote books in my spare time. Anyway, just so there's no misunderstanding—I'm doing this on my lunch time. Usually I go to the gym, heft a little iron."

It took me a while to see past those big blue eyes, that placid, moonlike face, and that fireplug body, to understand that Detective Inderlund was jerking my chain, and fairly hard at that.

"A hobby? That's what Russo said?" I flushed, doubly angry, that this question had come up twice in twelve hours. Damnit, *hobbies* don't include people breaking into your apartment.

Inderlund smiled, slapped me on the back, not hard, but in a way that got me moving toward the door. "So it's not a hobby, maybe. More like a special interest then?"

"What else did Russo say?" I was still mad at Russo, but I wasn't sure for what—that he had presumed to be so paternalistic of me as to ask this woman to play guardian angel? Or that for some reason he knew this woman well enough that he could ask a substantial favor of her?

Inderlund didn't answer right away, because we were bounding up the street toward the hotel. Or she was, anyway; I was panting along behind. The streets around the Van Horn were, well, colorful. We weaved around people arguing outside stores, old men on folding chairs playing cards and listening to blaring portable radios, kids playing tag and shouting, teens shrieking and flirting to the din of music boxes the size of microwave ovens.

"Russo said you're smart," Inderlund finally explained, when we had to wait for a light. "And lucky. But mostly what worried him, I think . . . he said, once you get an idea in your head, that's it. Stubborn as a Naples burro, was I believe how he put it. Here we are, the Van Horn. You got somebody particular you want to show that photo to, or just we start grabbing passersby at random?"

"Stubborn? Damn him!" I planted my feet, not willing to cross the hotel's threshold until I established my sweet reasonableness. "I'm not stubborn, I just . . ."

"Miz Cohen, if you're not stubborn, then I'm wasting my lunch hour. What Russo begged me to do this for, he said if I didn't, you'd probably come over here on your own and poke around anyway, more than likely you'd get somebody so ticked off they'd chuck you down the airwell, too. So I told him I'd come along. But what I don't get, how come you're so set on nailing this clown that's got the baseball bat for plumbing? He was maybe an old boyfriend?" She grinned artificially, to suggest it was a joke. It also suggested that maybe there was another old boyfriend running around under this conversation.

Which was a possibility far too complicated even to attempt to grasp, so I just jerked my chin in the direction of the hotel's dark doorway. "Whatever . . . I guess just ask around. I can't understand, though, why I'd need a *reason* to do this. I mean, you can't seriously tell me that *you'd* be anxious to have a murderer running around loose!"

"Ah, there's murderers and there's murderers," Detective Inderlund said gnomically, and then plowed ahead, into the gloomy hotel lobby.

Remember those montages on "Dragnet," when Jack Webb and Harry Morgan ask half of west Los Angeles some question? Shake of the head, new face, shake of the head, new face, shake of the head, right up to commercial break? This is not how it went in the Van Horn.

In the first place, English was not the language of choice for most of the Van Horn's guests, and not too many of them responded to Inderlund's Spanish, either.

"Cathtilliano," she explained with a grimace, exaggerating that aristocratic dialect's lisp. "Learned it college, and just about as useful with these Cubans, Colombians, Puetro Ricans, Dominicans and all as any other of my college subjects would be. Might as well try talking calculus to them, I suppose."

In the second place, most of the people we could understand seemed to have a few questions of their own, and considerably more urgency about asking even than I had.

"Cops, eh?" one harried-looking woman poked her stocking-covered head out to ask, even though Inderlund hadn't said so. She dangled a cigarette from her lips and a baby with eyes like a lemur from her hip; another kid, slightly bigger, sat rapt, with his back to us, in front of a TV that looked as though it might have been plucked from a trash heap. "What, you come 'round counting husbands again or something? Trying to take away our ADC? Why don't you go downstairs ask that fat-assed Indian owns the place where is the man who comes plaster the hole in my ceiling? Six month leaking down from the toilet upstairs, chunks of plaster big as pizza coming down on my kids, on our *food,* I got no place else keep our dishes and food and stuff, except in the tub and on the sill, make them kids something to eat, and all that shit . . ." She bounced her wide-eyed silent baby faster and faster in her fury, until Detective Inderlund excused us, and gently closed the door.

"Sure I seen him," one old fellow finally agreed, when Inderlund shoved the photo partway through his chained door.

"You *have?*" we both shouted, surging forward, making the old man retreat, a bewhiskered blinking turtle. Only the strategically placed tip of Inderlund's Air Jordan kept his door from slamming entirely.

"Listen, are you sure you recognize this face?" she said, her tone implying all the horrors the law holds for perjury. "You've seen this man in this hotel?"

"Of course," the man finally emerged, in an exhalation of vapor, the only parts of which I could name for sure being Wild Rose fortified wine, socks that had never been washed, and the sort of oral hygiene that would have blanched the black rinse out of my mother's hair. "He's a Rooshun."

Inderlund and I both glanced at one another, then looked away.

"A Russian?" the detective repeated.

" 'Course," the man nodded. "There's a bunch of them, they've got a tunnel on Broadway, they come through from that Kremalin of theirs, bent on destroying the world." He smiled, then looked about craftily. "They're robots, actually, most of them. That's why I live over here, 'cause the magnets scramble their wires."

"What magnets?" I asked, but Inderlund was already towing me along the corridor.

"Somebody ought to do something about them!" the fellow shouted after us, emboldened by our departure. "Damn dangerous, having all them machines about in our midst!"

"What magnets?" I still wondered, probably because I also wondered how much distance there was between the "Rooshuns" that old man saw under *his* bed and the ones I had been seeing under mine.

"Ah, it's probably got something to do with the Chrysler Building," Inderlund dismissed the whole subject with a glance at her watch. The last sands of her lunch hour were trickling away. "I don't know what it is, but there's something about that building, half of New York has hallucinations about it. Come on, two more floors!"

On the second of which, after we had already moved away from her door because by now we both silently agreed this whole exercise was pointless and so didn't wait if there was no immediate answer, we were called back by a woman of indeterminate old age, bent like a question mark, and with the bulging eyes of extreme high-blood pressure, but otherwise hale enough. What we could see of her room was also as hermetic as some kind of life-support capsule, but the smell was a considerably more unpleasant mix of old woman and parakeets; two of the birds chirruped and hopped about a large cage, jangling the bells on a red plastic mirror.

"Yes? Can I help you?" she asked.

"You're English!" I more accused her than asked, because it was so unexpected.

"I am not!" she said with as much outraged dignity as a bent old woman shorter than I am could muster. "October twelve, 1957, I took my citizenship, and there isn't a soul who can claim I've been aught but a Yank ever since!"

"No, but what I mean . . ." I did what I could to pluck my shoe from my mouth. "Your accent, you're not from . . ."

The woman's offense ebbed, but only a little. "An *accent* is it, dearie? I'm quite sure you wouldn't be calling this an accent, if you could but hear what some of our nig-nogs hereabout natter on in! But no, right you are, that's a good East Midlands you're hearing, and there aren't many about who speak it! The budgies excepted, of course, heh-heh."

Mrs. Brenda Morrisey, née Ploggins, late of Trent Overcoumbe, England, long ago stranded in America by widowhood, poverty, and a life that had gradually shrunk down to the narrow circumference of her birds and her books of Double-Crostic puzzles, which she galloped through as I would a bag of Fritos.

Or shrank so small, at least, until Simon Brent-Waterhouse moved into the Van Horn, and she had begun to "do" for him.

"Nice to have a countryman about, I suppose," I ventured, trying to understand how much there was to that ambiguous verb "do."

"Oooh, not just a countryman, he was proper Midlands hisself! Not from the villages, of course, educated he was. But a breath of home for all that! And very happy to have someone reliable to muck out for him, I can tell you. *Some* of the people hereabouts . . ." Her eyes boggled with unarticulated horror, at what her fellow tenants might steal, given the chance.

Bit by bit I managed to establish that yes, Mrs. Morrisey did have a good memory, and was in full possession of her faculties, and that, yes, she did take a very close interest in Brent-Waterhouse's comings and goings, and that, prim as she was giving herself out to be, chances were that she might not actually fall down in a dead faint, when I showed her the photo.

Still, I thought it worth warning her.

"I apologize, Mrs. Morrisey, about the photo, but it's the only one I've got. Try to ignore the . . . well, ignore everything but the face. Have you seen this person before, and if so, where?"

Mrs. Morrisey took the photo, glanced quickly at it, then stared at us, surprised. Detective Inderlund and I both made such serious faces that I nearly burst out giggling. Fortunately I did not, because Mrs. Morrisey was obviously waiting for one or the other of us to turn into Allen Funt, so she could wave at the Candid Camera.

When we didn't, she adjusted her apron and took a closer look at the photo. "Fancy dress ball, was this? Or undress, more like?" she added slyly.

"Mrs. Morrisey," Detective Inderlund began, but Mrs. Morrisey waved her right hand, to indicate the joke was over, then rummaged in her apron pocket for a cigarette, while her left hand brought the photo toward her face again, for more scrutiny.

Then she put it down again, her face now somber.

"So, Mrs. Morrisey?" the detective asked, while I toyed nervously with the belt of my raincoat. "Is that person someone you have seen in Mr. Brent-Waterhouse's room?"

Mrs. Morrisey made a lenghthy and fairly uncomfortable fidget of lighting her cigarette stub, but then admitted, "Yeah, couple of times."

"When, precisely?" Inderlund asked; her voice was so off-handed that I suspected she was excited. She had to have known at least that I was, because I was now digging my nails into her elbow.

"Dunno, exactly. Two, three weeks ago, perhaps, the first time. Difficult to say, precisely."

"Why is that, Mrs. Morrisey?"

"Well, middle of the night, innit? I hear the rap-rap-rap, wake up . . ."

"In *this* hotel?" I couldn't stop myself asking, unable to believe that the Van Horn was quiet enough at night to permit that.

Mrs. Morrisey fidgeted a bit again, before finally confessing. "Well, I watch, actually. Can't sleep, most nights, the insomnia something just awful fierce, so I watch. Pounding in the ears, don't you know, soon's I put my head to pillow. Used to watch out the window, but anymore there's so many guns, well, you can't trust you won't take one just by bad luck, can you? So I use the judas. Hard on my feet, but it helps me drift off . . ." She pointed up at the hard glass dot of the door's peephole, then puffed on her cigarette. The fit of her jaws suggested she wore a full dental plate, except not at the moment.

I was trying to imagine an old woman passing entire nights with her eye glued to the peep hole, but Detective Inderlund forged ahead, as if such a thing were perfectly normal. In her job, it may even have been so. "All right, so you first saw this man about two weeks ago. When was the last time?"

"Man?" Mrs. Morrisey asked, then looked at the photo again. "I don't know the man from Adam . . . even if he's dressed like him!" She cackled, pleased with her wit. Then, more serious. "No, it's the *girl* I've seen coming in and out." Then, that wicked twinkle in her Marty Feldman eyes again, she added, "And I must say *that* made a change for our Mr. Brent-Waterhouse! Till I saw her I thought Mr. B-W only liked his toast buttered one side, not both."

"Well, when was the last time you saw this woman enter Mr. Brent-Waterhouse's room, then?" Inderlund asked, professionally indifferent to this news, which had dropped my jaw to about my belly button.

"The last time? Well, it would be the night Mr. B-W did himself, wouldn't it? Not much point in her catting around once he's put himself out the window, now is there?"

12

WHY didn't I answer my door when the buzzer began ringing the next morning? Well, in the first place, I was working, for the first time in what seemed months. Yesterday's discovery, that Polina had been to visit Brent-Waterhouse the night he died, had loosened some kind of logjam inside me, set free some spring that had been under enormous tension. I had practically hummed my way home, had banged out a rough draft of the overdue book review, had slept, had fixed myself an enormous breakfast of egg, cheese, and bialy, and now was contentedly moving my executive heroine about her miseries in Manhattan.

I don't mean to give the impression that I *understood* what had happened that evening, how Polina had levered bag 'o guts Simon out the tiny window, and even less could I be sure of *why*.

However, just the fact that she *had* been there, and that it was because of *me* that the police established that fact. . . . Well, that vindicated my earlier hunch, that Simon had not killed himself, proved I'm not nuts. The rest was details, for the police to figure out.

And, in the second place, I didn't answer the buzzer because there was nobody I wanted to see.

Or so I thought, until I heard a key turning in the lock.

"Jesus! *Mother?*" I leapt up in irritation, immediately turning to guilt—she was letting herself into my apartment in the middle of a Thursday morning because I had gotten her fired!

"No, hey Midge, it's me . . . Mike," Russo said hastily, sticking his head in and grinning shyly. "Is it okay I come in?"

I smoothed my hair, checked my clothes, put my hands in my back pockets, remembered I didn't have any, because I was wearing a flannel nightshirt that I was given as a gag Hanukkah gift my junior year at Cornell, with a faded "I Slept Over at ZBT" arched across my breasts, that, in that faded, shrunken *schmatte,* might as well have been bare. "Golly, I was . . . I didn't . . . you could have *called.* . . ." The blush that had begun around my knees finally reached my face and went up through my hair. I crossed my arms and added, "I forgot you still have a key."

That was a lie. I knew Mike had a key; I just never had wanted to ask for it back, because . . ."

Well, because.

Russo stepped in, closed the door behind him, then held up my key, not quite showing it to me, not quite handing it to me. "Should have returned it, I suppose, but . . . anyway, here." He stretched forward and, reluctantly, I took the key, being shyly careful not to touch hands. Russo looked sad for a second, making me wonder whether he felt the same about that key as I did, that as long as he still had it things weren't *totally* over. He took a deep breath, rubbed his hands together nervously, straightened his back. Smiled. "Well, anyway, sorry to just let myself in like that, but. . . . I was gonna leave you a note, to say I was coming by later, talk about something, but then I heard the typewriter, so . . ."

I was touched, for a moment, happy that Mike had come, that he was in my apartment again.

Then I noticed the close way he was watching me, and started to wonder *why* he had come.

"Leave a note? Come by later? Talk about what? Is there something the matter?" My brain ran through a quick check of the few possibilities—my mother? His mother?

Russo pulled his overcoat a little tighter around himself, cleared his throat, then reached inside a pocket for a little wire-bound notebook. Just a prop, apparently, because after he flipped it open, with a one-handed, practiced ease, he never looked at it again.

"I talked to Bertie . . . about what you two did yesterday?"

"Yes?"

"That's why I came over, 'cause I figure that you've got yourself all wrapped up in this . . ." He waved his hand until he found the word he wanted, "thing."

"Brent-Waterhouse's murder," I said flatly, question disguised as assertion.

Mike ran his hand over his chin, the insistent sandy-brown beard rasping even in midmorning. "See, that's what I mean. Whether it *was* a murder . . ."

Panic took me by the throat. "What do you mean *whether?* That woman said Polina was definitely at Simon's room! And she's not crazy or ga-ga either! Polina was *there* the night he . . . died!"

Mike nodded, his lips tight. "She was. Same night. But about an hour *after* he died."

"Mike, come on, what is this? What do you mean, *after* he died? They didn't even *find* him until the next morning, how can they be so sure of when he died? And besides, that Mrs. Morrisey, she's got to be at least a *hundred,* how can you rely on . . ."

Mike laughed, not unkindly. "Can't have it both ways, Midge. Either she's a reliable witness or she's ga-ga!"

I glowered for a minute, then snapped, "Okay, so she's not ga-ga. But did she see Polina coming? Or going? How could she know that? And anyway, you still haven't answered me, how can you be so sure what time Brent-Waterhouse died?"

"Two thirty-eight. That's what forensics says the T-O-D was. And this Polina wasn't up there until around four."

"Oh, come *on, Mike!"* I think I maybe even stamped my foot. "I know something about forensics, *nobody* can be so certain that they can say 'two-thirty-eight.' Like he's an *airplane* or something!"

Actually, everything I know about forensics I learned from watching Jack Klugman on "Quincy," but still . . . he never says, "Yes, the woman died at precisely 11:17 P.M., E.D.T." I mean, it's always a range, right? Between something and something.

Mike shrugged, fingered some of the figurines along the mantle of my plug-in fireplace. "Well, actually, sometimes the lab guys can be pretty incredible. But in this case it wasn't so tough. Your friend landed on his watch and broke it."

I jumped forward, exultant with excitement. "Yeah, but who says it was working when he fell? Maybe he was wearing a broken watch! Or maybe somebody *set* it, so as to make you *think* . . ."

"Maybe," Mike said, with a dour face that told me eloquently there could be no maybes about it. Then he set back down the painted Russian Easter egg he had been fondling. "But he *was* alive about fifteen minutes before that." He looked at me, commiserating.

I squinted suspiciously. "How do you know?"

Mike sighed again, which I knew meant he had reached the part he hadn't wanted to tell me. But he did. "He came down to the lobby, and talked a bit with the guy at the front desk."

"The night clerk is certain it was Simon?"

Russo simply ignored that, since he knew as well as I did how many six-and-a-half foot *roué* Brits the Van Horn was likely to have had among its clientele. Mike went on, gingerly, "Brent-Waterhouse was pretty far behind on his bill, but he had talked the owner of the Van Horn into accepting some possessions as, like security. Until he could pay. Which he said wouldn't be long, of course. But it had already been long enough that the owner had started letting him use things sometimes. For business. Figured if he was going to get paid, he had to, I suppose."

I suddenly understood what Russo was driving toward. "My God, they found the typewriter!"

Mike looked relieved at not having to tell me. He nodded. "Your friend came downstairs, the clerk let him into the office, he typed a single sheet . . . just a couple of minutes . . . and then he went back upstairs."

I stared at Mike, unable to decide what I thought, what I felt. "Mike, it can't be, it just can't be!" I finally whispered.

Russo raised his eyebrows sympathetically, but added the details I hadn't dare ask. "The keys on that typewriter match the impressions on the note. Midge, the man typed his own note. Whether it was a *suicide* note or not, I don't know, but . . ." He picked the egg up again, hefted it a couple of times, before telling me the news I had already guessed. "Inderlund and Wolanski are satisfied, though, so I guess it is. A suicide note."

"OH, Mother, I don't *know* why this all frightens me, I just know that it *does!*" I slammed my fork down hard enough to make the ice in the water glasses tinkle, and people at the nearby tables turn, even above the blare of the Sicilian whistles and flutes. I could feel a flush creeping up my neck, but I glared at my mother, radiating warnings that I would not endure being jollied.

We were at our once-a-week-mother-daughter dinner, held today at the Alcamo, all tiles, painted platters, and an honest-to-god Sicilian painted cart for the antipasto table. These dinners had started last spring, after I met Russo, and my social life had suddenly turned terribly hectic. Pearl began to compensate for seeing me more rarely by "dropping by," just when Mike and I had reached the stage of the relationship where I was changing my sheets a lot. We had a couple of very close calls, until one day when Lieutenant Mike Russo, NYPD, had to get dressed in my closet, because Pearl had impressed upon me when I was about sixteen that there had never been any libido in her family.

Rather than let her discover that she was wrong, about *my* generation at least, in exchange for a promise to stop surprise visits, that's when I arranged this weekly soul-baring, at restaurants we took turns choosing, but I always seemed to pay for.

Now Pearl was drawing a gooey string of pimento and parsley flecked cheese from her bright-scarlet lips. For some reason, this evening she had decided hats were making a fashion comeback, and the black feather bobbing from the top of the earmuff thing she was wearing gave her a distinct resemblance to one of the quail from *Bambi*.

"I can understand, I mean some of the things that you describe sound perfectly *weird,* sweetheart, but . . . well, from what you say the police do seem pretty certain that it's a suicide."

"The police . . ."I snorted, deliberately indefinite, and began unrolling all the rollmops on my plate, savagely scraping the little bones and salt off the herring. I think maybe I was displacing a little, half pretending it was Russo I was flaying, not some fish. Russo's attitude, that I should give up my hysterical delusions and listen to the big smart cops, finally had made me so furious that I had thrown him out of my apartment.

Probably for the last time.

"Midge, sweetheart, the fish already, enough. Eat the poor things, don't just scrape them." Pearl delicately cleaned sauce from her lips, tried to blow the feather away from her eyes, and when that failed, tossed her head, setting the feather bobbing madly. "Margaret," she began again, in a voice that I knew meant it was lecture-time.

To which I was *absolutely* not going to listen.

"Mother, I don't care what you want to say, and I don't care what the police say. I was *there*, I saw him. At eleven o'clock Brent-Waterhouse was waving Polina's letter under our noses, cackling like a demon. I'm supposed to believe that three hours later he is so full of the milk of human kindness that he *voluntarily* types up and signs a renunciation of that same letter? HA! The only thing he was full of was cheap brandy, so much of it I don't even see how he was *walking* at two-thirty, let alone typing!"

"But the police are very sure?" Pearl was cutting her food with surgical precision, into pieces so small you'd think she was spoon-feeding a mouse, but she never took her eyes off me.

"I suppose that's what worries me . . . that they are so sure."

Pearl moved her head inquisitively, the feather bobbing pertly, fork and knife poised alertly.

I opend my mouth to explain, then shut it again, feeling like the sighted person who has to try to explain to the seven blind men what an elephant *really* looks like. Except that wasn't quite right—it wasn't an elephant, it was a Russian bear, and there was a creepy gnawing feeling at the bottom of my gut, under all that herring, that maybe the bear was about to bite my head off.

But Pearl wasn't going to accept silence as an explanation; I knew that, because she never did.

"Mother, I'm not going to argue with you, because you don't know anything about this. But you can understand at least that even *nice* people don't just suddenly renounce their worldly possessions, their savings, and their retirement funds—which is about what Polina's letter was for Simon. And even the time you spent with him at the office must have given you some idea how much Simon wasn't nice!"

Pearl very deliberately set her silverware down, "No, *nice* he wasn't. Even stupid old Mom could figure that out."

"*Mo*-ther . . ."

Pearl held up her hand, the expression on her face stern enough to startle me into silence.

"Margaret, let me finish. I may not have gone to college, and I may not write books, but I have survived very nicely on my own for twelve years now, so I don't think you have the right to talk to me that way."

"I didn't *mean* anything . . ." I stabbed miserably at my pasta, thinking how terrific this was—I now had one more person mad at me.

Pearl nodded, but wagged her finger again. "I'm not done. I wanted to say this too, no, Simon didn't seem a nice person. But he *did* seem a very shrewd person. One who knew his interests."

The way she said the last sentence, and the piercing way she studied me in silence, puzzled me for second. Then, with rising but confused hope, I understood she was saying she, too, doubted a Simon Brent-Waterhouse so filled with remorse and self-loathing that he decides to end it all, after a valedictory act of charity, setting free poor Russian authoress Polina Volkova from the consequences of the foolish thoughtlessness of youth.

"What you're saying is you don't believe either that he wrote that letter?"

My mother grimaced a little, disappointed, before explaining patiently, "Midge sweetie, the police are satisfied he wrote the letter, so he must have written the letter. But why would that mean he was *giving* it away? The Simon Brent-Waterhouse I met anyway, if he had something valuable, I think he would have *sold* it."

For a long moment I sat, stunned that I had missed so simple a point, and even more stunned that Pearl hadn't. It was true—Brent-Waterhouse wasn't a Samaritan, he was a blackmailer. And the whole point of blackmail is to hold the threat over whoever you are blackmailing until somebody agrees to meet the price you are asking.

And apparently, about two A.M. a week ago, someone had. And that someone would have been in Brent-Waterhouse's room, too.

My brain was beginning to riffle through the candidates again, just as it had done, so feverishly, for the past week. However, as abruptly as speculation had begun, it stopped.

Because what sense did it make that someone would *buy* Brent-Waterhouse's letter of renunciation, and then not take it with him? If you buy it, you have it, and . . .

And you have to present it! In court, or someplace! To prove that your right to Polina now supersedes Simon's! At which point you have to explain how you came by the letter, and what you paid for it.

And, I understood after another long minute, you have to reveal who you are.

All of which can be happily avoided, if Simon Brent-Waterhouse agrees to a convenient suicide, and the letter of renunciation becomes an artifact from the scene of the unhappy event.

I was happy for probably almost fifteen minutes, grinning with the satisfaction of a puzzle completed, and trying to minimize my mother's satisfaction at having filled in so much of it for me. We were waiting for the espresso and casserta that I had decided to celebrate with, when I remembered one other thing.

Whoever Simon Brent-Waterhouse's "customer" had been, only one thing stood between him—or her—and commission of the perfect murder, the murder that looks like a suicide.

Me. Margaret Rose Cohen. Whose address the whole world knows.

13

IT'S true that panic makes your brain move faster, but unfortunately it tends to focus on only about one or two things while it does. Like how long it will be until they kill you. Which is why it wasn't until the next morning that I understood that if Brent-Waterhouse had found a buyer for whatever he was using as blackmailing material, then his customer must have been right there in the room, to get the receipt. Instead of being content with that, of course, this customer had tipped Simon out the window.

Which is why, after lengthy consideration, I decided that the place I would prefer to start asking questions is with the *one* person whom I *knew* couldn't have been in Simon's room at 2:30 A.M. Wednesday last—because she was orbiting Jupiter someplace, courtesy of Dr. Kornbluth's Demerol.

Maybe it wasn't the most sensible choice, but it sure seemed the safest.

Susan Griswold's house was brick, glass, and weathered cedar, with a walled English garden to catch the afternoon sun and shield us from the wind off the Sound, which was wide enough at this point to make Bridgeport look romantic over there across the sun-sparkling waters. A teeny waterfall tinkled down into a lily pond, where plump goldfish lazed in and out of the shadows. A snowy terrier rolled in the gravel, then stretched out contentedly in a patch of sun at his mistress's feet.

All in all, about the sort of place you'd expect to find when you follow directions that begin with the phrase, "Turn left at the Stanford White gatehouse at the top of the hill."

We were drinking gin and tonics. Or, more exactly, Susan was drinking mostly gin, and I was pouring whatever it was she kept handing me into the ivy, because there were about fifty Friday-evening Long Island Expressway exits between me and Ocean Parkway. Even in midafternoon, coming out here, most of the way the traffic was so heavy I had felt like I was parallel parking at seventy-five miles an hour.

My reception at the Griswold-Pedlar house had been warm until Susan discovered I was lying—well, deliberately not correcting her mistaken assumptions, let's say—about having Simon's papers; then things had turned decidedly frosty for a bit, until the gin, and her obvious desire to talk, loosened Susan up again. Well, as loose as WASPs get anyway.

Susan was a Connecticut Griswold, which maybe was why she had not wanted to become even a hyphenated Pedlar, to say nothing already of a Korobeikin, and enough of that old Yankee money still stuck to her branch of the family tree at least to pay for this modest acre on the bluffs above Port Jeff. She was a little older than me, but a lot blonder; lanky, perfectly cut caramel and gold strands brushed from left side to right, baring a simple hooped earring of what I'm certain wasn't electroplate. A couple of inches taller, long legs in Talbot's cords, with a heather and sea mist Fair Isle sweater above. Susan Griswold was, in a word, who I had wanted all my life to be. A Yonah Shimel knish, dreaming of being a Fortnum and Mason's cream cracker instead.

Which is why it was such a struggle for me to keep looking sympathetic, as Susan Griswold explained how she had fallen into the clutches of Vitya Korobeikin just two years after I had managed to evade them.

"I don't even know what I was doing studying Russian, to tell you the truth. Annoying Daddy mostly, I suspect. God knows I haven't exactly *done* anything with my master's!" She made one of those noises that passes for laughter among WASPs. "But I did like it, and I was curious . . . any rate, curious enough to want to spend the summer there."

"On the teacher's exchange?"

"That's right," Susan nodded, her hair like golden parentheses framing a face whose tanned fabric was frayed white and threadbare in places, by stress and pain and gin. "Those tiny little rooms they stuck us in in that huge, huge building, and Moscow spread out down below, what you could see of it through the smog. You know, I've often wondered, if it hadn't been so hot that summer, would Viktor and I have ever happened?"

I had never been in Moscow in a summer, but the spring of my year there was hot enough to give me a sense of what Susan's long, grinding, eye-stinging summer would have been like, in a city, a building, a life that was built to withstand cold, not heat. Not only was there no air-conditioning, many buildings did not even have windows that could open, and the water was turned off for long, unannounced periods.

"So Vitya started taking me out to a place called Serebryanni Bor. Silver Grove, you know the place? Lovely long loops of the Moscow River, those great big pines with the scaly yellow trunks, the wildflowers. Close up, it was horrible, of course, broken bottles and rusty tin cans, and almost everywhere you looked someone had shat, but still . . . Vitya knew the good places, so we could usually find someplace where there was a breeze to catch, and then we'd swim a little, and sunbathe . . ." Susan took a deep swig of her drink, then looked over the top of the glass at me, a wicked look in her blue eyes. "And fuck," she added, laughing not quite hysterically, then shaking her head, "and fuck and fuck and fuck . . . Vitya is, well . . ."

Since the photo of Susan's husband in the buff had been burning a hole in my handbag all the way out Long Island, I had no need of more intimate description. "So you got married?" I put in brightly, holding up my glass, which as soon as she filled it, I sloshed onto the ivy.

Susan screwed the top back on the gin bottle, then nodded, with a faintly surprised look on her face. "We did. There, of course, because we had to for Vitya to get out, and then when he did, here . . . well, not *here* here. In America. At my parents' club, in Darien."

"That must have been hard, being married, but you were here and he was over there," I said, affecting sympathy.

"We were lucky, actually," Susan said, then jerked her head back, as if surprised she had said that. She smiled, bitterly. "At least lucky is what it seemed then, anyway. Vitya got his papers in about a month. Too young for them to want, I suppose . . ."

I played with the outer seam of my jeans, trying to conceal the thoughts that my face undoubtedly was betraying. I had known of people who had waited as much as twelve *years* for a spouse to get permission to emigrate, and waits of a couple of years were not uncommon; the *only* explanation for Korobeikin's speedy emigration was that his bosses wanted him to be here.

Which Susan's further maunderings seemed only to confirm.

"To think back on it, I don't even recall that Vitya actually proposed, it just sort of *happened*. Days at the river, then nights we'd go to somebody's dacha, or wander around the city. He'd buy me flowers at the peasant market . . . big sunflowers, with green spiders crawling on them, or those, what do you call them, red, with petals like they're plastic?"

"Zinnias?"

"That's it, zinnias. And then one time we rented a boat, at a park out by the television tower thing. *Hundreds* of people, all rowing about on this scummy little teaspoon of water, bumping into each other and swearing the most terrible things. Poor Vitya tipped us over, and I ended up with impetigo!" Susan laughed uproariously, spilling some of her drink onto her slacks. "Damn!" she sat up, plucking the material from her thigh.

"Was he a dissident?" I asked, struggling to balance an as-sumed off-handedness against Susan's growing inebriation.

"Dissident? Oh, God, no, those were the most *tiresome* peo-ple," Susan waved her hand dismissively, silver bracelets clank-ing one on the other. Her silibants were delicately fuzzed. "That's one of the things I liked about Vitya, it wasn't always that gruesome gloom and doom. We had fun, we laughed, we danced . . ."

For a second, I wasn't sure whom I was angrier at, Vitya the bald-faced liar, who had been a dissident for me, a good-time-Sasha for Susan, and who knows what for whatever girl or girls had come between Susan and myself (Vitya the marine biolo-gist? Vitya the folk singer?), or Susan, who found the struggles of a people trying to remove an iron heel from their necks "tiresome." I thought for a moment of lecturing her, but de-cided against it. For one, she didn't seem the lecturable sort. And for two, she was sinking faster than the afternoon sun.

I decided it was maybe time to get a little more direct. "Susan, it was you who gave Victor my phone number, wasn't it? And my address?"

The sun was just about to land on Connecticut, and Susan

was nearly looking into it; the reddish-gold burnished her hair, but it also made her skin look ancient, the crows' feet almost creased around her eyes as she squinted. Gin, slyness, or the pleasure of private memories made her slow to answer; when she did, and she turned to look at me, her face looked older than my mother's.

"Yes to the second, no to the first. But even Vitya can figure out how to use a phone book," she said acerbically.

"But why?"

"You said you had that little whore's letter," Susan smiled, the first hint of a slur audible.

I nodded, waited. That much I had known. The more important part, though, was the part I was waiting for, and she wasn't saying.

"Were you actually working with Simon?" I finally decided to prompt her, in as neutral a way as I could think of.

Susan laughed, but said nothing. Instead she sloshed her drink around in the glass, running it up the sides. Then she tried to drink, and the swizzle stick swung around, hitting her in the nose. She raised her head, tonic dribbling down her chin.

"Well, what did you want the letter so badly for, then?" I tried. "After all, you had Victor call the next day, and come over to my house . . ." Then I remembered the housecleaning I hadn't wanted. "And the woman who cleaned my apartment!"

Susan grimaced, her eyeballs a mesh of red capillaries in the last of the sun. It was as though the alcohol was kneading her now, her features becoming ill-defined and lumpy, and she waved her hand feebly. "Fuckin' goddamned hairy dwarf, I don clean my *own* goddamn place, and he stands over me and *makes* me, even do the *toi-let!*" Susan nodded, staring at me as if she had the distinct impression she was making sense.

I snorted a laugh cruel enough that it seemed prudent to convert it into a fake cough. Good for Sasha! I thought with satisfaction, staring at those long, perfect Griswold fingers, which Sasha had forced to bruise themselves, scrubbing away at the lime scale on *my* bathroom tiles.

My pleasure faded as more of the implications of what Susan was saying grew upon me. Such as that, for instance, whatever Polina's letter meant to Susan Griswold, it had been important enough to send the poor woman out imitating a charwoman, less than a day after a serious dental disaster. I flirted for a moment with thoughts of what a bastard Vitya was, that *he* hadn't gone to imitate a cleaning service instead of his injured wife. Something of that calculation rang false, and it took me a moment to realize what—how much sense did it make that if Vitya and Susan were working together to get that letter, *first* they would try breaking and entering, and only *afterwards* try telephoning me?

"*You* wanted that letter, didn't you?" I understood. "For yourself, I mean. Not for Victor, for *yourself*."

Susan's sloshed smile was pushed from her increasingly distorted face by a growing, if fuzzy, anger. Red blotches blossomed along her cheeks, as she struggled to sit up. "It's my letter, damn-it," she muttered. "Eighty thousand bucks I paid that sonofabitch for it last spring, and now that goddamned queer limey son of a bitch has the *balls* to claim that was an option . . ." Her effort to pull herself higher in her chair failed, and she slumped down, chin all but on her breasts.

Not precisely thrilled at the prospect of nursing a foundering souse, I glanced about the garden; through the sliding double glass of the patio door I noticed the dark young woman who had opened the door for me earlier, Mexican or Italian or something, now smiling and chattering as she led two children up to the door—both of them early elementary-school age, to judge by their sizes and by their bright backpacks. The woman grasped the handle, but looked out at us before opening the door; as soon as she saw Susan, she turned the kids smoothly around and shepherded them off into another room, which I could just see beyond the Florida room. A second later the frenetic pink-and-blue of TV danced over the visible door frame, and then she came back out, bearing the backpacks. About five minutes later she returned, now carrying two trays of what looked like supper. After that first glance, the maid never looked at her employer again, carrying on smoothly without her.

All of which made it pretty plain that this was not the first afternoon when mama had gone down with the sun.

I rocked gently on the springs of my garden chair, listening to Susan's ragged, gin-thickened snores, and trying to sort out these new bits of the puzzle. His sun-warmth gone, the terrier got up, snuffled about the garden, and then came over to nudge me with his nose. Absently I scratched his head, and thought about Susan's $80,000. Apparently invested in Sirin, and part of the general cascade of money tumbling down into the black hole of Simon Brent-Waterhouse's profligacy.

But what had Susan been buying? Polina's book, presumably, except how could she have known of it last *spring?* And what would she have known then that would make worth paying eighty grand to get it? *Eighty grand,* for heaven's sake! Two-thirds of my entire inheritance from Great Aunt Dora, handed to Simon Brent-Waterhouse like it was cream cheese on a zwei-back!

Even odder, Susan Griswold would have paid that chunk of cash to get rights to a book that her husband all but owned in the first place; if Polina was to be believed—which it wasn't wholly clear she should be—then the book was Victor's idea, not hers. So why would Victor's wife *pay* to get the rights? The immediate, obvious answer—that she and Victor were trying to out-hustle Simon—seemed unsatisfactory, because Polina hadn't told Simon about the book until *after* she got to this country. Which was this fall, and the money had been paid last spring.

And so *much* money! I gnawed at that for a while, and maybe too hard, because suddenly the terrier yipped, snapped his teeth at me, and grumped off to another corner. I folded my hands and rested my chin on them, smelling the lanolin of the terrier's coat on my fingers as I thought about $80,000. For Susan to get her money back, Polina would have to make at least $800,000 in royalties, which meant Polina's book would have had to sell something like a quarter of a million *hardcover* copies.

Okay, maybe it could happen. There have been stranger best-sellers than the book Polina was going to write. On the other hand though, if there is any business *less* certain than picking bestsellers, it would have to be something like peddling donkey basketball franchises, or perhaps computer-picking lottery numbers. But even if all that *did* happen, all that would just bring Susan back to zero. Even I knew, this was not an investment.

Susan was now drowsing, her head slumped down onto her bosom, the hank of blond hair trailing a question mark over the Fair Isle sweater. I could have woken her, but my fraternity-house experience back in college told me it was probably better just to let her snooze; waking a drunken date to take you home had been one of the surest ways to get barfed on. Besides, with the sun gone, the garden was cooling down rapidly, which would probably rouse her. I continued to bounce gently on the springs of my chair, thinking, and shivering slightly.

Nor were all the tremors a product of the cooling air, either.

I watched Susan, who was beginning to mumble, probably a sign that the cold was getting to her. She had about $600 worth of casual clothes on her body that I bet didn't come from Loehmann's. Like the old joke says, God made WASPs so there'd be somebody to pay retail; what's the fun of discount, if there's nobody out there in the same blouse as you, except that they paid $300 for it in September, and you got it in March for $12.95? Her jewelry? A couple thousand, at a guess. The house?

Who knows, with Long Island real estate these days. Say a million, if you could find a buyer?

Okay, on the one hand that all meant she wasn't particularly going to miss the eighty grand. On the other, I was pretty sure that one of the reasons why the old rich *stayed* rich was that they didn't throw their money around. If Susan had spent that sort of money—indeed, if she had cared enough about it to drag herself from a dental sickbed and imitate a charwoman—then clearly she was intending to get *something*. The question was *what?*

My first answer made sense for only about five minutes, that this money was some sort of joint effort by her and Victor to pry Polina loose from Simon's clutches. For one thing, Susan seems to have given the publisher the money last spring, while for Victor the letter had apparently come as a surprise, after Polina's arrival, this fall. For another, what sense did it make that Susan had broken into my apartment first, and only *then* had her husband telephoned, to find out whether I had Polina's letter?

The problem with logic is that it leads you to conclusions that seem to make no sense—such as now, when the only conclusion I could draw from Susan and Victor not being allies in the search for Polina's letters was that . . .

They were rivals?

It was a crazy thought, and yet . . . Victor had married his wife on Party orders. That photo, of him and Polina, both in a state of nature that the camera made unambiguously clear, Victor had found exciting. Victor, who had brought Polina to America. Polina, who was determined to marry Victor.

Victor and Polina. And Susan.

I stopped bouncing, stunned by the realization that all this might be no more than a classic triangle. Susan loves Vitya, Vitya loves Polina . . .

Suddenly, a number of the loose chunks of the puzzle seemed

to clump together, like iron filings around a magnet. Vitya may never have loved his wife, but he appeared to have no ambiguous feelings about her money; if he was running off with Polina, then obviously he would be wise to get control of her literary rights, so as to ensure himself as much of a dowry as possible. And Polina too, whatever her affections for Vitya, surely her respect for his citizenship was sufficient to make her willing to go great lengths to rectify the error of her youth.

But *what* lengths? Murder?

I toyed with versions of what it meant that Polina had been at Simon's room the night he died—was she *joining* Vitya there? Ensuring he had done his job? Picking up the paper he was to have paid for? Gradually, though, I saw problems growing. Such as, what would Vitya have *paid* for Polina's letter with? Susan Griswold had apparently paid Simon $80,000 and *not* gotten the letter; why would Simon have taken less from Vitya? And surely, Vitya could not have offered an even larger sum; my bet was that most of what bulged in Vitya's pocket was Griswold money, not his own.

The real problem was what Susan had wanted the letter for—she was no publisher, and somehow I doubted she was an ardent democrat, anxious to help the peoples of Russia cast off their totalitarian yoke.

After almost an hour of thinking about it, in the darkness gathering above Port Jefferson, I was left with only one explanation that made sense. Susan wanted to get control of Polina's book *solely* because that book was important to Victor.

And Susan wanted to deny it to him, or at the very least make him beg. I watched the ruby lights of the ferry chugging across the Sound, and wondered . . .

What was that final dinner *meant* to have been like?

I remembered Simon's arrogance, his boasting. Victor's grim desperation to keep Polina away from Brent-Waterhouse's control, to pass the book to O'Connell. O'Connell, who didn't want the book, but whose publishers insisted he take it.

And Susan, had she not cracked her tooth. Susan, who had apparently not told Simon that Vitya was her husband, nor told Vitya that she was going to be at the dinner. Susan, who apparently believed that the letter of rights was hers, or at very least, would stay in Simon's hands, solely for purposes of denying her husband something he wanted. To punish him. To *hurt* him.

In front of the woman who had taken her husband away.

Susan shifted in her sleep, snorted, saliva running out the corner of her mouth. I stared, fascinated, at her long fingers, wondering at the strength of her arms, her legs, wondering whether she could have somehow dumped Simon out that window. Crazed with pain, and drugs, and alcohol . . .

Perhaps.

I stood, shivering, wondering what to do. I had come out to Port Jefferson hoping to eliminate a suspect; instead I had added one. Vitya remained a spy, possibly a murderer. Polina, too. And now Susan Griswold.

I looked around the garden, feeling guilty, and scared, though about what I wasn't quite certain. I tidied up our drink glasses, wondering for a moment whether I should wake up Susan, or just leave, with a smile for the indifferent housekeeper.

But I didn't do either, because just then, I realized that I had overlooked something about that horrible evening with Simon Brent-Waterhouse.

14

IT had been an ugly dinner, which I had blundered into only because of my mother's desire to have a grandchild. And, honesty made me add, because of *my* desire, that if I had to bear a grandchild for my mother, I might as well have it in London, with a fancy flat in Mayfair to bring it back to, and maybe one of those Mary Poppins-like nannies to help me raise it. These were good reasons why when that evening turned out to be the big disaster it was, I simply assumed that the fault must be mine, somehow. Which makes sense, because who in his right mind is going to figure that a man who at eleven A.M. doesn't know you're alive nine hours later is going to set out deliberately to slice your ego up and serve it as sushi?

Which I suppose is why all week I had been seeing trees, not forest. Failing to notice that the whole *purpose* of Simon's little dinner party was turning out to have been to make his guests miserable.

Victor wanted to publish Polina, and couldn't, because of the letter. Polina wanted to *be* published, big and lucratively, with Victor as her agent, in order to become Mrs. Green Card, and it was the same letter that kept her in Simon's thrall.

What made me feel like I was sitting there with my feet in Susan's fishpond, though, was my swelling certainty that the trick Simon had intended to play on snoozing Susan here was, if that was possible, even nastier.

At least, it certainly sounded like the cuddly, loveable Simon I had been learning about all week, to lead Susan into hostessing (and presumably paying for) a dinner that would let her humiliate her husband in front of his new woman friend, only then—when Susan was gloating on the very pinnacle of her revenge—to shove her down into the pit alongside her husband, by announcing coyly that he had changed his mind. That he wasn't going to sell Polina's letter after all. Which is what I was now sure Simon had been planning to do.

Thus creating miserable Victor, miserable Polina, and miserable Susan.

So how could it be that O'Connell wasn't supposed to have been Miserable No. 4?

The problem I gnawed at for ages though, unable to make sense of it, was that O'Connell and the others, or Polina and Victor at least, seemed to be on opposite ends of the misery teeter-totter. If Simon made Victor and Polina miserable, by keeping Polina's letter, then O'Connell would click his heels for joy. No matter how great Piper-Wilkey's desire for Polina's memoirs, as long as Simon had that letter, then O'Connell could maneuver comfortably between what his publisher wanted and what he wanted—that the book should just disappear. On the other hand, if Simon were to make O'Connell miserable, by passing the literary rights back to Polina or Victor, then at least the other two would be happy. Susan, poor souse, looked to have been slated for misery in either case, so it was probably a lucky thing she had cracked her tooth.

Which made no sense, because the one thing I was absolutely convinced of now was that Brent-Waterhouse's plans for that evening were that the only one who would go home happy was himself.

Unfortunately, it was the sound of tires squishing over gravel, on the other side of the brick wall, which plucked off the last of my blinkers. Pedlar, arriving home from work, I realized, with a snatch of guilty panic, because I wasn't supposed to have been sitting in his garden, watching his drunken wife contract pneumonia.

I leapt toward the garden gate, when the thought hit me, that I hadn't been supposed to be at that dinner, either.

What I mean, I didn't *have* to have been there. Of course, for a week I had known that if Susan Griswold's tongue had pushed her olive another quarter inch in almost any direction, I would have spent last Wednesday evening being miserable at home alone in Brooklyn, instead of being miserable with company, over in Manhattan.

What years of living with Pearl had blinded me to was that just because Susan had happened to bring her shattered tooth into a dental office run by a full-time, one-client marriage broker, that still did not necessarily mean that Simon *had* to ask me to replace her as hostess.

I mean, Simon *could* have said no to Pearl, correct? My mother, when she sets her mind to it, can be very persuasive, but what I had learned about Simon Brent-Waterhouse over the course of this week made it perfectly clear that poor he might be, but schmuck he wasn't. A man who had made a fortune swindling Russian dissident writers could certainly have fended off Pearl's assault of prematrimonial guilt.

Which had to mean that Simon had *wanted* me at that dinner. More exactly, since he didn't know Midge Cohen, that meant he had wanted *someone. Anyone.*

The question was why.

I didn't know, yet. But the bits and bulges of possible answers that I could glimpse looming out of the murk were enough to scare hell out of me.

Which is probably why Victor Pedlar went about two feet in the air, when I barked, just as he swung open the glass door letting onto the garden.

"Vitya, who in the devil is O'Connell?"

Pedlar stood blinking at the French doors, raincoat still over his arm, tie loosened; except for the look of blank surprise on his weary face he seemed every inch the Long Island commuter just returned home. He glanced from his wife, who was struggling soddenly with her chair, to me, back to her; then quickly back to me.

"Vitya?" he cocked his head.

"Christ," I brushed my hair back nervously, "how many girls *were* there, back in MGU? You don't remember me, talking in the showers, all that dissident bullshit you fed me?"

Pedlar studied me for a moment, his eyes hard-blue things that made me wonder whether I hadn't guessed wrong, not about who he was, but about putting my cards on the table right then. No choice, though, since I couldn't think of any good quick lies, about why I would just happen to be drinking gin in Victor Pedlar's garden that particular Friday afternoon.

My shivers grew worse, so I added, "I know you, Vitya, I know what you are." I tried to match his hard, cold glare.

The staring contest lasted another moment, then Vitya shrugged, and put his briefcase and coat onto an empty chair.

"Come on, help me get her upstairs, would you? I hate for the kids to see her this way." He went to his wife and took her left arm.

Not really thinking, I did the same on the right, and the two of us managed to hoist Susan to her feet, and began stumbling her into the house. She wasn't out cold, but she couldn't have walked. Consciousness seemed to come and go, slurred complaints to Victor, attempts at bitter jokes, clumsy efforts to snatch her arms away from us, all punctuated by alcoholic blackout.

"How much did she have?" Victor grunted at me, as we maneuvered her through a plant-filled sunroom, across a glittery-papered dining room done with a Korean–style table and hutch, beneath an enormous modern design chandelier. We were heading for a set of free-floating stairs, at the top of which presumably was the bedroom.

"I didn't think it was so much," I was having trouble coping with my half of Susan; she was bigger than I, and Pedlar was a lot taller, so that the weight all seemed to run downhill onto me. "I was pouring mine out, but . . ." I adjusted my hold on her with a jerk, then realized what that sounded like. "I don't mean I was trying to get her drunk or anything, I just mean . . . well, I've got to drive back, and so I didn't want . . . but maybe five drinks?"

We had mastered the stairs and were dragging Susan along a thickly carpeted hallway. None of the rooms seemed to have proper doors, just louvers, all propped open, showing that upstairs was as ritzy as down. The master bedroom was about the size of my apartment.

Pedlar was not exactly brutal—just very efficient—as he flopped his wife onto the huge bed. She lolled, smiling, her eyes closed, murmuring indistinctly. Pedlar's jaw knotted as he jerked her shoes off, then covered her with a quilt that had a sort of Frank Lloyd Wright design on it.

"Five drinks with you," Pedlar said bitterly, still staring at Susan, sprawled on the bed. He looked up. "Three quarters of a bottle since lunch then. There wasn't even any gin in the house when I left."

I didn't know whether that was question or statement, so after a moment, I put a question of my own. "The drinking isn't because of the tooth, is it? The pain and everything?"

Pedlar punched the big gold cufflinks from his sleeves and rolled up the expensive striped cambric. "More like the opposite, she broke the tooth because of the booze."

"So she's been drinking a long time?"

"As long as I've known her, but . . ." His thoughts wandered somewhere private for a moment, then got back to me. He wasn't smiling when he looked at me. "All right, you're here. What do you want, because I've got to go see my kids now, so we can all pretend again that Mommy isn't feeling well, so she's taking a nap."

His tone surprised me, because it sounded genuine. But then I suppose even spies must have some attachment to their children. Even if he hadn't, revulsion at Susan, now slobbering on the bed, would not have been difficult to feign.

"Is the drinking worse?"

He shrugged. "I don't know if it's that, or just . . . it catches up with you, you know. Susan's mother, she was fine, and then it was like six months, and she was gone." He clicked his fingers, except no sound came. He tried again, this time with success. Then he looked at his wife again, and sighed, for the moment at least sounding exactly like a man who suspected he might eventually be widowed, with two young children still to raise. He might be a spy, and his love for Susan might never have been more than an assignment, but those children were genuinely his.

The tender green shoots of my sympathy withered, though, when he looked at me again and snapped, now in Russian, "All right, you say you know what I am. So what am I?"

"We're on 'tu' again? That means you remember me?" I

snarled back, hoping that that was a live-in housekeeper that I had seen downstairs, and not someone who went home when Little Loonies came on the TV.

"Remember, don't remember, you're in my house. In my bedroom, in fact," he leered. "So maybe the familiar *is* appropriate, eh? What I'm more interested in, what do you care about that evening with O'Connell? You still pretending you have a business interest in Sirin?"

"Pretending?" I began automatically, then realized I couldn't very well lie myself out of this. "Okay, I was pretending," I tossed my head, waved my hands. "But you jumped out of the bushes at me!"

"Jumped?" Pedlar grunted, then shrugged. "I wanted to talk to you, and you wouldn't return my call."

"Talk about what? Really, I mean," I asked, my throat tense.

Victor shrugged, said nothing, turned away angrily. He stalked over to more louver doors, which he flung open, to expose a walk-in closet that was pretty much the one that I hope to be assigned in heaven, if I am a good person on this Earth. Save for the measly yard of space that was plainly Victor's, that closet looked like a small Midwestern Loehmann's. Yards and yards of sweaters and tweeds and good woolens, all in colors and cuts that Mary Tyler Moore would wear, scores of Charles Jourdan and Coach and Bally shoes, all of them designed with that incredibly elegant understatement that, if I ever popped the $600 it takes to buy a pair, I would carry them in my hands, so people could see the label.

"Jesus," was all I could manage. About the same thing as I said on our honeymoon tour, when me and my ex, Paul Blank, chanced to stumble into Notre Dame Cathedral, just as sunset hit the stained glass windows.

"Capitalism in the stage of primitive accumulation," Victor sneered, in Russian, obviously understanding my awe. He was angrily tossing bits of his jewelry into a caddy on his dresser, then unbuttoning his shirt.

"Well, isn't that why you married her?" I asked, still too stunned by the closet to pretend.

"What do *you* know about why I married her?" he snapped, the threads of his shirt protesting as he snatched it off his torso. A handmade tattoo of a grinning skeleton peeked over the top of the silk undershirt, and thrust a bony hand in the direction of Vitya's left armpit. Then, with a savage jerk, Vitya undid his belt, sucked in his gut, and undid his trousers, letting them slide to the floor.

"A lot, Vitya, I know a lot," I replied, studying him distractedly, in that blank way that television catches your eye, if someone else has it on when you come into the room. Vitya had put on some weight since the photo, I registered absentmindedly, but most of it hadn't gone to unpleasant places.

I suppose it was the photo that made this intimacy seem so matter-of-fact, this standing in his closet watching Vitya undress. I had been carrying him around in a state of nature for so long already that getting down to boxers and undershirt just made him seem more natural. However, Victor didn't know that I had been seeing so much of him lately, because suddenly he snatched a pair of jeans from a hanger and held them in front of himself.

"Do you *mind?*" he asked, his face a mix of anger and speculation.

"I've been talking to Polina," I blurted, which I guess was part explanation and part apology, because I blushed, and backed out of the closet, sliding the louver behind me. "About you," I added through the back-lit slats.

Victor emerged a minute later, much more recognizably the Vitya Korobeikin of Moscow State University—blue jeans, plaid shirt, sneakers. And a guarded, smoothly blank look.

"About me? What about me?"

For a shiver of a second I had a vivid sense of where I was—halfway out Long Island, in the bedroom of a Soviet spy. It was dark now, and nobody knew I was here, and there were a thousand places practically within spitting distance that could hide the dead body of stupid, nosy Margaret Cohen—the Sound, and the scrub pine forest, and the concrete molds for pouring 998 bridge abutments, condominium complexes, and new Toys R Us.

Then the shiver passed. Christ, this was just somebody's *house*. There was a housekeeper, and two kids, and Susan (drunk maybe, but there she was anyway, groaning away on the bed). Not to mention neighbors. It was all too *normal*. Like you can't have vampires and ghouls in Levittown, right?

"About Moscow, and the Komsomol," I said, trying to be as blank as Vitya. "The old days," I smiled.

Maybe Victor's eyebrows went up a half notch; if they did, it was his only reaction.

"We were members together," he finally conceded, stiff in his offhandedness.

"What about all the dissident crap you handed me?" I asked, my anger of before replacing my momentary fear. If there is one thing I *really* hate, it is when people lie to me.

Victor eyed me again, as if not quite sure he could place me, then shrugged. "You had to belong to the Komsomols then, or they threw you out of the university. Everybody lied back then."

"You're lying *now!*" I shot back, before I could be surprised by my own nerviness.

Victor dropped his head slightly, and his eyes widened, then narrowed, like a bull taking the measure of a matador, just before charging. "Interesting . . . about what am I lying?"

"Goddamnit." I turned on my heel and started for the door. "I'm not going to stand here and play word games with you, Vitya. Maybe you think it doesn't matter what kind of lies you live, and maybe you're right, it doesn't! But what I can't understand is why you'd be so damn *stupid!* If you didn't want anyone to know you're a Soviet spy, then why in the devil did you bring Polina *over* here?"

If I hadn't been wearing leather bottom shoes, or the stairs hadn't been made of such well-polished wood, Vitya never would have caught me, but it didn't seem to make a lot of sense, breaking my neck while trying to save it. I was tugging on the front door before I felt Victor's hand close over my wrist. I turned fast, scared to death, but ready to try to do as much damage to him as I could.

"Daddy! Daddy!" two little voices said behind us, and we both froze. "We didn't know you were home!"

A girl, about seven, and a boy, a little older, were leaning over the back of a huge, C-shaped settee, the TV a vivid frenzy of cartoon animals behind them. I saw TV trays, and plates, and a ketchup bottle, and somewhere further on, the enigmatic but concerned face of the housekeeper.

I felt Victor's hand squeeze harder, for a second, then loosen. His breathing was forced, but under control. He straightened, smiled to the kids, almost genuinely.

"I said hi, but you were watching the TV," he managed. Then, to me, "These are my kids, Steven and Roberta."

"Hi!" they chorused, both a little artificially. Young as they were, they seemed to have learned that keeping a distance between appearance and reality was a crucial skill in their household.

So what makes me better than them? As artificially I smiled back, "Hi! My name is Margaret . . . your father and I know each other . . ." I looked at Vitya, whose face was rigid with fright. "From my college days," I ended, taking a pity on Vitya that I didn't understand myself.

Probably he didn't either, but he appreciated it nonetheless. Suddenly his smile was real. He touched the two kids, tousling their hair, then turning them around and shooing them back toward the television.

"You kids have eaten already? Well, how about Ramona gives you some dessert, and then . . ." Looking over his shoulder at me, "Margaret, maybe you will stay and share supper with me, eh? Ramona!" he shouted at the housekeeper, who was hovering at a kitchen bar the far side of the television. "Can you fix up ice cream for these two, and then maybe something for the two of us, in the dining room?" Then, his face somber and his eyes trying to look about four inches into my brain, Victor said, "I think that we have to talk."

"SOMETHING" turned out to be scallops and fettucine, followed by green salad, and now cheese. My attempts to refuse wine had failed, and we were halfway through a second bottle of a Montepulciano that was good enough to make me forget I would probably have to sleep in my car.

Actually, if it hadn't been for the knowledge that Susan and Roberta and Steven and even Ramona were all breathing peacefully in the dark of that big house, there would have been another possible sleeping arrangement hovering in the air, because once Vitya had shrugged off his outer shell of big, tough businessman, there proved to be a sad, bewildered, and worried boy inside. Much like the boy I remembered, from all those years before, to whom (or so it seemed to me that evening) I had been more attracted than my (then-married) memory had let me acknowledge.

I don't know if it was the wine, or talking Russian, or the illusion created by being with this person whom I had thought a friend more than a decade before, that somehow that decade had never been—which made me feel younger and less time-worn than I in fact was—but by the time we were doing Camembert, crackers, and green grapes even Vitya's admission that he really truly was a secret agent was not helping me keep him at arm's length.

Because he didn't *want* to be an agent anymore. That was why he had brought Polina over, in fact.

"Of *course* I did that for them, marry Susan, chase after girls like you." Then, showing that his time in America had trained him well, he stopped, smiled, apologized. "Sorry. *Women* like you. I thought it was my Komsomol duty!" he exclaimed, waving the wine bottle before pouring. "To learn about the enemy, and to use the enemy's weakness as our strength! And what an honor, to be chosen for a mission behind enemy lines, I couldn't believe it! My parents were so proud and happy . . ."

"You told them?" I popped a grape into my mouth, savoring the squish of the juice, which I washed down with a mouthful of the puckery wine.

"Well, no, I couldn't, of course . . . except in a general way."

"What were you supposed to do over here? Blow things up or something?"

"Why don't better I tell you what I *wasn't* supposed to do?" Vitya stretched back in his chair, contemplating the wine he was slowly circulating in the fishbowl-size glass. He ran his other hand over his brow, as if that would somehow clear the burdens piled upon his head. "I wasn't supposed to come here and fall in love."

"With Susan?"

"With America," he smiled ruefully, then began to talk in a disjointed way about how the Soviet scales had dropped from his eyes, one after another. The food and shopping and huge glass buildings, sure, but more, too. The PTA, for example, people voluntarily banding together to help the teachers do their jobs better. Halloween, and neighborhoods that organize parties, so that little kids will have somewhere safely scary to go. Storekeepers that want to chat with you, even if you don't buy anything. The car dealer who won't *let* you buy an option for a new car, because he considers it not worth the price.

And his children, who went to ballet classes and kung fu classes and who begged to hang out at the local malls with their friends and who dreamed of Nintendos and birthday parties at Disney World.

"They are *free*, Midge," he finally slapped the table in his frustration that no other words would explain more fully. "There is no one standing behind their words, looking over their shoulders. They do not study hard in school, and they wear torn clothes, and they shirk their chores, because *they fear nothing!* They believe that whatever happens, whatever life sends, it is theirs to rise above. They are born into a world that they are meant by man, God, and the universe to inhabit. They *trust*, damn it. In themselves, in me, in life. Injustice to them is that I will not let them go to a PG-thirteen movie, which all of their friends have seen. Persecution is demanding that their rooms be kept tidy."

"Americans *are* spoiled," I murmured in agreement, thinking of people, families, whole nations which had disappeared overnight, on Stalin's political whim.

But this was not what Vitya meant. "No, no! It is Russians who are spoiled, ruined. *Crippled*. Russians fear everything, and so we do nothing, we lock ourselves in our cells like obedient prisoners." Then, looking uncomfortably like an understudy for Raskolnikov, Vitya hunched forward, grabbed the wine bottle, and studied the label intently, before glancing over at me, eyes dark and hollow. "There is a joke. An American, a Frenchman, and a Russian are sharing a cell. Way back under the straw, they find hidden a vodka bottle. They open, take a drink, and *poof*—a genie. It is a magic bottle, and they each get one wish. The Frenchman, he says, 'Take me back to Paris, I have a date!' A cloud of smoke, and he is gone. The American says, 'New York, I have important business!' *Poof.* Now it is the Russian's turn. He picks up the bottle, shakes it, thinks, 'There's still vodka left, and we were having such a nice talk.' 'Okay,' the Russian says to the genie, 'bring the other two back.' Eh?" Victor grunted inquiringly. "You like that?"

I laughed, a shade falsely, because I wasn't certain the joke was funny. Still hunched, and incredibly Russian-looking, Vitya poured the last of the second bottle into our glasses, then smiled one of the sharklike grins I recalled so well from our Moscow days. "Bring the other two back, and we can all rot in jail together. That is what they are trying to do to you. To *us*, I mean. . . and that's why I asked Polina to come. I could think of no other way."

Sipping the wine, whispering as he had in that shower so many years ago, Vitya told me of his increasing despair, watching the West fall in love with Gorbachev, watching even more horrified as we slowly bought the idea that the new rulers of Russia were democrats. "Democrats, ha! They are gangsters, like the old gangsters except worse! A man who calls himself a communist and who looks like Stalin, a man like that you must fear, a child knows that! But put a man in a nice haircut, a pair of West German eyeglasess, a good suit, have him tell a joke about Lenin . . . and the West decides this must be a democrat, to whom we must give truckloads of money, or else some un-named 'dark forces' will sweep them all away. It is like the man holding his pistol to the head of his own children—give me money or I shoot! And we give! We give!"

"Yeah, but I don't understand." I rubbed my head, which felt woolen and numb. "Why Polina? Why couldn't you just . . ."

"Tell all this myself?" I suppose the expression Victor made was a smile, but it looked more like his mouth sliding open as enormous weights squeezed his head.

Victor's attempt to gather an explanation, which seemed to be costing him enormous effort, was suddenly interrupted by Susan, his wife, who stood silhouetted at the top of the stairs, before descending into the candlelit intimacy of the ground floor. She had changed into a silk nightshirt that was cut high enough to be sexy, but seemed more clinical than seductive, because of her matted hair, streaked makeup, and veined, flaccid body.

"Victor! Who the goddamn hell is that? I've told you how many times, no bringing your little love trophies back here!"

Infinite weariness dusted over Korobeikin, like a shower of stifling ash. "Susan," he said, more like he was identifying a bug than greeting his wife. "How wonderful, you've slept off your liquor."

Susan crossed the hallway and stalked slowly into the dining room. At first I had thought her slow approach was meant to be menacing, or reproachful; but the closer she came, the more I suspected that she was having problems with her coordination.

Vitya was watching her approach with undisguised loathing. I watched him, wondering how a marriage can go so wrong. Paul and I had bored one another at the end, so that we could go for days at a stretch without having a thing to say; never had there been this *hatred* between us, though.

Murderous hatred.

The glare of Vitya's stare could have melted holes in a can of beans, and I did not like the way his thumb was flicking back and forth across the sharper side of his dinner knife. I glanced at Susan, who also looked ready to go for his eyeballs—or perhaps mine—with her fingernails. In a disjointed, panicky jump cut of thoughts, I tried to imagine marrying someone for whom you had no feeling, living a lie every day, in service of a higher cause. A higher cause that only an idiot could have believed, even then. What would a man feel like, as the woman turned into a sponge, and the cause turned into an international laughing stock? So why not simply walk away from it? Hang up his trench coat and become just a literary agent, not a secret one?

The answers flung themselves at me so fast and incoherently that I could no more see their true shape than I could have swatted fruit bats in the bottom of a cave. What I knew, though, with a force that nearly made me redeposit the evening's scallops on Susan's Rosenthal china, was that Vitya *couldn't* just walk away; he had to *rip* himself away from shackles with which his former masters still bound him. I swallowed back a nervous gorge, and tried to imagine what those shackles could be—friends in Russia still? his parents?

And then I understood. The shackles weren't *there*. They were *here*. In this house, sleeping somewhere upstairs.

Vitya's kids.

Whom if he divorced Susan, he would lose. Whom he would lose if he went to jail, as a spy; espionage must still be illegal, even if the country you were spying for had gone out of business. Whom he would probably lose even if he was simply *exposed* as a spy, because Susan, and the Griswolds who hovered behind her, would surely not endure that public humiliation.

So why not simply keep quiet? Because . . .

"Jesus, Vitya," I breathed, the realization making my knees so weak I sat again. "You're not an ex-spy, are you? They're still making you work!"

Fortunately this was still in Russian, which kept it private between me and him. Vitya glanced at me, nodded, then grinned sharkishly. "Why not? The boss is still around."

Just then Susan's legs gave out, and she fumbled sideways into a chair, then slid off to the floor with a *whumpf* and a muttered curse. Vitya stood, flinging his napkin into his plate in disgust, then coming around the gleaming table to help his wreck of a wife to stand.

The boss? I felt as though the huge smoked-glass and bronze chandelier over my head had just flicked on. And then had landed on me.

15

MAYBE I was wrong. In fact, I hoped I was wrong. *Prayed,* even.

Except I knew I wasn't, which was why I drove back into Brooklyn feeling like my brain was bobbing in mulled wine. I did the entire LIE—ten lanes of solid traffic doing seventy-five mph, bumper to bumper, and everybody with his high beams on—in such a distracted state of mind that when I finally nosed my old VW into one of my favorite no-parking but also no-towing spots (the loading dock of the Waldbaum's that closed), I blinked in surprise, uncertain how I had gotten there.

That mental numbness was nothing compared to what it was doing to my brain that I was now thinking what I was thinking about Peter O'Connell.

I mean, my God, *Peter O'Connell.*

Translator of dissidents, biographer of Kostoglotov, Mac-Arthur genius, distinguished chairholder at Queens, PEN activist . . .

This is a man who I now suspected was Victor Korobeikin's KGB master?

Ever since that possibility—no, I had to admit, with a nauseated lump in the pit of my gut, that *certainty*—flashed into my head, I had been trying to fight off a conviction that all this must be symptoms of some kind of hormonal madness caused by not having children, precisely the terrible fate that my mother had always warned me I would meet, if she were to die without grandchildren.

Except . . .

Look, not only was everybody at that dinner supposed to be miserable, they were all supposed to make each other miserable, right? Milk-of-human-kindness Simon had invited Polina to make Susan miserable, and Susan to make Victor miserable, and O'Connell to make Polina miserable, and so forth.

So who was supposed to make O'Connell miserable, and how?

The who I had understood right away. Victor. The how and the why, that took me the rest of the night, and even then it was just a guess that I set out to check Saturday morning, about as soon as the sparrows and pigeons were out of bed.

"MIDGE, this is crazy! *You* are crazy! You should never have started up with that policeman, he has made you insane!"

"Sasha, damnit, when I want my head shrunk I'll go to a doctor, not some lousy plumber with burnt umber and cobalt blue in his beard! Just answer my question, is there anybody you know who works at Queens?" I had not actually put my head to pillow until after two A.M., and the glare of the headlights I had stared into all that way home had left me with a headache and a foul taste in my mouth that, if I hadn't known that nice young ladies don't drink to excess, I might almost have sworn was a hangover. Certainly I was in no mood to submit to my janitor's advice mongering, even if we had shared table, bottle, and sometimes even bed at various points in the past. Sasha was an emigré, and I had come to him strictly on emigré business.

"This isn't a fish market! Why are you shouting?" He waved his hands, then snatched for his pajama bottoms, which had started to slide off his bony hips.

"It's almost nine, Sasha, the only one I'm waking is you. And what's the matter, since when do we conduct our business in the hall?"

"Ah, well . . ." Sasha sort of blushed and looked away, his bristly black hair and beard all tufts and clumps. He bunched the waistband of cotton bottoms tighter with his left hand, gently closed his door completely with his right.

"You have your key?" I smiled sweetly.

"SHIT!" Sasha slapped himself on the head, starting the pajamas on their slither southward again.

I laughed, maybe a little too loud, but feeling as if I had won a round in some obscure game. "It's okay, ring your doorbell, and Karla will let you back in. Then get dressed, come upstairs, and we'll talk. I'll even fry salami, potatoes, and onions for your breakfast, if you want. I bet Karla doesn't fry your onions, does she?"

Somehow that sounded so lewd that we both laughed. And I was still smiling, even humming to myself, when Sasha finally appeared at my door, showered, dressed in a clean shirt, and very suspicious, in a flattered sort of way.

"Nu?"

"Nu yourself. Sit and eat, while I talk."

"These are green onions?" he sidled to my table, not entirely convinced I wasn't going to swing my spatula at him.

"There's another kind of onions? Of course, sit, eat," I laughed, enjoying my own imitation of a *yiddische mama*, though not quite certain why I was in such a good mood, except maybe for the three aspirin I had gagged down with the last of my orange juice. A mood I was not going to ruin by explaining *why* I wanted Sasha to find me somebody to talk to at Queens College, who might know something about Peter O'Connell.

Fortunately for me, you don't get to be a plumber in Leningrad if you don't have a natural talent for cultivating acquaintances in all sorts of unlikely places.

"You are interested in this man . . . professionally?" Sasha cocked a thoughtful eye at me, as he stroked his beard with his fork hand.

"You mean am I interested in him romantically?" I plopped a splat of eggs on Sasha's plate.

"No, no," Sasha blushed, meaning that that was what he had been wondering. "As a translator, perhaps, or . . ."

I put down the cooking utensils, untied my apron, and then slid into the chair opposite him. Even if it was only Sasha, whose bearded, bright-eyed face made him look like the second cousin of a Scotch terrier, it was pleasant to have somebody to look at across the breakfast table. I curled around my coffee and smiled, "No, see, that's just the point. What people say is, he's unapproachable. What I need is a fly on the wall!"

"A fly on the wall?" Sasha didn't seem to notice that his beard-stroking was getting egg and onion all along the left side of his face.

I smiled, reached across the table to wipe his beard with my napkin. "It's an idiom. What I mean is, somebody who is too small to be noticed, and so will see the things that other people do not."

"A fly on the wall," Sasha repeated, his smile growing as the expression sank in, and he savored it. Then he jabbed at the air with his fork, tracing a spatter of breakfast along my kitchen wall. "I've got such a fly for you! *After* I finish these most excellent eggs!"

"MOUSE" might have been closer to the mark, for the slightly stooped, round-eyed, tremulous creature we trudged up to the apartment above a shuttered Coney Island Avenue antique shop to meet, after the nearly forty minutes it had taken Sasha on the phone, wheedling, cajoling, and sometimes threatening, to arrange this chat.

Ester Zalmanovna, no last name given, had big, luminous brown eyes, hunched shoulders, and the quick, nervous gestures of someone who expects to be slapped arbitrarily and without warning. Her apartment too seemed timid—tiny arrangements of plastic flowers in the sort of grotesque Japanese–Occupation period vases that crowd flea markets, and I never could figure who buys, and Soviet reproductions of classic Russian paintings, the colors muddy and glum like mid-March in Moscow, and a small bookshelf crammed with Russian-language collections of authors like Nataniel Gavtorn and Gerbert Vells and Villiam Tekeri. And, as with most of the Jewish refugees from the Soviet Union, there were the obligatory signs of Russian Orthodoxy. A few time-abraded metal icons and Orthodox crosses, a guttering lamp in a faceted red-glass cup, a dusty palm frond stuck behind a lithographed icon, varnished onto wood. The only item in the entire room that suggested Ester Zalmanovna's life was anything more than a chapter in a Soviet-produced reader for second-year language students was a big painting on black velvet, the kind they sell out of vans at gas stations, which hung above the couch; the face might have been the Statue of Liberty, but the sideburns and the guitar suggested the painting was actually of Elvis Presley.

Ester Zalmanovna recorded language laboratory tapes for Queens College, reading the grammar book exercises onto audio cassettes. Not much of a job, but she was terrified of losing it.

"Ester, darling," Sasha cajoled, "there is nothing to fear! Midge is my oldest and dearest friend in America, and if she makes a promise, *I* make that promise!"

"Sure, and then Mr. O'Connell finds out that I have been speaking with you, and I am down at Court Street again, filling out papers for Public Assistance!"

"But I'm not asking you to *do* anything," I said as reasonably as I could manage. "And I'm not trying to harm Mr. O'Connell. I'm simply trying to understand something. Such as why he wouldn't want you talking to me, for instance."

"This is for a book she's working on," Sasha said, his voice grave.

"For a book?" the woman's voice was suddenly timbrous, with that exaggerated respect only the Russians seem to muster for the printed word. "You are a *writer?*"

I squirmed with my usual embarrassment, but Sasha took my arm, as if he were holding me up to auction. "Midge is a very important American writer. She has written *three* novels, and now is at work on her fourth!"

Ester Zalmanovna adjusted her goggle-size glasses and tucked her elbows even tighter to her knees, before asking shyly, "And perhaps there is a place in such a novel for me?" She blinked and twitched her nose, lacking only the green pea in her mouth to complete the resemblance to someone of whom Peter Rabbit would inquire how to get out of Mr. McGregor's garden. But what else would you expect of a person who would feel her life was more real if she could somehow be transformed into fiction?

Hating myself, I smiled and said, "Sure, especially since the project is just taking shape. In many ways, you might even be the perfect, well . . . I mean, that's why I asked Sasha to bring me here, because I'm interested in how little people see big people, and the big people don't notice them at all, don't care about them, aren't concerned about their problems."

"Like Gogol," Sasha pitched in, his face so solemn it was all I could do not to guffaw.

"Or Dostoevsky," I added, feeling sleazier by the minute.

However, Ester Zalmanovna apparently had always known that she was the heroine of an unwritten Dostoevsky novel, for she began nodding energetically. "Of course, the smug satisfaction of those who are full, and the gnawing hunger, the wounded pride of those who are not!"

"You see!" Sasha patted Ester Zalmanovna's knee encouragingly, then sneaked a wink at me.

Feeling I had to salvage a shred of self respect, I asked, "Mr. O'Connell is . . . full?"

"And how! He is the older brother of God!" Ester Zalmanovna's eyes took on a glint less mouse and more rat. "It isn't even that he doesn't listen to other opinions, for him there is no such *thing* as another opinion. There is only error, and truth. *His* truth!"

Bit by angry bit, Ester Zalmanovna spun us a tale that anyone who has ever worked in a university—or maybe anywhere else, for all I know—will have heard a thousand times. She had arrived in America almost a decade before, charred with the indignation and insult of Soviet life, only to find that life in America, for all its glitter, lacked the lofty moral seriousness of existence in Leningrad. As many of the early émigrés had, Ester Zalmanovna had eventually found her refuge in a Russian department.

Or did until O'Connell arrived, nine years later, with a monthly paycheck that looked like Ester Zalmanovna's net income for the whole year, and a mandate to "professionalize" the department.

Which meant, in essence, to fire people like Ester.

Not surprisingly, the woman's picture of O'Connell was venomous, but I confess I only half-listened, because the complaints were as familiar as they were scathing.

Then Ester Zalmanovna finished the preamble, and moved on to current grievances.

"And then after all of that trouble . . . can you imagine, *me*, with a *tsertifikat* from Leningrad University, *me* he wanted to make sit for the lousy American MA! . . . then suddenly, alongcomesthis*boyfriend*," she sneered so much contempt into the word that it made my ears feel soiled even to hear it, "his *boyfriend*, for whom *Dr.* O'Connell tries to make a chair as well. *Dr.* O'Connell has at least his doctorate, but *this* one . . . *this* one has only a master's, and is a crook besides! And *he* is a chair, while I, with my *tsertifikat*, I must join the bag women sitting unemployed at the bus terminal?" Ester Zalmanovna's mousy gaze burned with indignation.

I shook my head, trying to clear it of this sudden fog of confusing information. "Wait, wait . . . O'Connell has been trying to get someone else a job at Queens?"

Ester Zalmanovna's rage had been thriving on my silence; my sudden question startled her, and made her wilt. Sasha glowered at me, and my heart sank, wondering whether I hadn't just frightened the rabbit I needed back into its hole, forever.

Luckily, Ester Zalmanovna's outrage proved larger than her considerable timidity.

"Not just a job, a *chair*. A distinguished professorship! For a man who has never written a word of his own. And, of course, the bureaucrats at Queens, the same sheep in pinstripes who bleat to us each spring that there is no money for raises, no money for raises, these sheep are now saying, 'Oh yes, he has published so many important writers!' and 'His services to world literature' and blah-blah-blah! What they do not know, and what I know very very well, *bitterly* well, is that he is a thief, not a publisher. Worse even than a pickpocket!"

I took a guess, but it wasn't a wild one. "Simon Brent-Water-house?"

"My fiancé, in Leningrad . . . do you know Vladimir Solo-vetsky?" she addressed Sasha, for a moment.

"Volodya Solovetsky? Sure, who didn't know Volodya!" Sasha beamed, then darkened a bit. "But I hadn't known that . . . I mean you were going to . . ."

Ester Zalmanovna flushed, blinking rapidly. "Well, perhaps not precisely *fiancé,* but Vladimir was a man whom I admired deeply, an artist of very great soul, a poetic gift such as only a Russian may possess . . ." She stopped and sighed. Then, eyes aglitter, the feral mouse returned. "Vladimir gave a manuscript to Simon Brent-Waterhouse . . ."

When she had been silent a moment or so, I finished for her, "And Simon stole the royalties?"

Ester Zalmanovna looked at me with the dolorous face of the Madonna in an icon that has been venerated until it is half-erased. "He published half of Volodya's poems under someone else's name!"

"He stole the book?!" I was surprised and puzzled, unable to think of any reason on earth why Simon would publish some-one's poems as his own.

"Worse," Ester Zalmanovna said bitterly, "he didn't *notice.* It didn't matter. It was a *mistake.* A little, what is it Americans call it? A *boo-boo.* Which cost an enormously talented poet, a gift from God himself . . . this *boo-boo* cost him his life!"

"But Volodya *drank* himself to . . ." Sasha blurted out, before managing to stop himself, his eyebrows apologizing sheepishly to me.

Ester Zalmanovna's glance smoldered with scorn. "And just what do you suppose drove him into the embrace of the white fever, eh?"

The accusation of manslaughter by induced alcoholism was easy to ignore; even without Simon Brent-Waterhouse's editorial indifference there were plenty of reasons to drink yourself to death in Russia. Her accusation of Brent-Waterhouse's mistake rang true enough, though; even in the days when Sirin Press had seemed heroic to me, I had always been conscious of a certain editorial, well, *flamboyance*, perhaps?—chronic typoes, an inconsistent standard of accuracy in translation, and, on one occasion at least, a novel that had been printed inside out (the last two hundred pages first, followed by the first two hundred—and what's more, virtually no one noticed). Disposed to honor Sirin for its literary heroism, I had always allowed such blotches as the necessary companion of Brent-Waterhouse's almost singlehanded battle to preserve Russian culture from the Soviet overlords.

Clearly, though, to Ester Zalmanovna such slipshod editorial practice was infinitely worse than if Simon had stolen anything as base and negligible as money.

However, that O'Connell had been trying to hire Simon was not only news, it seemed nuts. If *anything* had been clear at that one dinner, it was that little love was lost between O'Connell and Simon Brent-Waterhouse. And if Ester Zalmanovna's intimation that O'Connell and Brent-Waterhouse at some point had been what my mother might call "romantically involved," was *anything* more than a snide exaggeration, well didn't that make it even *less* likely that O'Connell would try to hire Brent-Waterhouse? I mean, I confess that I am perhaps not the world's greatest expert on homosexual relationships, but it seems to make sense that, the details of the plumbing apart, those sorts of relationships would probably be a lot like the kind I used to have, back before the Darkness of Bran descended over my love life.

I mean, I didn't even *hate* any of the people I used to be intimate with, and I certainly can't see myself bending heaven and earth to get any of them a prestigious job just like mine, in the very same Russian department.

Shifting my weight about on Ester Zalmanovna's threadbare and sprung-bottomed sofa, I began to understand that I was looking at matters the wrong way about.

Yes, it made no sense for O'Connell to try to get Brent-Waterhouse a distinguished chair at Queens. However, it made a *lot* of sense for Brent-Waterhouse to *force* O'Connell to try to get that job for him.

Sirin Press was $700,000 in the hole, so Brent-Waterhouse didn't even have anything to liquidate. Neither was he likely to escape by setting up some other publishing entity, or even by selling off other literary properties he controlled; any money he made that way was likely to be litigated down into that same maelstrom of his debt. Nor had Simon seemed the type to enjoy hard tack and iron rations; that wobbly belly, carnation-red nose, and endless appetite for alcohol suggested a man who would do almost anything to secure a snug warm burrow in which to live out his golden years.

And, provided you have tenure and your university isn't about to go bust and you can refrain from moral outrages so flagrant that deans are forced to discipline you ("flagrant" here usually meaning things like attempting intercourse with a horse on the stage during the graduation ceremony), well . . . what burrow can be cozier than a university? Especially for a distinguished chair? A couple of seminars, some orotund bloviation, and lovely long weeks of doing nothing.

Well worth a bit of serious blackmailing to obtain, all things being equal.

The bright sun of morning, the after-effects of the Montepulciano, and a certain tendency to assume that my intuitions and hunches were as nuts as most people took them to be all had ground last night's conviction that O'Connell was not only an agent, but the man who was running Victor, down almost to nothing, leaving in its place a huge incredulity—how could a man as distinguished as Peter O'Connell be a Soviet agent?

But if he wasn't, I now wondered, what else could Simon have been blackmailing him about?

That O'Connell was homosexual? If indeed he was? Nowadays, and especially in a university, this seemed exceeding dubious grounds for extortion. Not much better than threatening to expose me as heterosexual; in fact, what I was told by the few of my old colleagues with whom I more or less kept up suggested that in the sacred groves of academe the latter state was now held in much lower general regard than was the former.

So what else was there that might drive O'Connell to expend goodwill and influence so copiously, trying to secure a distinguished professorship for a man he had seemed to loathe?

Even an imagination as cursedly fertile as mine, which had gotten me into trouble abundant over the years, could come up with only the one explanation: O'Connell was a Soviet agent, and Brent-Waterhouse was threatening to use Polina's book to reveal it, unless he were to receive a substantial *quid pro quo*.

Trembling, I interrupted Ester Zalmanovna's further rehearsals of the wrongs she had suffered at Queens. "This position, this distinguished chair. For Brent-Waterhouse. What has happened with it, since . . . well, since . . . ?"

Ester Zalmanovna shrank back into her timidity, puzzled by my question. Seeking guidance, she looked from me to Sasha, who murmured, "Brent-Waterhouse is dead."

Her myopic eyes opened in surprise, then closed again, as a grin slowly grew across her face. The woman let herself sit back into the chair on whose lip she had been perching, tense.

"Dead?" she finally asked, with an appreciative shake of her head at fate's ironies. Then a question crossed her face, like a sudden cloud. "But if his friend is now dead, then why has Dr. O'Connell been so cheerful this week?"

16

ESTER Zalmanovna's information, that O'Connell had been trying to get funding for a chair in Slavic, was the detail that suddenly brought the whole puzzle into focus, making sense from what had been a jumble of patterns.

I mean, think about it. Driven into a desperate corner by debt and the specter of eventual old age, Brent-Waterhouse hits upon the perfect blackmail. Once tenured, Simon would have been invulnerable, to lawsuit and ex-lover alike.

Which is precisely why such professorships are so difficult to get, especially for someone of Brent-Waterhouse's offbeat credentials. I don't know exactly how much arm-twisting, cajoling, and skullduggery O'Connell would have had to go through to arrange that sort of post for Brent-Waterhouse, but my sense, based on years in college teaching, was that disarmament talks with Iraq would have been a piece of chocolate chip babka by comparison. At a guess, securing an endowed chair for Brent-Waterhouse would have cost O'Connell every shred of influence the man had, and maybe a good bit of his money as well.

This was not an effort that O'Connell would have been quick to put himself through even if he *liked* Brent-Waterhouse, so he must have been very sorely tempted to face down Brent-Waterhouse's threat, to bluff it out, daring Simon to publish Polina Volkova's book himself, in the hope that the general obscurity of Sirin Press would protect him against serious harm.

Which must have been why that dinner had been convened, for one final tightening of the screws, to convince O'Connell he had no choice but to capitulate to Brent-Waterhouse. I was a hastily acquired stand-in for Susan Griswold, whose role (of a wealthy private investor) did not even require that I understand I was playing it. There *had* to be such an investor, if O'Connell was to know, completely and finally, that there was no other escape; either O'Connell arranged the cushy academic position that Simon wanted, or Polina's book was going to be published, one way or another.

What Simon intended that dinner to demonstrate was that however Polina's book appeared, it would be in a way that guaranteed no one in America would miss the sensational revelation that MacArthur genius, PEN activist, and dissident champion Peter O'Connell was in fact—and had always been—an agent of Moscow intelligence.

It was a perfect scheme, very much in the spirit of Simon Brent-Waterhouse. And O'Connell had apparently gotten the message, slinking back to the Van Horn sometime later that evening, to get Polina's letter, as a receipt for price paid. But O'Connell would have discovered a final nasty surprise there, that instead of giving up the letter from Volkova, as O'Connell had expected, Brent-Waterhouse dashed off that renunciation of his claim on Volkova. The "suicide" note.

Why one, rather than the other? I wasn't sure, but even the little time I had spent with the two Englishmen told me that negotiations between them would have been like porcupines mating—a precise operation, with a constant likelihood of pain. Presumably O'Connell had tried to hedge his capitulation at the last minute, and Brent-Waterhouse, to insure himself until he actually had a firm offer from Queens College in hand, had substituted the "suicide note" letter, which he had typed while O'Connell waited.

And O'Connell, expecting the original letter, and now goaded beyond endurance, had chucked Brent-Waterhouse down the airshaft.

Which illustrated the only weakness that I could discern in the entire fabric of Simon's plan. It was the flaw common to most blackmail schemes—blackmail stops when the blackmailer is dead.

Meaning that I had found my murderer.

The problem was, now I had to prove there had been a murder.

"THIS really is all they eat at a Russian banquet?" Walter asked me, his shirt collar open and his hair in dark damp ringlets; left ankle tapped furiously across right knee as he shoveled in another forkful of salad, chased by a chomp of black bread. "There's no main course?"

"Usually there is, but it's real plain, just meat and potatoes. Rabbit most times, or maybe duck. I had chicken once, I think . . . but chicken is harder to get. More expensive, cause you have to feed them grain. You ready to try some of this eggplant salad?" I spooned huge blobs onto Walter's plate as I asked. "And this the Russians call meat salad, even though it's all potatoes and egg." Over his protests I dumped a little more glop onto his plate, because I didn't want Walter getting totally drunk. Trying to manage this impromptu "Russian party" that I had conned Walter into was giving me some retroactive sympathy for what Saturday nights must have been like for those poor ZBT boys, at their fraternity parties back at Cornell, trying to intoxicate us college girls toward a copulation that would be successful, but also somehow distinct from necrophilia. Like they had wanted me to be then, I now wanted Walter drunk enough to say yes, but not so drunk that he wouldn't be able to do what he had said yes to.

Except it was company I wanted, not copulation.

"No! No, no, no!"

"Aw, come on, Walter, it's not like I'm asking you to *do* anything, it's just that I need . . . well, like a witness, I suppose. You just come with me to the Van Horn, and . . ."

"*Witless* is more like it, if I go with you to that hotel! You have any more of that with the pepper?" He extended his vodka glass across my food-laden kitchen table. "Anyway Midge, have you got any idea what it's going to be like up there, especially on Saturday night? I mean, we are talking major *New York* here. People *eat* people in this city."

"Of course, of course!" I hastily poured a syrupy ribbon of incredibly expensive vodka from the frost-rimmed bottle, then put a token splash into my own glass; not having proper Russian vodka glasses, I had put out the bigger sherry glasses, and Walter was already beginning to show the results. "Here, take a little more of the caviar too, it's *great* with the vodka. Black caviar is even better, but God, who can afford it? Anyhow, you're wrong. It's Milwaukee they eat people in. New York is where they stuff people in ice chests and leave them by the freeway."

"Very funny. You should go maybe on the television, or to one of those comedy clubs," Walter said, taking about four spoons more than "a little," making me cringe even though it was just roefish caviar, because it was not as if I could afford *any* of this—the $20-bottle of vodka, the smoked whitefish, the sliced sausage, the roe.

But what choice did I have? Inderlund and Wolanski, the two detectives who had decided Brent-Waterhouse had committed suicide, would have found my discoveries, and my new suspicions, about O'Connell and Korobeikin confusing, demented, and—the adjective I think I dreaded most of all—*cute*. I could have asked Sasha, the janitor, to come over to the Van Horn with me, but in the first place he had only just barely begun speaking to me again after the debacle that my last serious request for help had caused, last spring, and in the second place, if it came to testifying in court . . .

Well, who was going to believe a Russian émigré, who even in a tie and jacket looked like a Scottish terrier, except that he also had paint in his beard and bushy eyebrows?

And why not Russo?

Why not ask Russo to come to the Van Horn with me, to show Mrs. Morrisey the photo that was on the back dust jacket of O'Connell's biography?

I asked myself that a lot. However, as sorely tempted as I was to pick up my phone, and no matter how much sense it seemed to make—Mike is a cop! Mike is strong! Mike is a detective!—I always came to the same conclusion: A girl who valued her independence so much that she would strip buck naked on a beach to prove it really would be being a hypocrite if she ran to ask for help and protection from the very man whom she had humiliated by doing so.

Which left me Walter.

Whose face at that moment was shining as Marcel Proust's might have, if Proust's childhood had been spent in Lublin, and instead of madeleines someone had given him roast eggplant salad.

"Christ, I remember this stuff! My grandmother used to make it! But I think maybe she used more garlic . . ." Walter said through a mouthful big enough that not all of it fit; olive oil dribbled out of the corners of his lips. Then, after a swallow that hurt my throat just to watch, Walter touched my hand, dropped his voice about a quarter octave, and said, "Midge, where you *shouldn't* go is that far into the Upper West Side, especially on a Saturday night! I just don't want you to get *hurt!*"

"Walter, that's exactly what I don't want, too," I said matter-of-factly, after passing Walter the breadplate, as a way of making it seem like I hadn't really snatched my hand away. I was surprised, that Walter should sound so concerned, but after a moment I was also encouraged, that maybe Walter was at least a little inclined to share my suspicions of O'Connell. After all, if Peter O'Connell was even half the things this week was leading me to think he was, then I was risking coming a whole lot closer than I really wanted to at the moment, to finding out if I was famous enough to get my obituary in the *Times.* "So that's why we have to find out, was O'Connell *there* that night? Look, if I'm wrong, then so what? Who's to know we even asked, right? But what about if I'm *right?* If I'm right, and O'Connell went to Brent-Waterhouse's room that night, then O'Connell has been getting away with *murder . . .*" I brushed a loose swatch of hair back behind my ear, shuddering because I suddenly realized the reality of that familiar exaggeration.

"But *Jee*-sus, Midge!" Walter now brushed his own forelock back, then brayed his "aren't-*you*-a-dope?" laugh. "This is Peter goddamn O'Connell we're saying is a run-amok Kremlin *goon!* Human rights committee at PEN, MacArthur genius . . . I mean, why don't we go all the way, and decide it was Salman Rushdie who pushed Brent-Waterhouse out the window, on orders from the Kremlin? Or Mother Teresa?" Then, a little unsteadily, he held up his fourth shot of home-peppered vodka. "You're supposed to raise the glass like this when you toast, right?" Walter beamed, his face flush, beneath tiny seed pearls of sweat. Looking grave, Walter spoke to the book-sized glossy of O'Connell that I had propped against the vase into which I had jammed Walter's gift of three red roses. O'Connell had posed himself over a chessboard, as though he were waiting for you to make your paltry, feeble move; his thinning hair was combed carefully to disguise a bald spot, his chipmunk cheeks were lined by an inch-wide, close-clipped beard, and his glittering eyes glared out, through the A of raised, touching fingertips. There were so many bookshelves, oriental rugs, and pieces of Biedermeier furniture behind him that the photo could have been taken in the study of Sigmund Freud. "To ummm . . . To Midge!" Walter boomed at the photo. "May her . . . uhh literary imagination grow as bountifully as her ummm . . . well, regular imagination!"

I accepted this muddled gallantry with a bow of my head and what I hoped was a sane, reasonable, and very pretty smile, then clicked glasses and we both bottoms-upped. Walter banged his glass down, then with a flourish munched the caviar and cracker, the sweat now trembling plumper on his crimson brow.

"Christ, Walter, okay, so I'm wrong. And you can laugh at me until my hair turns blue and we've both got wrinkles like an elephant, all right?" I refused to give up my point so easily. "But what if I'm right? Isn't *national security* important enough for you to at least *check*? It's not like anything will *happen*. We go, we show Mrs. Morrisey O'Connell's picture, and then we come home! *Careful!* You get that eggplant on your jacket and the oil will never come out!" I jumped up for a cloth, with which I began scrubbing at the elbow Walter had just put down in the red-orange-blue Sicilian bowl near the table's edge.

He yanked his arm away, so I handed him the dishcloth. Walter scrubbed vigorously at the spot, which seemed only to be getting wetter, not cleaner. He quit with a sigh, looked at me, his eyes mournful. "Goddamnit, I never should have gone into

Barneys, I *knew* it. Thousand-buck raw-silk jacket, that they marked down to three fifty. I swear, every time I go into that damn store I do that, blow like half my paycheck on something, and then the first time I wear it I do something like sit on a park bench they just painted. It's because of that goddamn Hamilton I work with, he could walk through a fertilizer factory in a white suit like Tom Wolfe wears, and it would be cleaner when he comes out than when he went in. He doesn't even *sweat!* And me? The shirt I'm going to buy stains itself when it's still in the store! I sometimes wonder if I'm really made for this business." Walter mourned his jacket a bit longer, then studied me again. "We just show that picture," he pointed at the book jacket, "and then we come back here?" A bright glimmer of concupiscent hope had kindled in his eyes.

I hastily amended my last phrase. "What I meant, I'll drop you off right in midtown!"

The spark of hope faded, and Walter looked confused. "Why midtown? You mean like at the paper? It's midnight Saturday, what do you think, there's going to be a stop-the-presses book review?"

"I thought at your apartment, actually," I said, maybe a little too tartly.

"My apartment? I live at my mother's. In Scarsdale."

"Your *mother's?*" I gaped at him, and was surprised to see he was blushing.

"Yeah, well . . . just till I find someplace," he said uncomfortably. "You know what rents are like."

I laughed, but to make it seem as though I wasn't, I dumped the last of my bottle of Stolichnaya Crystal into Walter's glass, then raised my (empty) glass inquiringly.

"Come on, what's this going to cost you?" I ventured, trembling. "You'll come with me to the hotel, I'll do all the talking. And if I'm right, well . . . you could testify. About what Mrs.

Morrisey says, I mean . . . the police would believe you. Working for the paper and all . . ."

Walter looked pained, then thumped his glass back onto my kitchen table. My heart began to hammer; if Plan No. 1 fell through, I had no Plan No. 2.

"*Je*-sus, the paper! I can't have the paper mentioned!"

"Okay, no newspaper, then. All I'm asking is, we go up to the Van Horn, I look around, and then we come back, okay?"

I could tell that Walter was thinking hard, and for a second my mouth went dry, with the fear that he would still refuse. But then a big grin spread across his face, and my heart began hammering. He lifted his glass, clicked against mine. "Son of a bitch. Let's do it! What the hell, how did they use to say it? *Smert shpionam!*"

I winced at Walter's mangling of the Russian, but clicked my glass to the toast. "Death to spies!" I agreed.

17

EXCEPT who exactly was the spy now? And who was going to be dead? I wondered. Even my VW seemed to be smarter than I was; at least it flat-out refused to start, and pretty soon even the battery quit listening, contenting itself with disapproving clicks.

So I got to worry until the inside of my mouth turned to shoe leather while our Jamaican-driven gypsy cab, a blue Chevrolet with brown doors and a red trunk, its fenders so battered that the car looked like it had taken part in some David Letterman stunt, bounced and rattled us from Brooklyn over to Manhattan, and then up the West Side Highway, headed for the Van Horn.

Which, when we reached it, was on the other side of Amsterdam Avenue; our taxi yanked a U-turn that all but tipped us over.

"Van Horn, mon," the rasta driver announced, ivory-yellow eyes watching amused as Walter and I disentangled ourselves from the heap his driving had thrown us into.

"You wait," Walter said, his voice tight with tension. "We won't be long."

"Wait *here*, mon? I doubt that be wise," the driver shook his thick, stiff dreadlocks.

Walter leaned over me, to point at the street. "Wiser than assuming you're going to get another fare out of this neighborhood, isn't it? I mean, *look* at this place!" Then he added, muttering in my ear, "Midge, I swear to God, I thought you were crazy before, but this is *dangerous.*"

"*Wal*-ter!" I managed, even though he was quite right. By day the Van Horn had seemed merely seedy; by night it looked like the most rundown Hilton in hell. In the autumn sunlight the kids dashing around pretending to machine-gun each other had appeared pathetic and touching; now the kids on the sidewalk— and there were several, even small ones, despite the hour— looked diabolical, or maybe demonic, watching us with wide-eyed, silent, and probably exhausted calm.

I write mysteries, and I read them, watch them on television. Once I even went, at Pearl's insistence, to one of those mystery-package weekends for singles, at a resort in the Poconos that had dreamed up this staged murder-fest as a way of filling an off-weekend between the last of the Fall Foliage Frolics and the first of the Wild Winter Weekends. All of this, with the exception of the wheezy overweight accountant who had elected himself to be my constant partner throughout that weekend in the Poconos, is entertaining, and intellectually stimulating and not terribly different from what I had been doing all week, chasing Pedlar and Polina and Susan Griswold around the city. Until now, as I stared at the Van Horn, when I began to understand that this was *real*. I stepped out of the cab, trembling.

"Fifty bucks, mon. That buy you fifteen minute wait time."

"Fifty?!" Walter yelped.

The driver grinned. "Like you say, you think you get another cab, this place?"

Muttering, Walter paid, while I forced my numb feet to move me toward the doorway.

Walter slapped an arm around my shoulder, making me jump about two feet in the air. "*Jee*-sus," he repeated. "A *fifty* . . . but looking around, I'm beginning to think maybe it's worth it."

Walter's attempt at good humor cheered me up enough to at least enter the hotel. The television in the lobby was still spewing good times at an audience of three or four indefinite creatures, only one of whom still had the energy to lift his bottle-in-a-bag to his lips. Maybe the set didn't even have an off switch.

Walter pursed his lips. "Nice place. You think maybe they offer some kind of getaway package? You know, 'live the urban nightmare!' something like that. And then you and me could make a dirty weekend of this, eh?" When I stared at him, startled, he waggled his eyebrows in a burlesque Groucho Marx leer.

"Well, at least they've added fresh urine to the elevator since I was here last," I whispered back, then tiptoed past what had been the next hurdle I was fearing—getting by the front desk. Except it wasn't much of a hurdle; the caged reception area was lit, and there were papers scattered about the desk, but the place was empty, with a serious-looking lock to secure it. We started up the stairs.

Saturday night at the Van Horn was like a cross between a carnival haunted house and early episodes of "The Honeymooners." We trudged upward, flinching at the moans, shouts, laughter, and snatches of argument which ricocheted up and down stairs and hallways made murky by the light of rare twenty-five-watt bulbs, some of which were so old they had been painted, two or three times.

I puffed and trudged, paying no attention to the few people I passed, so that they would think I knew where I was going. I did, too, though I swear the distance between floors must have doubled since the last time I had come to the Van Horn.

"Mrs. Morrisey," I panted, tapping gingerly at her door, when I finally reached the sixth floor. I squinted into the peephole, feeling sweat prickling down my back. As far as I could tell, the peephole was closed. "Mrs. Morrisey!"

"One fifteen in the morning and the woman doesn't answer. I'm astonished. Can we go home now?"

"Shut up, Walter. Mrs. Morrisey, please, it's Margaret Cohen, I just want to ask you a question." I put my ear to the door, hoping for some giveaway floorboard squeak or long-held exhalation. Mrs. Morrisey's room seemed to be about the only one in the Van Horn that was quiet. Maybe she really *was* asleep, I wondered, knowing somehow that she couldn't be out; when I had been here with Detective Inderlund the woman's room had breathed the never-unoccupied, fetid air of a hamster cage. Or maybe Mrs. Morrisey was *worse* than asleep? I suddenly wondered, which put enough adrenalin into my blood stream to double my pulse. I straightened up, looking up and down the narrow hall, with no idea what to do next. I looked at Walter.

He looked back, his head starting to shake as he understood the question I hadn't even asked. "Oh no, no! I am *not* going to try to knock the door down! As it *is* I'll probably lose my job, I sure as the *devil* will not go to jail for . . ."

"I never asked you to break down her door! I was just . . ."

"Just nothing! You're nuts, and this whole evening is nuts!" Walter backed slowly away. "Hell, *I'm* nuts! Goddamn sixth floor of a welfare hotel in the middle of the night, to show a picture of a murderer to a woman who isn't even there! I am never drinking vodka again! Come on, you leaving with me, or am I going alone?"

Walter was halfway down the short hall, almost at the stairs, when someone's head emerged from a door further along.

"Murderer?" a familiar voice asked. "There's a murderer here?"

"Mrs. Morrisey!" I shouted, before managing to hush myself. "Mrs. Morrisey!" I galloped down the hall, gesturing to Walter. He had paused, undecided, at the stairs. "Mrs. Morrisey!"

The woman straightened as best she could, her Marty Feldman eyes bulging even more with fright. She nearly shut the door, but then, apparently recognized me.

"Ahh! It's you, the filth with the dirty snapshots!"

"Filth?" I stopped at half-stride, confused and a little hurt.

"Sorry, sorry. Copper, I should have said, don't have much to do with the police over here, but I do remember how your kind *hated* being called 'the filth' back home. Don't really know why, to tell the truth, it was just a name, no harm done."

"No harm done?" Walter hissed at my back. "Impersonating a police officer is a *felony*." His 'f' got the back of my neck wet.

"I *didn't* impersonate anybody," I snapped at him, then, doing the best I could to pretend that this was a simple social call, I said, "Did I remember the wrong room, Mrs. Morrisey? Isn't this . . .?"

"Poor old Mr. B-W's room? Quite right it is, quite right! Mine now, though." She threw wide the door, with a proprietarial flourish, then stepped aside. The faded flowers of her quilted bathrobe unfurled as she waved at the room, which now looked—and smelled—as though it had always been hers. Stacks of puzzle books, the pink shag rug under the small table, now topped with the two caged parakeets, the ancient television on the nighttable the mirror of which had had the "suicide note" stuck to it, even the stink of AirWick and Salem cigarettes.

"It's the windows, don't you see?" Mrs. Morrisey pointed at the side-by-side sashes. "Look out on Amersterdam Avenue, they do, so I can watch out there now. Not quite as safe as the peephole, perhaps, but ever so much more interesting than that side street was. That nasty sepoy didn't want to have me take poor old Mr. B-W's room, but I promised him I'd make him no end of fuss about the scandalous things that go on here, and in the end he left me have it. The budgies are *ever* so much happier here, aren't you dearies?" She stepped over to tap the cage of the two fluffed-up parakeets, who looked very grumpy at being awake.

Taking her move to the cage as invitation, I stepped in, then motioned Walter to follow. After a moment, scowling, he did. Mrs. Morrisey eyed him curiously, then said. "He more filth? I mean, sorry . . . coppers."

"Mrs. Morrisey, I apologize for coming so late, but, well, I knew that you're a night owl, and so when something came up, I just thought . . . I mean I suppose I should have waited, or at least called . . ."

"Called? No phones, remember?" she said, seeming proud of that, as she patted the pockets of her bathrobe. Finding her cigarettes, she lit up, cigarette tucked in the left corner of her toothless mouth, so the menthol blue smoke could escape out the right. It gave her face an unsettling resemblance to that of Popeye the Sailor.

"Mrs. Morrisey, as I said, I am sorry to bother you, but you were such a big help the last time I showed you a photo, I was hoping that maybe you wouldn't mind if I asked you about just one more photo."

"Another of your dirty snaps, is it?" she cackled, holding out a slightly arthritic hand. "Now who would you be handing about in a state of nature today, eh?"

I held up Peter O'Connell's empty book jacket. "Did you ever see this man visiting Mr. Brent-Waterhouse?"

Mrs. Morrisey glanced curiously at the title page, then snorted as she flipped it over, to glimpse the photo. "*Visiting* is what they call it now, is it? Couple of middle-age fairies wrestling for pixie dust in the linens? And that's visiting? Right you are then, 'visiting' there was!"

The trembling of my hand made the photo quiver, but I think I had my voice under control as I asked, "Well then, do you recall the last time you saw this gentleman come to the hotel?"

Rather than answer immediately, Mrs. Morrisey cocked her head at me, and shifted her Salem across her frog's mouth with her tongue; for a moment I thought she was going to swallow the cigarette, like a particularly juicy bug. Finally she smiled, before saying, "I believe I do, miss, and me budgies do too, don't you sweets?" Mrs. Morrisey tinkled a little bell in the parakeets' cage. The birds sidled about on their perch, but then settled back to sulking.

"So when was this last visit then?" I finally could stand the smirk no longer.

"About eleven o'clock, I expect. Before eleven thirty absolutely, because me and the budgies we just hate to miss that Arsenio's first monologue."

I knew Mrs. Morrisey was playing deliberately simple, but I wasn't sure about what. Impatience made me dig my nails into the palms of my hands, but I sounded like sweet reasonableness itself, asking, "But what *day* was that, Mrs. Morrisey?"

The old woman smiled at her private joke. "Why, today, of course. Did I forget to mention that?"

She had, of course, but it wasn't so hard to understand why; like most people who have only themselves, and maybe some parakeets, for company, Mrs. Morrisey was pleased to take full advantage of this unexpected audience, by spinning out our conversation as long as she could. What I still can't figure out though is what *my* excuse was, that at first I only snapped at her.

"No, no! Last Wednesday! Was this man here last Wednesday?"

Of course he had been, which I must have known, because already I had dug my nails so deep into my palms that I drew blood.

Looking a bit miffed to be hurried through a conversation, Mrs. Morrisey nodded. "Arrived around one, I would suppose, and left an hour, maybe an hour and half later," Mrs. Morrisey puffed on her cigarette, no hesitation of memory at all. "Saw him going the one way and then back the other, didn't I?"

"Did you hear fighting, shouts, anything like that?"

"In this bedlam?" she looked scornful. "The nignogs in this place could drown out the Last Trump. No, it was like a regular thing, Mr. O'Connell come tripping along the hallway on his little fairy feet, and then, some hours later and the worse for drink, he'd come slithering back."

As he had last Wednesday. At virtually the exact moment that Brent-Waterhouse's watch had stopped, because the publisher had fallen onto it, from six stories up.

I felt weak. Almost weak enough to sit. Walter must have noticed, because I felt his hand at the small of my back.

"Midge?" he inquired, almost intimately.

"It was him," I said, as softly. "He was here. O'Connell."

"Good. You did good, kid," Walter patted me. "Except why was he here tonight?"

Since I was obviously withering as a conversation partner, Mrs. Morrisey was happy to assume that Walter's question was meant for her.

"He said he thought he must have left a business paper of some sort over here. Very sorry to bother, but could he rummage about in Mr. B-W's things, because he'd looked everywhere else, but just couldn't seem to turn this scrap up anywhere. It's all one to me, as far as I know the whole pitiable lot is to be chucked anyway," Mrs. Morrisey disdainfully waved the back of a veiny and crumpled hand at the three cardboard cartons into which Simon Brent-Waterhouse's effects had been stuffed, still stacked next to the cigarette-scarred dresser, in the space where the door swung open.

"Did . . ." in order to talk I had practically had to scrape my throat clear, "Did . . . he find it? The paper?"

Mrs. Morrisey shook her head. "Looked through all that, poked about, even stuck his head out the windows, but nothing. Made him *angry*, it did." Mrs. Morrisey rolled her Ping-Pong–ball eyes, smirked.

Walter shook his head, irritable. "No, no . . . that's not what I meant . . ."

Feeling ill, I held up my hand, to stop him. "It was the letter he was looking for, Walter. O'Connell was trying to find Polina's letter."

Now his irritation turned on me. "I *know* that, what else would he be looking for? What I wonder is, how come it was *tonight*? I mean, chrissake, that fat limey publisher went out the window ten *days* ago. So how come it's only *tonight* that O'-Connell comes looking for it?"

I didn't know, and then—suddenly, like an army boot in the belly—I did. I didn't ask permission of Mrs. Morrisey; I just sat on her bed, although the loose hammocklike springs nearly dumped me out again.

Why the letter? Because that letter might still let its bearer own Polina's book. Which meant control Peter O'Connell's life.

But that had always been true. So why *today*? Why not any of the other nine days between Simon's death and now?

What had changed?

Me.

I had spoken to Vitya. And Vitya must have questioned his wife, to find out why I was there. And once he found out that Susan had intended to be her own nasty surprise for him at that dinner, Vitya would have reached the same conclusions I had. After which, if I were him, I would have called O'Connell.

Which would have let O'Connell understand that his blackmailer might be dead, but the blackmail could still go on, unless O'Connell got control of Polina's book, once and for all.

The easy way to do so was to find the letter. The hard way, but maybe ultimately the surer way, was to get rid of Polina.

Less than three hours ago O'Connell had apparently drawn a blank at the first of these choices.

"Walter," I looked up, suddenly gripped by that icy, logical calm that comes only when you are really, truly in a terrible, terrible mess. "Listen, go call this number," I recited Russo's telephone, "and then take the cab downtown, to the Bristol Hotel. Room 1478."

I think it must have been my voice, because Walter actually took a couple of obedient steps backward, before stopping. "What do you mean, I should go? Who's this phone for? And what's at the hotel? And anyway, what about you? I'm supposed to just leave you here?" He crossed his arms, shook his head. "Uh-uh. No way."

So, feeling almost as though Pearl had taken over my body, and Walter was me, a four year old who refused to pick up her blocks, I rose, said a polite good night and thank you to Mrs. Morrisey, who looked cross at losing her company, and then led Walter out into the hall.

Where I tersely explained about Russo and Polina.

"Come on, Midge, what's with this guy in the Bronx?" Walter's nerves made him sound peevish. "If we want police, just call 911. And what am I supposed to tell Polina?"

"Walter, Russo is a long story that I don't want to tell you now, but he's a cop, and he'll come. Polina you can tell whatever you want. Tell her you're in love with her, tell her you can't live without her. Just make sure she's not alone. And *please* go and call RIGHT NOW!"

Walter opened his mouth, to argue, then shut it again, took a couple of steps, opened his mouth again.

"Walter, O'Connell has at least a two-hour head start on you," I said, as gently as if I were saying "so long." Then I brushed by Walter and started up the staircase. He nodded, face grim with purpose, and started down the same staircase. Then he stopped, and shouted up after me.

"Wait a minute! Where in the hell are you going?"

I leaned over the worn wooden banister, Walter barely visible through the steel railing. "To find Polina's letter, I hope."

"You know where it is?"

"I think so. But wish me luck anyway."

18

THE ninth floor of a hotel with a chronically busted elevator was every bit as spooky and deserted as I would have expected. It was impossible to tell whether anyone lived there, partly because of the hour, partly because of the dead bulbs in the hallway fixtures, and partly because of the piles of junk that had been dumped indifferently everywhere. Broken beds, cardboard boxes, forgotten bedsprings, plaster-covered lathing. . . . Even a couple of barrels of toxic waste wouldn't have seemed out of place, in what I could make out of the jumble in the faint light that had survived a trip through the filthy glass of the skylight. I scrambled over, around, and under piles of things to get from one end of the hall to the other, but found no stairs to take me higher. The squeaks and scrabbling little feet among the junk were doing nothing to lessen my inclination to start screaming, burst into tears, or both; instead though I forced myself to look again, as calmly and carefully as I could.

Because there had to be *some* way up there, to get access to that airshaft.

At first, even though Mrs. Morrisey was able to place O'Connell at the scene of Brent-Waterhouse's death at the precise moment the publisher had died, and even though I was absolutely certain that O'Connell had killed him, I still had had one question.

How had he killed him?

How does a man almost too short even to reach that bathroom window force somebody sixteen inches taller and at least a hundred pounds heavier through it?

About thirty seconds later I realized the answer.

He doesn't.

Brent-Waterhouse must have been *leaning* out that window, and O'Connell merely gave him a push. And why would Brent-Waterhouse have been leaning out his bathroom window?

The original of Polina's letter would have been hidden somewhere that would have made it impossible to find, yet kept it immediately at hand, depending on the course of the evening's negotiations. Obviously Brent-Waterhouse had been dissatisfied with whatever O'Connell replied, because he had substituted the second letter. Perhaps that was not good enough for O'Connell. Or perhaps it seemed to be, and Brent-Waterhouse had thought the other man was gone.

Whether he had meant to check the letter's safety or to fling it in O'Connell's face, Simon had gone to where he had hidden it.

Somewhere out in the airspace. To be reached only by leaning through the bathroom window.

Of which O'Connell had been quick to take fatal advantage.

I didn't know precisely where that letter was now. Still taped under the sill, perhaps, or in a bag on a string, or maybe stuck under a wire or clip of some sort. Or maybe it had fluttered down, to join the muck and junk at the bottom of the shaft.

However, I was going to find out, just as soon as I discovered the access to the airshaft.

A second and more careful look, aided by the feeble light of my keychain flashlight, found the black square of an access hatch half hidden in a corner where the hallway bent around some structural detail, with three iron handholds set in the wall beneath it. I suppose that the idea had been that any workman who needed access to the roof would have a stepladder that would get him up to the rungs, while any one else would have been unable to reach.

That is, if someone hadn't already built a rickety tower under it, of the junk cluttering the top floor. Two broken chairs on top of a desk, on top of a crate. I breathed hard several times, trying to drown out Pearl's voice, which was ringing in my inner ear—"My God, Midge, you'll kill yourself!" Then, trembling, I slung my purse across my body, wondering for not the first time why we women have let ourselves be saddled with that damn clumsy bag; couldn't somebody dream up an easier way to keep credit cards, driver's license, old kleenex, spare tampons, leaking pens, and lint-covered sourballs on one's person?

The pile of junk shuddered but held as I made my way slowly to the uppermost chair. Tense, frightened, I straightened slowly, half hunched under the hatch cover. The penlight showed me that there had been a simple hasp to keep the access secure, which somebody had ripped free with a pry bar. Now the hasp dangled from shattered wood, the lock still clutching it uselessly shut.

Kids, I supposed, gingerly pushing up with my shoulder. The hatch gave, reluctantly. Grunting, I pushed harder, but my tower of junk slipped downward, instead of the hatch going up.

Stinging sweat was blinding me, and my jaw was clenched so

tight my teeth ached. Not daring even to move on that rickety scaffold, I glanced around, wondering how badly I would be maimed when it all fell. The pile shuddered again, so I gave a final, scared-stiff shove, my right hand on the top wall rung.

With a *skreek* of rusty metal and rush of night air, the hatch flipped back. I stuck my head up, just about eye-level with the roof, a pebble-studded tangle of pipes, wires, and chimneys, glopped over with solidified tar, littered with bottles, bird droppings, paper, and other urban leftovers.

It proved a devilishly difficult thing to do, and I broke off one of the heels that I wish I hadn't been wearing, when I jammed it trying to scrabble up those rungs, but finally I succeeded in belly-flopping myself over the sharp, tin-metal lip of the hatch opening, where I lay for a moment on the damp, biting pebbles, panting and staring at the yellow night sky over Manhattan. Vowing that in the next life I would *not* cheat on push-ups in high school gym. Chin-ups either.

Finally I got to my feet.

The view from on top of the Van Horn was different than from the street, but it wasn't a lot prettier; despite the coils of razor ribbon which glistened on the parapets, kids had clearly made themselves a world up there. Cigarette butts, condoms, broken bottles, and graffiti on any surface that would take paint, in huge convoluted designs that might have been letters, or might not; the number of colors and the care with which they had been spray-painted said that at least the kids hadn't been hurried as they defaced the building. The graffiti seemed much more, well, *complete* than it does on the overpasses, subway cars, buses, and the other more public large flat surfaces of the New York, which I guess they have to vandalize on the fly. I listened for a moment, fearing suddenly that despite the hour perhaps I would not be the only person on the roof; however I heard only cars in the street below, shouts from somewhere, distant music.

Hobbling because of the broken heel, I gingerly made my way to the ladder, the top of which arched its rusty way over the knee-high parapet around the airshaft. First shaking the ladder to satisfy my doubts about its firmness, I held tight, and peered over the lip.

The scaly rust on the ladder felt about like the inside of my mouth, when I stared down into that tiny black rectangle. Had it been utterly black, I might have convinced myself the airwell was nothing to fear; as it was, lit here and there by bathroom lights within, the airshaft appeared to spiral straight down to the bowels of perdition.

"This is crazy!" I told myself loudly, hoping to convince myself to turn around, and go back home.

"Even if two of us have reached the same conclusion?" somebody asked behind me.

I think if I hadn't been holding onto the ladder, I would have gone over the lip, into the airshaft. Instead I lurched, threw myself back, turned around. My heart felt like it was trying to batter its way up my throat and fly away.

"YOU? You're supposed to be at Polina's!"

Peter O'Connell stepped around the chimney he must have been standing behind, his shoes scrunching on the gravel. He was all in black. Including gloves. He nodded, smiled. The sulfur-yellow street lights glittered on his contact lenses.

"Miss mmm Cohen, isn't it?" He laughed, dryly. "I must say you gave me a start, when that doorway thing let out its shriek! I could just *imagine* the sort of desperadoes who might be up on *this* roof, at *this* sort of hour!"

Desperadoes like you, I thought, but didn't say. My mouth wasn't working. The hatch opening was between us, but O'Connell was closer to it. Even closer, after he took another step. He dusted his gloves off.

"Why should I be at Polina's?" he asked mildly. "I mean, since we both obviously agree that her letter has to be here?"

"DON'T COME ANY CLOSER!" I shouted, waving my right hand in warning, but still clinging tight to the ladder with my left.

"All right, but why ever not?" O'Connell asked, but he did stop. Maybe twenty feet from me. But only five from the hatch. "So tell me then, why should I be at Volkova's? Because that's where Simon's letter is? If that's the case, then why are *you* here?"

"Because . . . because . . ." I stammered, glancing wildly about. The hatchway wasn't going to do me any good. Jump to another building? It was about fifty feet to one parapet, less to the other. But there was a coil of razor ribbon along each. Plus which I had no idea how long a drop I might have to the next roof. Or whether there was an alley. "Because Polina . . . you don't need the letter if . . ."

I clung trembling to the ladder, another moment, then, because I had no other choice, I swung right leg, then left leg out over the abyss. One step, two steps.

And suddenly I was standing over eight stories of empty air.

O'Connell took another step closer. "Where on earth are you going, Miss Cohen? And what do you mean, I don't need the letter? If I didn't need the letter, do you think this would be my choice of a Saturday night?"

My calves were spasming and the gritty rust of the ladder dug into my fingers. My heart no longer seemed to pound in separate beats, but rather to be one trembling ululation; even so, I was a little less addled than I had been when he first spoke. At least I now realized that it would be pretty stupid to tell O'Connell he should be off killing Polina instead of me, because right at the moment it would have been awfully easy to do both.

At least it would be pretty easy to start with me.

"Look, you're up here," O'Connell still was speaking as if this were a cocktail party. "So that means you have some idea where the letter is. It's not at the bottom, I can *tell* you that. I've looked."

"It's . . . uh . . . not here at all. It's at a lawyer's. The letter is with Simon's . . . DON'T YOU COME ANY CLOSER!"

O'Connell's face had gone grim as he strode toward my ladder. I had nowhere to go but down, so I did, shaky step by shaky step. The bolts that held the iron ladder to the brick of the hotel shuddered in complaint, sending down a soft shower of flaky dust.

"Look, you've caused quite enough trouble with your misrepresentations already, young lady. And just where do you think you're *going*, anyway?" O'Connell leaned over the parapet to ask; I could see his head round against the muddy yellow of the night sky.

"To the police!"

O'Connell laughed; the noise already sounded hollow, down in the airwell. "There are no police down there, that I can promise you!"

"Is that why you pushed Simon down here!?" I shouted back, now climbing more energetically.

Why had I not let Inderlund and Wolansky do this? Why had I not at least waited for morning? Why had I sent Walter away?

"Pushed Simon? I never pushed Simon, I can assure you!"

I was down perhaps a story already, and descending quickly. Maybe that's what gave me the courage to shout back up, "Sure you didn't push Simon! And you're not a Russian agent, either! Right?"

O'Connell said something muffled, that sounded like a curse. Then a vibration rang through the ladder; I could feel one foot, then the other as O'Connell started after me.

I climbed faster, the rusty ladder ripping at my fingers.

There were ten pebbled-glass windows per floor, two on the narrow side where the ladder was, four right and four left of me, and, I suppose, two behind me. Most were pitch black, but some were already glowing diamonds of light, as lights were being switched on. One or two of the bathroom windows flung open, and heads poked out, knocking objects from the sills, down into the airshaft. A child's yellow bath duck, a box of cornflakes. Flowered cardboard tubes of bath scents, a stack of soda cans, or beer.

Witnesses! People! Shouting!

I began to hope I might not die, but I kept slithering downward anyway. Furiously, because the ladder was banging and jumping about under O'Connell's weight. I tried not to look down, concentrating instead on the blank, gooey bricks that were about six inches in front of my nose. Blank wall, then the next floor. Seventh floor, sixth. Simon's window, Mrs. Morrisey peering timidly out.

There were too many people now! O'Connell couldn't do anything to me! I exulted, but I kept climbing downward.

Fifth floor.

The bathroom window under Simon's was dark, but the glass was wide open. The narrow sill looked almost like a drinks cart. At least a half-dozen bottles clustered on the narrow tile sill, most of them dark with syrupy alcohol—cheap whiskey, sloe gin, fortified wine.

It looked like the hospitality room for an SRO hotel, I thought, as I slithered past.

Or tried to. Because just then a man popped his head out of the window with the bottles and blinded me with a flashlight beam that felt powerful enough to dent my skull.

"*Ladrone! Ladrone!*" he shouted.

Stunned with surprise, I clutched the ladder tighter with my left hand, to be able to throw my right arm across my eyes. That spun me out to the left. Close enough to let the person who had been hiding in the darkened bathroom window immediately to the left of the ladder grab my jacket.

Startled, and terrified, I let go of the ladder.

19

AFTER that, things got a little confused.

Whoever grabbed me hadn't expected to suddenly bear my whole weight, but at least he had a good grip. We slithered down another half story while I pulled him slowly through his bathroom window. Screaming my head off and flailing wildly, I somehow managed to snag *something* as I fell past the ladder. This nearly yanked my arm out of its socket, but even that wouldn't have stopped me, if I hadn't also had the good luck to get my purse strap stuck.

I stopped falling with a jerk that almost cut me in half, but at the moment I wasn't complaining. In fact, I breathed feverish thanks to every saint and deity that might accept petitions from nice Jewish girls that I had listened to my mother, when she insisted I pay the extra for the Coach bag; if I had bought the beaded opera bag I had also been considering, I would already have been dead or crippled at the bottom of the airshaft.

My involuntary companion in freefall was also clutching me tight; when I stopped falling he was swung down into the ladder. *Hard.* I heard a clang that would have stunned an ox, except that both of us were far too terrified to pass out.

The man moaned, but we both held, for a silence about as long as a mouse whisker is wide.

Then there was a shrill metallic shriek, a shower of brick dust.

The bolts holding the ladder had decided they had had enough. With a nauseating shudder the ladder first collapsed into the near wall, and then, slow as in a nightmare, it peeled away from the top of the airshaft. There was a pop, a blinding blue flash. Somewhere above I heard a scream, then a solid *thump* as the ladder wedged against the opposite wall. Whoever had popped out of the bathroom window had let go of me, and I was dangling free, tangled in my purse strap.

"*Santa Maria,*" someone whispered from somewhere behind me. Which made me realize I had maybe better do something about improving my grip. I thrashed and flailed, and finally managed to get myself so the ladder was between me and the ground. Only then did I look around, to see my unexpected companion. He was ash-faced, his eyelids clenched tight, and his lips moving furiously, wiggling a pencil-mustache up and down in time to what I was certain was the Hail Mary. In Spanish.

Then I looked up.

O'Connell was hanging limply, torso wedged through the bars of the airshaft ladder, legs dangling. I couldn't tell for sure, but he didn't seem conscious. On the other hand, he did seem firmly attached to the ladder.

I exhaled, slowly, gripping that rusty iron ladder as tightly, and as gratefully, as if it were a lifeline. Which it was, in a way.

The ladder had wedged diagonally in the airshaft. We were about four stories up, and while there was no guarantee that the ladder wouldn't fall sideways, for the moment, as long as no one moved, we seemed safe.

I don't know exactly how long we froze there, afraid to move a muscle; being in stark terror and extreme pain does not make time appear to fly. I lay on that cool metal, gradually becoming aware of the other noises echoing up and down the airwell. Shouts, questions, screams.

A noise like popcorn popping.

And a smell, damp and smoldering. Like rain-dampened leaves burning. Or the woodstove in my big kitchen up in the Victorian in Dryden, New York, the first time my ex-husband and I fired it up each September.

Trembling, I clung to that ladder, almost sleepy, almost cozy, as the terror and adrenalin faded. I shut my eyes, thinking of that kitchen, and popcorn, and autumn, and being safe, and having someone to hold me and protect me . . .

Then I realized that wherever the fire smell was coming from it, it wasn't a country kitchen, and it wasn't a barbecue. I opened my eyes, and looked down.

Already the smoke was thick enough to make it hard to see, but the sparks of arcing electricity were so vividly blue that I could see them even through the oily gray clouds that were billowing sulkily up toward us. When the smoke shifted, I could see the snapped power line, which writhed slowly among the cluttered junk, like a snake with a broken back.

The smoke clawed into my eyes and throat, reminding me that what we were dangling in might as well have been a chimney.

"Cut the power!" I screamed, gagging and retching. "Cut the goddamned power!"

Abruptly someone did, and the eye-searing blue of the sparks disappeared. Which turned the airshaft into a landscape by

Bosch, a velvety smothering black of writhing bitter smoke, lit only by the dull red of smoldering junk.

Eyes streaming, trying not to breathe, I began to back down the ladder. Fumbling my way backward along the slant of the trembling ladder, I indicated with kicks and shouts that the man behind me should do likewise. The ladder quivered, people shouted, hands waved out to us, extending unreachable assistance. Somewhere, above all the hubbub, I heard the wail of approaching sirens.

In the end, though, it was Jesus who actually saved me.

Ramone's friend, the one with the flashlight.

I was already dizzy and despairing, no idea where we were, when that beam cut through the smoke, like one of those swords from *Star Wars*. Somewhere in that cone of light was a pole, jabbing out toward us.

At first I thought that someone was trying to knock us off the ladder, which is probably why I almost kicked the man who later introduced himself as Ramone in the face, when he grabbed my ankle. Gesticulating with one arm, shouting instructions at me in Spanish, of which I understood not a word, Ramone grabbed one end of the stick, wrapped a rope of some sort over his wrist, and disappeared.

Numb, tears streaming down my face, coughing, I kept creeping downward. A second later the flashlight beam stabbed me, and the pole poked at me. Now the two men were waving at me, imploring me to grab the pole.

I did, looping my wrist through a rope that was wired into a kind of noose at my end of the stick, like a dog-catcher's lasso. Then there was a little testing jerk, I jerked back, and suddenly, the pole yanked me off the ladder, and snatched me up toward the window, like a fish on a gaffe hook.

The two men pulled me over the window ledge so roughly that it may take me the rest of my life to get the slivers out of my belly, but I was inside, sobbing safely on the tile floor of somebody's bathroom.

"O'Connell!" I choked. "Somebody get O'Connell!"

"NICE perfume, Midge. You smell like a burnt marshmallow." I was startled by the soft voice at my elbow. Walter, studying me closely. "But you're okay at least, kid?"

I smiled wanly, surprised by how happy I was to see him. I shook my head. "Not really, but at least I don't *look* like a burnt marshmallow. What's the matter, how come you're here? Polina wouldn't believe you loved her?" I pulled my blanket tighter around me and shivered. Walter hugged my shoulder. I think it was meant as a joke, but at the moment I was pleased to accept any affection the universe might offer, no matter how grudgingly. I leaned against him.

"Looks like you *tried* hard enough to toast yourself into a marshmallow, though. I mean, assuming you had something to do with that?" Hugging me, he pointed his chin at the crowd on the other side of Amsterdam Avenue.

"I don't know . . . but *they* think I did," I circled my head, pretty much indicating the world around me. We were with about a hundred other people, huddled on the far side of Amsterdam Avenue, watching four fire trucks and a half-dozen police cars spin their red lights over enough dripping hoses that the sidewalk looked like spaghetti, with firemen for meatballs. Two ladders were up against the outer wall, and another around the corner, and firemen dressed like astronauts were walking in and out of the Van Horn's front door. Radios squawked, glass shattered, firemen shouted.

Walter studied the scene, then me, his look puzzled. Then a half beat later, he smiled. "Polina? You mean why I didn't stay with her? I was . . . I just couldn't figure how I was supposed to make sure she wasn't in danger, plus I was worried about you, so instead of doing like you asked, I told your cop friend you wanted that he should bring the two of us up here. Fast."

I straightened up, looked around. "Mike is here?"

I felt Walter's arms drop away from me. "Your cop friend? Yeah, he should be, anyway. We all came up here together."

We both studied the crowd of police and firemen. As we watched, two men in white emerged with a stretcher, which they put into their orange-and-white ambulance. The driver shut the doors, and the vehicle pulled away, siren shrieking.

Russo, I saw, had been standing behind the ambulance.

He was talking with several other cops, including Lieutenant Wolanksi. Wolanski was jabbing his finger into Mike's lapel, his face angry. Mike was nodding, reluctantly, his face looking as if it were made of cast iron.

I was so tense I felt like vomiting. Instead I said, through chattering teeth, "That was O'Connell. That they just took away. In the . . ."

When I didn't say anything more, Walter laughed, a little forced. "So *now* he was here."

It wasn't just cops across the street. There was a tall man in a camelhair coat, thrown over pajamas. He looked Indian, or perhaps Pakistani. The manager, or the owner. The two Hispanics were there, too. Ramone and Jesus. Explaining themselves with a great deal of waving of arms.

And, I saw, when the group shifted a little, Polina.

I felt as if someone had squeezed my heart in his fist.

"Now?" I croaked, doing my best to pretend I was paying attention to Walter. "What do you mean *now?*"

I must have sounded dreadful; Walter stepped back as if I had tried to bite him. "All I meant was, you thought he'd go to Polina's hotel, but instead he was here. But the time when she was looking for him here, he wasn't. He was somewhere else. Maybe at her hotel?" He forced a laugh.

"Polina came *here,* expecting to see O'Connell?" I repeated, ideas beginning to spark in my head again. *"When?"*

"That's what she said, anyway." Walter peered at me, then shook his head. "You're starting to think again, aren't you, Midge?"

I ignored that. "You said she said she came to the Van Horn, looking for O'Connell? When?"

"That night. The night the Brit died. You told me that old lady had seen her over here that night, but after Brent-Waterhouse died, so I asked. You know, to have something to say, while we were waiting for your cop to show up. She told me she was looking for O'Connell, not Brent-Waterhouse. The publisher's room was wide open, so she went on in, but nobody was around, so she left again. She's the one who stuck the other letter on the mirror. With bubble gum."

"Why?"

"To show she'd been there, I guess."

"No, why was she looking for O'Connell?"

"She didn't say," Walter looked across Amsterdam at the group, then back at me. "Is it important? I could try to pry those guys away from her, if you'd like to ask her yourself."

I didn't answer. Polina had *arranged* to meet O'Connell? Whom she had *expected* to be here?

I watched her now, from across the street. She was wearing a leather jacket, shimmery spandex tights, the cloche hat that did nothing to restrain her curly hair. The men were all beaming at her, jostling one another out of the way to stand closer to her. I couldn't hear, but I could easily imagine her every charmingly broken word. Her gawky, vulnerable gestures, her eye-catching, bizarre clothing, her gift for intimacy, making each man in that little group feel she was his alone.

In need of his protection.

Polina, who had pulled herself up, by her garter straps I guess, to the very pinnacle of Soviet society, and who now was about to transplant herself to America, by whatever means necessary.

At that moment I understood how completely I had been had. By Polina.

Sure, Brent-Waterhouse had used Polina's book to blackmail O'Connell; but who was it who had told him about the book in the first place?

I remembered Brent-Waterhouse's arrogant pleasure that night, his assurance that he had the world on a very short chain. Because, by viciously manipulating Victor Pedlar and Susan Griswold he had maneuvered O'Connell into promising him the endowed professorship he coveted, at Queens.

And ripping the letter into bits, that had been nothing more than theater. A final cruelty, to raise O'Connell's hopes that he was unexpectedly free of Brent-Waterhouse's hooks, so as to dash them even lower, by making clear he wasn't.

Except that he didn't know Polina had already turned the advantage against him, by permitting O'Connell to top the bidding. Which she had come over to the Van Horn that night to do, in person, and so give O'Connell the exquisite pleasure of watching Brent-Waterhouse's face as his blackmail scheme deflated in front of him.

But she came too late; the publisher had out-finagled the professor, as a reward for which he had gone down the airshaft, and the professor had scooted out the door.

"My God . . ." I breathed softly, then hobbled off across the street on my one broken heel, my face grim with purpose.

"Lieutenant Wolanski," I said, when I came up to the group clustered around Polina, "I want . . ."

Except I didn't get to say what I wanted, because Wolanski turned to me with a glower that could have clabbered milk. Sleeplessness hadn't done anything for his looks; the early morning light made the detective's scalp seem pale green through his buzzcut, while the bags beneath his eyes puffed a bruiselike sepia.

"Hey look, everybody! It's Miss fucking Marple!" Wolanski shouted. "Glad you could join our little early-risers meeting here, *Mzzzz*. Cohen," he said with sour cheer, then popped an obscenely pink rectangle of gum into his mouth; he masticated with such deliberate fury that I was pretty certain he was wishing it was me he had between his teeth, and not the gum. "So, you want to tell us something?"

"Midge, listen, watch what you say now . . ." Russo stepped forward, his face looking worried and pulled, as if he were being tugged about a dozen different directions. "This could be, you know . . . serious."

Meaning, I understood, don't incriminate yourself. I opened my mouth, then closed it again, confused.

Wolanski blew an egg-sized bubble, then pinched it off, removed from his mouth to examine, then popped it back in, where he squashed it with his tongue. I found the whole display revolting.

"No, come on, the lady wants to talk, let her talk. I mean, all your friends over there probably wondering why it is they're on the sidewalk, instead of in their beds, right? Ted Mack is dead, right? So this stunt couldn't have been for 'Amateur Hour,' and nobody has said nothing about this being in video tape, so I don't suppose this all was to get you on 'America's Funniest Home Videos'? No? So do you mind telling me just why in the blue hell you decided to spend this particular Saturday night burning down a hotel in the middle of Harlem, hmm, *Mizz* Cohen?"

My ribs hurt like hell, I was still half scared out of my wits, and I was badly confused by everything that happened, but I was damned if I was going to let Wolanski patronize me. "I was looking for evidence, Lieutenant. Evidence. That you people missed. And I didn't burn down the hotel. Did I? I mean, it didn't burn down, did it?" I waved vaguely at the brick hulk behind him, which might have reeked of smoke and had several leaky canvas hoses running in through the lobby door, but which was still very much *there*. "And even if it did, it wasn't me . . ." Mike's face went a gloomier shade of cast iron, so I shut up. Then, if only because she would be easier on the eyes than her partner was, I looked around Wolanski for Bertha Inderlund.

"Bertie will be here, eventually," Wolanski understood. "Still putting on her little feminine touches, I imagine. You *gals* understand that sort of thing. You prefer to wait until a member of the great sisterhood of the fair sex shows up? No problem . . . except I gotta tell you, you're making a mistake if you think Bertie's going to be some soft kind of fluffy little puff dollie about this . . ."

"About what?! I haven't *done* anything!" I shouted. "O'Connell chased *me* down the ladder, and it was the ladder falling that must have snapped the wire! Nobody's even been *hurt*. Have they? I mean, except maybe O'Connell . . ." I looked at Mike, who shrugged, looked away. Toward Polina. I felt a chill in my stomach.

"O'Connell will be all right," Wolanski sniffed, after a minute's struggle, making it seem as if this admission were physically painful for him. "Lucky he's wearing so much leather, though. Guy went right through the line, with his back I guess. And lucky for you, too. That wire had got stuck to your ladder, you'd have been sitting on an eight-story vertical hibachi."

"And the hotel?" I nodded, feeling as though my point were somehow being made. "Nobody hurt in there either, right?"

Wolanski shrugged, pointed his chin across the street. "Everybody spends a night outside, so maybe a head cold or two, and the rooms will smell of smoke for a while, but . . ." he smiled, but not with any amusement. "Probably that'll be an improvement, most cases. Actually you might even call this a lucky kind of fire. Substandard wiring illegally placed in an airshaft that not only doesn't meet fire code but is stuffed full of flammable junk besides . . . well, a *real* fire could have ended a *lot* worse."

Here the owner opened his mouth to say something, but Wolanski silenced him with a glance.

"So, since nobody was seriously hurt . . ." I began, my voice sweet reason itself, even if my knees were trembling violently underneath the blanket.

Wolanski slapped his thighs angrily. *"I'm* hurt, damnit! You think I *want* to get out of bed, come over here to the middle of cowboy country before even the rats is out of their holes, because of some damn dizzy lady thinks she's a master sleuth?" Wolanski shouted. "And this whole hotel up out of bed and a twelve squad cars full of cops that might better be out busting crack dealers or escorting diplomats or otherwise making themselves useful? Four goddamn fire trucks and an ambulance? You want me to sit down and figure up for you the exact dimensions of the hole this little midnight excursion of yours has put in poor old Mayor Davie the Dink's police budget?"

"Killed, I should have said. Not hurt. *Killed.* Like Simon was."

"You listen to me, and you listen good. I like Mike Russo a lot, and there's plenty of rules I'm happy to bend, as a favor for the man. But bending is one thing, breaking's another. Two more years snuffling 'round scumbag hotels like this one and my pension's vested, at which time the last these five boroughs is ever going to see of Gabe Wolanski is his two hind pockets, as he disappears down the Garden State Parkway. I'm heading *south.* Become chief of PO-lees in some redneck southern town, get me an Aunt Bea and a Barney Fife, and live just like ol' Andy Griffith, catch more fish than criminals. And you know what?" Now Wolanski threw an arm around Russo's neck, heavily enough to make Mike wince. He looked miserable as Wolanski pulled him nearer; then Wolanski spoke to both of us, looking from one to the other. "You two aren't going to fuck that up with some dumb stunt that gets this bimbo killed. Understood, the pair of you?"

"Great!" I snapped back, furious. "And so what, we're all supposed to just *sit* there with our thumbs up our noses, until *Barney Fife* finally figures out it was O'Connell killed Simon?"

"Uh, Midge . . ." Mike shook himself free of Wolanski, then stepped toward me, touched my shoulder. His eyes were cold green now, with none of that yellow undertone I loved. His skin was pale, almost marble. Like his touch, hard and cold.

But Wolanski didn't let Russo explain whatever he was trying to tell me. He turned his back, raised his arms to heaven, to shout, "*Jee*-sus! O'Connell didn't kill Simon!"

I snatched free of Mike, ran to the other side Wolanski, so as to be able to shout directly into Wolanski's face. When I was so close I could smell his garlic-and-bubble-gum breath, his sour skin, his buzzcut pomade, I yelled, "O'CONNELL KILLED SIMON! BECAUSE SIMON KNEW HE WAS A RUSSIAN SPY!"

Walter snatched me from behind, and Russo stepped in front of me, to separate me from Wolanski.

"Shit." Wolanski sounded as disgusted as I felt. "You dumb broad, *nobody* killed Simon."

"Yeah, well, now I suppose you're going to tell me he killed himself!"

Instead of answering, Wolanski barked something at Ramone and Jesus, who were hovering on the edges, studying our group with the sort of concentration that only people who don't understand a language can muster. Whatever Wolanski said to them set the pair jabbering and bickering, until Jesus went back into the hotel. After a second he returned, sheepishly offering Wolanski the stick with which he had yanked first Ramone, then me, through his bathroom window.

Wolanski snatched it so fast I thought he was going to hit me with it. I cringed, wondering how many years in Sing Sing I would get if I were to slug him back.

"In a manner of speaking, he did. See, it appears security here in the Van Fleabag isn't as tight as some of the guests might desire," Wolanski said, instead of hitting me. He glanced portentously at the Indian owner/manager, who again shuffled awkwardly, mouth opened to offer an explanation, until Wolanski scowled him into continued silence. "And Jesus here was getting tired of somebody all the time stealing his booze. There is usually a certain amount of pilfering among the fellow residents, but this booze thing was different. Jesus says that for the last three months, he's been losing about a bottle, bottle and a half every couple days. He didn't catch on for the longest time, because the *bottles* are never missing. Just the booze."

"You actually *understand* them telling you all that?" I asked. I shouldn't have.

Wolanski's face puckered. "Meaning a dumb fucking Polack such as myself is lucky enough to just know English, right?"

"I didn't mean that, Lieutenant, I was just . . . I mean . . . well, I've been listening to them yammer at me ever since they tried to kill me, and I *still* can't figure out why they did that."

Wolanski laughed, but this time it sounded genuine. "That's about what Jesus here is saying, too!" Wolanski pointed his pen at the older man, the one who had had the flashlight; he nodded politely, smiled some big white teeth. "They couldn't figure out what happened, they spring their trap and BANG . . . *you're* in it!"

"Trap?"

Wolanski waved his pen at the two men. "When he finally figured out he wasn't crazy, that somebody really was stealing his booze somehow, Jesus accuses his young friend Ramone of doing it, except Ramone swears up and down that he doesn't know anything about it, and they argue back and forth . . . got pretty ugly, I gather. So Ramone looked around, and found *this* in the bottom of the airshaft."

Wolanski shook the pole at me, then asked something in Spanish. The two men answered excitedly, pointing at the top of the stick, where the loop was.

"They said there was even still a broken bottle neck in the top," Wolanski translated. "So Ramone brought the stick back up, and they set up their trap, waited three, four nights. Figured whoever had been using this stick to swipe bottles would either be trying it again with a new stick, or maybe would sneak down to look for the old one. Either way, they figured Jesus would be able to present his bill. Except when Ramone jumped out and grabbed you, you let go . . ." Wolanski started sputtering again, like he'd never heard anything funnier. "And like Jesus says, your tits was so big they pulled the both of you down the airshaft!"

I don't think that part was supposed to be translated, because Jesus and Ramone blushed, Mike looked uncomfortable, the cops grinned, and Wolanski was nearly in convulsions.

And me? I could feel a slow, burning blush spreading upward from my shoulders, singing upward through my hair. But not because of my chest.

Because at last I understood.

Drunk—still or again—Simon had treated O'Connell to some of the booze pilfered from Jesus, celebrating their agreement that never came, because O'Connell was stalling for time, waiting for Polina to arrive. But then the two had quarreled, and O'Connell had left in a huff, as Mrs. Morrisey described. After which Brent-Waterhouse had tried to return his stolen bottle to Jesus's window ledge, even though he was far too drunk to attempt to do so.

Simon really *had* killed himself. By accident.

He had fallen. Simon Brent-Waterhouse had simply *fallen*.

I began to cry, big gelid tears carving slow furrows through the grime on my face.

"But he's still a spy," I blubbered. "O'Connell . . ."

I felt Walter's hand, reassuring and steady on my back. For a second I leaned into it, and then noticed Mike's stony face. I sprang forward, to grab Polina. "Ask her! She knows Brent-Waterhouse was blackmailing O'Connell about being a Russian spy! That was why she came over to meet them here! She was even *helping* Simon blackmail O'Connell, at least until she switched sides!"

Polina ripped my hand from her arm with a sudden snarl, as if she would have preferred it to be strips of my flesh she was pulling away, then looked around, her eyes wide as those of a cornered animal.

Which is when I understood *why* Polina had switched sides.

"Oh my God!" I stammered, switching into Russian. "O'Connell promised to marry you!"

Polina's eyes narrowed, the green smoldering through her barely open lids. When she growled back at me, her Russian was like a noise I imagine tigers would make while they mate.

"Whores don't work for promises, Margaret. He didn't promise to marry me. He *did* marry me."

I sagged backward; only the fact that Walter was still behind me kept me from falling.

"But . . . but," I stammered, in what language now I'm not even sure, "but O'Connell's homosexual!"

Polina smiled bitterly. "He's worse than that. He's *English*."

In other words, for all her street smarts, all her high Party whoring, Polina had ruined her own intricate plan, fooled at the last moment by counterfeit coin. O'Connell only possessed a green card, and his wife would not automatically be granted the same.

For a moment I could do nothing but gape at Polina, as stunned with pity as I was with awe. Awe, that this apparently coltish, gawky woman could move, plan and act with such ruthless, clear-eyed purpose. Pity, that the accident of her birth as a citizen of that dismal chaotic swamp of a nation had forced her to such terrible designs, simply to achieve a life that ungrateful I usually took for granted, if indeed I wasn't complaining about it. And pity too, that Polina had failed. Gone backward, even, because now Polina was farther away from her green card than ever. Her husband, after all, was a Soviety spy.

Then the last little piece fell into place. I smiled, wiping tears and smearing grime all over myself.

"The letter was real, wasn't it? The one you tore up. You made Simon give it to you . . ."

Polina said nothing, but I didn't need an answer. Confident that his scheme had finally worked, Brent-Waterhouse must have returned the real original to Polina. Her price for helping him arrange that bit of letter-ripping theater at the restaurant, maybe.

Which is why Simon had not had it to offer O'Connell later that evening, and so had typed up that "suicide note" instead. Which O'Connell did not understand, and so—pressed by Victor, who had been pressed by me—he had come looking for the letter tonight.

As a result of which we all nearly burned down the Van Horn.

What a pleasant little dinner that had been, I thought, so tense and exhausted now that I was quivering, almost gagging.

"Are . . . are you okay, Midge?" Russo stepped forward and took my elbows. He studied my upturned face, rubbed at something on my cheek with his thumb. "You don't look so good . . ."

"Will you take me home, Mike? Please?" I whispered.

20

"STILL raining?"

"Mmmm." I answered, running my finger along the top of the window frame, as I looked out at Ocean Parkway, which was purpling into a rainy evening. The mulberry trees were beginning to drop their leaves, which fell to clog the gutters and make the sidewalks slippery.

"September . . ." Mike said, after a longish silence. I heard him stretch, and waited, wondering whether he was getting up. He wasn't, though; he had simply been shifting position. I cinched my robe tighter, and looked at him. Hands behind his head, he was studying the ceiling, not the silk Dior dressing gown that I had paid $120 for in April, because he had said he liked me in magenta.

"Almost October, really . . ." I tossed in, after another long silence.

"That's right."

Mike continued to stare at the ceiling, so I stared at his torso. The four neat round bundles of stomach muscles, like a turtle's belly. The corrugations of rib. The nipples, like chocolate M&Ms; the golden hair, so fine it was almost invisible, like a body stocking, but stiff somehow too, like a good bath loofah, when he rubbed against me . . .

Our reunion hadn't been a success.

I mean, okay, for a *while* it had been a success, maybe. Mike had brought me home from the Van Horn, sobbing in the embrace of his bucket seats. He had scolded me, a little, but he had also helped clean the grime and smoke off me. Strong, gentle, *familiar* fingers had checked the angry yellow-green bruise that ran from my left hipbone to my right shoulder. Checked for other breaks, injuries, sprains. . . . And when he was convinced that nothing was broken, he had . . .

Well, you know.

And that had been good too. Very good.

After that I had slept.

Until about a half hour ago, when a nightmare—of falling—had woken me up screaming, stiff as the dead, and half scared out of my wits. Mike had still been there, then.

Staring at the ceiling. Like he still was now.

So what was I expecting?

I didn't know, exactly. Conversation, anyway. And it didn't *have* to be about marriage and having kids and giving up writing and just being normal, either. That would have been *wonderful*. But just a little giggling would have been okay, or just even running his fingertip along the line of my nose, Mike saying something about how he had missed me.

Instead . . .

Well, he didn't hug me. He *patted* me, asked if I was all right.

I said I was. We cleared our throats. I asked if he wanted anything. He said he didn't.

The weather. We talked about the weather.

Well, what did I *want* from Mike?

I didn't know that, either. Love would have been nice. Marriage? Up until maybe two hours ago, I would have said yes.

But right now, I would have settled for the two of us not being so tense with each other that we didn't even *talk,* because we knew that in ten minutes it would turn into a fight.

I think that must have been what Mike wanted too, because when my phone rang, we both leapt as if electrocuted.

"It's probably for me!" he shouted, rolling over to grab the bedside phone.

"For *you?* Why would it be for you?" I grabbed his hand, halfway to the receiver, which rang again.

Mike jerked his hand away, sat up, looking uncomfortable as he pulled the bedclothes tight around his waist. "Umm, that Russian girl . . . I told Wolanski to let me know what her situation was, if she needed help or anything. I gave him this number."

Ring.

That meant Mike had *expected* to stay here. I smiled, tentatively. "You said you'd be here?"

Mike looked sulky. "Christ, it's no big deal. I gave him *lots* of numbers. Said try my mom's, try here, try my Uncle Gino's coffee shop . . ."

Ring.

My smile disappeared. "Hold it, you're so worried about Polina that you gave Wolanski half the phone numbers in New York City?"

"Chrissake, Midge! The poor girl is a *guest* in this country, and now she's got nobody looking out for her, when she's into shit maybe up to her *neck.* So Gabe and I . . ."

"So you and Gabe are ready to let that Russian remora get a

hold on your ass that she won't relax until one or the other of you's standing just to the left of her, in front of a church altar someplace! And you want to know something else?!" I snatched up the receiver, just as it began its fifth ring. "It isn't going to matter to her *one bit* which of you two it is, either! So live with *that*, buster! Hello?"

"No problem," Mike scowled at me, then swung his feet out of bed. "Gabe is already married."

"Midge? Hi, sweetie, is someone there? Is this a bad time?"

"God good almighty, so is Polina!" I muttered, fuming as I watched Mike pull on underwear, then jeans. "Hi, Ma, look . . ."

"Okay, it's a bad time, I can tell. So just tell me one thing, you're all right?"

"I'm all right, why wouldn't I be all right? Ma . . ."

"Because it's Sunday evening, and you didn't call me since Friday morning. That's why you'd be not all right."

"Mother," I started, in what I hoped was not an unkind but clearly preemptory tone, "I am thirty-five years old, I own my own apartment, I pay my own bills, and . . ."

"I didn't ask, are you a grown-up. I asked, are you *healthy?* Is everything *all right?*"

"It's a long story, Ma . . . look, I'll . . . I'll call you back."

"Don't bother, don't bother. You're busy, you have your own life."

Mike was throwing on his shirt now, searching with his feet for his shoes. He hadn't once looked at me, since I had yelled at him.

"Ma . . ."

"I know you don't have the time now, but when you do, call me, because I want to tell you about this new bran I just got, something one of the women at the health club was talking about . . ."

"What health club? Mother, you're not in a health club."

"See, Midge, sweetie, that's what I was going to talk to you about. Because I was feeling like you. I mean, like I think you are feeling like. I mean, I don't *know*, but . . . anyway *I* was feeling like I was losing some of my *zip!*" Here Pearl clicked her tongue, making me shudder. "So, three evenings a week now, I started doing water aerobics. And that's where one of the women told me about this new product, it's really delicious, with raisins, and bits of prune and apricot all diced in, and even oat bran. And it *works!*"

This is middle age, I thought, watching Mike tie his sneakers, put on his jacket. When your mother discusses bowel blockage with you.

"But that's not what I was going to tell you about it. It was because on the back of the box there's this whole great text, like a philosophy really. About how to make your life so you live healthier. Exercise, eating the proper foods."

"Meaning, eat lots of their cereal," I interrupted nastily.

My mother sounded tart. "Just say so, if you want me to hang up. But of course, naturally they mean that too. It really *is* very good, you know, Midge. But the important thing, and the reason I was going to talk to you about it . . . the other thing they suggest is . . . well, attitude."

"Attitude?"

"Yes, that you can live a lot healthier if you have a healthy attitude. If you try to be cheerful, not brood on things, don't let things get you down. Try to have fun. Say *yes* to life!"

I looked away from Mike, who was waiting, politely enough, for me to get off. So he could say good-bye.

I bit my lip. That didn't work, so I turned to the wall, because tears were trembling on my lower lids again. I had been wrong, about when middle age is.

Middle age is when you have made such a mess of your life that you have to take advice from a cereal box.

"Anyway, I was going to talk to you about that," Pearl ended lamely. "And I guess I did." She laughed, then paused. "Because I was wondering . . ."

A man. My mother was going to fix me up again. I could feel it coming, like someone was ramming a dirty sock down my throat. I would have screamed, but . . .

"I was wondering. Because there was a message for you. On *my* machine."

"On *your* machine? Nobody's got *your* number for me except . . ."

"Somebody named Walter? He said . . ." she was clearly looking for her pad, from which she read, " 'Hey, kid, the paper can't wait forever for that review. So, I was thinking, maybe you want to talk about it, if that would help get something started. Get some juices flowing.' " My mother left her script. "Is that supposed to be dirty?"

I smiled, sniffed. I remembered Walter, our lunches at Cornell, with their steady undercurrent of silly double-entendres. "It's ambiguity, Ma."

"Ambiguity," Pearl pronounced, as if it might give her lesions. "Anyway, then the message ends, 'Anyway, I'll be at Hyman's around six. They've got a stuffed derma and buckwheat Sunday buffet that's to die for. Stewed fruit to follow.' So what I was wondering . . ."

"He's Jewish, Ma, he's Jewish," I was smiling broader now, running my fingers through my hair, wondering whether if I called a car service to take me back to the city, that would give me enough time to wash it again, and still make it to Hyman's in time for the stewed fruit.

"Jewish, schmooish," Pearl snapped. "What I'm wondering, he's single?"